EVIL VILLAIN

THE ROYAL COURT BOOK 3

REBEL HART

EVIL VILLAIN

THE ROYAL COURT - BOOK THREE

REBEL HART

1

___

CHERRI

Waking up in the mornings now made me sadder than it used to.

At least when I woke up in Deon's bed, it smelled like him, but it'd been eight months since he'd last been there, and his scent was officially gone. Any clothes he left behind were clean and smelled only of laundry detergent or the gathered mildew from being untouched for more than half a year. If I wasn't staying with his mother, I'd be inclined to say that I didn't have anything left of him, but at least I still had his smile through hers.

Even if she didn't smile much these days.

"Good morning, sweetheart." Ciara was standing at the kitchen counter and looked back over her shoulder to smile at me when I walked in.

"Would you like some eggs? We have leftover ham, so I could put some ham in like you like them?"

"That sounds really yummy, thank you," I replied.

Sinking down into one of the kitchen chairs, I noticed that the microwave said it was just past seven in the morning.

Eventually I'd have to leave and face my life.

Ciara's deep red hair was pulled back into a messy bun with wisps hanging off of it, and her eyes were sunken and sallow. Though she had never been a particularly large woman, she was borderline emaciated from how little she'd been eating as of late, and whatever energy she did have from the little bits of food she ate were going into worrying about her son.

I couldn't blame her.

"You're having some too, right?" I asked.

"I've already eaten," she replied.

Without responding, I scooted my chair back from the table and walked over to the sink, I looked into it, seeing it totally bare and bone dry, then I looked over at Ciara. "Really? Out of your hand?"

She glared over at me. "What are you, my mother?"

"I might as well be," I said. She was cracking eggs into a bowl, so I walked over, picked a few additional ones out of the carton and cracked them into the bowl. "There. Enough for two."

A huff of frustration puffed out of Ciara's nose, but she didn't say anything back, just resumed mixing the eggs with a little bit of milk and some seasonings. I returned to my seat and rested my head on the table, knowing that Deon would want me to be making his mother eat, at least a little bit. If he knew she was starving to death while he was missing, it'd make everything worse.

I was making a list in my mind of everything that I had to take care of, starting with leaving my current accommodations and ending with going to my new ones. It would require a chat with my parents, and probably my brother too, though I was dreading that the most. I also had to face my friends, to whom I'd been absolutely awful for the past six months.

"Ugh," I opted to say out loud. "It's gonna be a long day."

Ciara snickered from over near the oven. "What makes one of the first days of summer vacation for a rich girl a long day?"

One place Ciara and I differed was in our pocketbooks, but nearly everything else was the same. I used to live in the same rundown neighborhood as her until my dad got promoted and we moved to

South Postings. Being back in her house in North Postings felt much better to me. I missed being in a house where you actually crossed paths with the people you're living with.

"Well, first—and this is bad news for you and me—" I started, and Ciara looked over at me. "I think I'm moving out today."

She scoffed. "So much for sixty days' notice." Then she chuckled. "I'll be sad not to have you around anymore. Are you going back to your parents'?"

"No," I said. "I'm actually—prepare to lose your mind—going to stay with Nathan."

Ciara's eyes widened. "What?"

My cheeks puffed up as I took in a huge gulp of air, and deflated as I sputtered out. "I'll wait until the eggs are done. I've got some explaining to do."

Ciara's eyebrows went up, but she took my excuse and returned to the eggs. Like me, Ciara always maintained that Deon was still alive. When I lost my mind a little bit after his disappearance, my parents kicked me out and I ended up going to stay with Ciara. I hadn't told her that, as of a week ago, I had confirmation that Deon was alive out there somewhere, even if I didn't know where. There was no guarantee he was going to survive his battle with Connor. There was no guarantee any of us were going to survive. Ciara was better off with false hope than worrying herself even sicker that her son was maybe tied up in a chair somewhere being tormented by his own father.

Eventually, Ciara finished putting together the ham and eggs and set a couple of plates down on the table. She then got some coffee and a bottle of water for me and brought them over and set them down as well. She sat down across from me, and we each took a few bites of our food before I finally cleared my throat.

"So, these past six months living with you have been so amazing," I started. "I'm really going to miss you, but I wasn't myself. I was… mourning, and it made me treat my friends terribly."

"Mourning?" Ciara said. "Deon's not dead."

"I think that too," I replied, "but at this point he's gone, and as far as I know, he isn't coming back."

"Did Nathan tell you this? Is that where it's coming from? He's pressuring you into moving in with him or something?"

"No. Nathan actually thinks he's alive too, but none of us has any clue where he is or anything… My old friend group, The Royal Court, they've had a tough six months and we all just really need to hunker down together and treat ourselves well after the time we've all had. It won't just be Nathan and me. Sicily will be there a lot too, plus all of my other friends, and Nathan has a new girlfriend now. A girl he's *always* been in love with, named Nikita."

"After what he did to you, suddenly he's a good guy?" Ciara asked.

She was referring to the fact that, by all accounts, Nathan raped me. I was far from the last person that was going to make any excuses for a man that assaulted me, but the man that was in that bathroom that day, pointing a gun at me and forcing me down to my knees, was *not* Nathan Loche. He was Connor Loche's darkness in Nathan Loche's shell.

"What he did wasn't okay, but he was just as much a victim to Connor Loche as me or you. Maybe even more because you were able to fight back, I was able to leave, but Nathan had nothing. Connor tortured him, Ciara. For all intents and purposes, he tortured his own son. It's not his fault. I've forgiven Nathan for that. Truth be told, I forgave him for that before Deon even went missing. I knew it wasn't him."

"That's why you went to save him from Connor?" Ciara asked.

"Yeah, and I know you won't believe me, but Nathan loves Deon. He loved Deon when he went to live with them, and even when Deon came home, Nathan tried in his own way to extend an olive branch. It was covered in Connor's shit, so it didn't work, but he did try. He'd be just as happy to see Deon again as we would be."

Ciara sat in silence for a few minutes, took a few bites of her food, took a few sips of her coffee, and then sighed. "So you're going to work with Nathan to find Deon?"

"Well, if we hear anything we'll follow it, but we don't have much to go off of right now," I lied. The truth was, we had more than a couple of threads to pull on, but Ciara didn't need to know that for now. "I'm going to go and talk to my parents. Give them a much needed apology, then I'll be headed to Nathan's."

"I understand," Ciara said. "I'm going to miss my roommate."

"I'm gonna miss you too, but I promise to check in often, and who knows, maybe this time next year, we'll be sitting around a table with Deon, laughing about all of this nonsense."

A small smile came to Ciara's face. "I certainly hope so."

I took my time finishing breakfast and talking with Ciara, then I packed up the clothes I had, gave her a huge hug, loaded into my car, and started it up to leave.

Ciara leaned into the driver's side window and petted a hand over my hair. "You'll be careful, won't you, sweetheart? Sometimes I think you forget that you're still just a kid."

"I will, I promise," I said.

She pulled back, and I gave her one final wave before backing out of the driveway and officially leaving North Postings for a while.

It'd been a while since I'd last driven down to South Postings. My family lived there, ever since my father got promoted, and all of my friends lived there as well, apart from Sicily, who lived in Postings Proper not far from the high school. The time between when Deon first went missing and the beginning of winter break, I just sort of went through the motions, but I officially started to lose it during the break. I'd stay out all night with Sicily, sometimes not coming home, and eventually my parents started to lose their patience with me. All they had to do was see my new, dramatic look and learn that I wasn't going to *any* classes when school resumed after winter break to tell me that if I didn't shape up, I was gone.

They kicked me out a week after that.

Fortunately, Ciara took me in, and at least from

the standpoint that she was suffering in the same way I was, I was far more respectful of her home than my own parents', which was far from fair. That was where I planned to start my apology. They wouldn't get the full, honest story, because I wanted them to have deniable culpability if shit hit the fan, but I'd tell them enough to explain.

I'd have to deal with Gus too, but I was dreading that more than my parents.

Even though I had a key to the house, I knocked when I got to the front door. My heart was pounding faster than I expected it to be. They were just my parents, that was it, but that didn't make me any less nervous.

The door opened and my mother was standing on the other side. Her face flashed a variety of emotions all in the span of about six seconds—shock, relief, anger, love, frustration—all emotions she was entitled to. "Cherri," she finally got out.

"Hi mom," I said, and the more normal tone of my voice must have instilled some confidence that I was better than the last time we spoke, because she smiled a little. "Um... I'm here to apologize, and explain. Can I come in?"

Instead of a verbal response, my mom reached out and curled her arms around me. She dragged me into a hug, squeezing me tightly, and I hugged her back with the same veracity. I'd always been very close with my parents, and being without them those past six months had been awful.

It felt nice to be back.

"Come in," she said. She released me and led the way in. "Should I call Gus or just your father?"

"Just Dad for now," I said. "Gus is going to be a whole different battle."

She looked back over her shoulder at me. "Yes, he will."

We walked into the kitchen, and I sat down on one of the stools at the island. My mom continued through the other exit back towards the hallway leading down to my father's office. It was a little strange being back in the kitchen, with its marbled granite countertops and dark brown cabinetry. For some reason I was looking for differences, as if things would have changed drastically.

It was only me that had changed.

"Cherri." I looked up and my dad was rounding the corner into the kitchen. He led with his arms out wide, and the tears that I didn't realize I was holding back broke free.

"Daddy." I leapt down off the stool and met my dad's embrace, burying my face in his chest, and letting my emotions spill out. "I missed you."

"Aw, baby," he said in his comforting, dad-voice

timber. "I missed you." He let me go and used his thumbs to flick away my tears. "I'm happy you're home."

"Come, sit," I said. "We've got a lot to talk about." My parents did just that, each sitting themselves down at the island, and I walked around to the other side so I could face them both. Standing allowed me to fidget as I pushed myself to begin my apology. "I, um… I owe you guys an apology. You're wonderful parents and you didn't deserve the way I behaved these past handful of months."

"I just don't understand," my mom said. "You're a good young woman. I think what upset your father and I the most is that we didn't raise you that way."

"You didn't," I said. "A friend of mine… died."

"Who?" my father said. "Not Avery?"

"No, none of my friends from these past few years. A friend of mine from South Postings."

"Deon?" my mom asked.

I nodded. Imagining his smile and my heart breaking. "Yeah."

"We saw him on T.V.," my dad said. "I was unaware you were spending time with him again."

Deon's name and face had been in the news right around the time he went missing. Connor attempted to frame him for Miss Abrams' death, but not much else about Deon had been released. As far as they knew, Deon was a kid I stopped hanging out with four years ago, and then they didn't hear anything else about him.

"It's complicated, and a lot of it I'm not in a place to discuss, but we'd been speaking again. We were going to be together before… it happened."

"What happened to him?" my mom asked.

That was the only part of the story I'd planned that I hadn't quite figured out. Anything too permanent would result in their later disbelief if Deon *did* come home again, but anything too vague would make them think I was lying again.

I went for the only thing I could say honestly. "I don't know."

My mom and dad exchanged an uncertain look. "How do you not know? If you can't confirm *how* he died, how do you know that he died?"

"His mother told me," I lied. "Naturally, she didn't want to discuss the details. We'd only just recently reconnected so…"

My mom stood up and walked around the kitchen island and pulled me back into a hug. "Sweetie, I'm so sorry. Losing someone is never easy."

"Thanks, Mom."

She leaned away a little, but kept her arms

fastened around me. "Where have you been staying? It's time for you to come home."

"Just… another friend, but…" I looked over at my dad who was watching me with sympathy, and then looked back up at my mom. "I'm not moving home."

"What?" my dad said. "Cherri, I know we had to put our feet down, but this is your home. We can see that you're remorseful, and that's a difficult thing to go through. We can help you through it."

"My friends, the ones you *do* know, we've all had a really hard second semester. Now that we're all graduated, The Royal Court is going to kind of hole up together and spend the summer relaxing. We've earned it, I think," I said.

"The Royal Court?" my dad said. "You're going back to them? Are you… reuniting with Nathan?"

"No," I said exasperatedly. "He's got a new girlfriend. A woman he *actually* likes. Nikita. We will be at his house, but we'll all be there. Avery, Alistair, Colette too. Kyle, Brayden probably. Even Jaxon. It's a recovery for the six months we all lost."

"Okay, sweetheart," my mom said. "You go. We trust you."

My dad scoffed. "Rebeccah. She should be at home."

"She's been away from home this long and has done fine," my mom responded. "It'll be good for her to be with her friends." She looked down at me with a hiked eyebrow. "If you're being honest, that you're sorry to your father and I, you can prove it by continuing to be responsible. Check in often. Take care of yourself."

"I will, all of that," I said, then looked at my dad. He stared back at me, still uncertain, but then he nodded. "Thank you, daddy. I love you."

"One other thing," my mom said, bringing my attention back to her. "You need to go make nice with your brother."

I looked over in the direction of the hallway, which would lead to the staircase to the second floor. "I'm really dreading that."

"You should be," my father said. "He's heartbroken."

2
____

CHERRI

There was loud, rock music playing from Gus's room, and I couldn't help but laugh. It seemed we dealt with our problems in a similar way —if there are longer things around us, we can't be left alone with our thoughts. I attempted to knock, but it didn't even sound like there was any shifting inside, so I grabbed the handle and opened the door.

His room still looked mostly the same, and the kid himself was sitting in his haptic gaming chair, staring up at his large 50" television screen, playing a video game. His head sat a little higher against the back of the chair than the last time I'd seen him. Even in just the six months since I'd seen him last, he'd grown at least an inch. He was only nine, but it felt like time was flying by.

I was mad at myself for missing so much.

"I'm not hungry, mom," Gus called without even looking back. "Dad brought me a breakfast sandwich this morning. I ate most of it, I swear."

Skipping meals too? This kid was a chip off the ol' block.

"I know from experience that not eating when you're sad is bad for you," I said.

Gus' head flipped backwards in my direction and his eyes got a little wider. "Cherri."

"Hey kid," I greeted. "How's it going?"

Gus looked at me for a few more minutes and then turned back round to face his game again. "Fine."

Ouch. No elated hug, not even a smile. My dad didn't lie; Gus was upset. Instead of pressing, I walked over next to his chair and sat down on the floor. He didn't look over from his game, but he shifted uncomfortably in his chair. I waited until it seemed like he was at a safe spot in his game, then I held out my hand for the controller. He looked down at my hand, but then flopped it in, and I took control of the person on the game.

"So, what do I do?" I asked. I'd never been much of a gamer, but it was one of Gus' favorite things to do and I used to play with him a lot before I moved out.

"That sword in your hand is actually a key," he said. "Those little black things, you can hit them with it, and you're trying to find something to unlock with the key."

"Ah, a key that is functional both as a sword and an actual key, how useful," I said and then I laughed, but Gus didn't join me, and eventually my smile faded.

It was so much worse that he was *angry*. It was like he'd forced himself to write me off and didn't know what to do now that I was back again. I'd gambled with my very rare and precious relationship with my little brother. I hated that so much.

I followed along the path, striking any of the enemies that I could find, and then in the distance on the level, I saw a keyhole focused in the middle of a fountain. I started to charge forwards, but all of a sudden, the game went into a cutscene, and a much bigger monster than the ones I'd fought came falling from the sky.

"Whoa!" I yelped, then I handed the controller back. "Here. I don't wanna cost you the game."

Gus took back over, expertly making short work of the bad guy, then he sweetly offered the controller back to me so I could use the key and unlock the hole I'd found. It sent the game into another cutscene, and at the end of it, it gave me an option to save the game, which I did, then I turned the game off and moved so I was facing Gus instead. He didn't put up a fight, but wouldn't look at me, which hurt me more.

"Gus, look at me." He didn't look up, so I reached out and grabbed his hands. "Gus. I know you're upset with me. I want to apologize."

"You don't have to say sorry," he replied with a heartbreaking tone in his voice. "You just went away for awhile, that's what mom said."

I ran a hand through my short half-brown and half-blond dyed hair. "Yeah. I was having a hard time and I just needed to deal with it."

"I hope you found something to help," he replied. "When I'm sad, you help me, so if I couldn't help you, I hope someone else could."

It was like a knife straight to the heart. In his own nine-year-old way, he was asking me why he wasn't good enough to help me through what I was going through. Thinking of him going to sleep every night wondering why I didn't come to him when I was sad killed me. He deserved a better explanation than the one I had. He put his faith in me, and I essentially told him he wasn't worth mine.

"Gus, you are who helps me when I'm sad. I don't know why I didn't come to you. I think I was just so confused with how sad I was. Have you ever been so sad that nothing makes sense at all?"

He shrugged. "Just when you left."

Oh man, the kid was aiming straight for my throat. How was he making me feel so terrible without even trying? "I'm sorry, buddy. I'm so sorry. You know how much I love you, right?"

He nodded, though still sadly. "Yeah."

I smiled. "Do you know what extortion is?"

He looked up at me with a tilt of his head. "No?"

"Sometimes, people do bad things, like me when I left you and made you sad, and sometimes that means that good people, like you, can hold that over the bad person's head to get a few things they want," I explained.

"It sounds like that would make me a bad person too," Gus replied.

"Well, yes, in most situations, but in this very specific situation, no. I deserve to feel guilty for hurting you and upsetting you, and you deserve to be spoiled a little bit because I did those things. So anytime you want something, you just call and extort me for it."

At that, Gus finally cracked a little smile. "The

new game in that series we were just playing came out."

"Then I'm buying it for you," I said. "Can you download it directly?"

His smile widened. "Yeah, but will you play it with me?"

I nodded. "I promise I will, but I can't do it right now. I'll get it for you right now, but I have a few more people I have to apologize to. You weren't the only one I hurt."

"Will they get to use the extortion thing with you too?" he asked, and I laughed.

"Probably," I said, then I opened my arms, and Gus flopped forward out of his chair, onto his knees, and into a hug. "I love you, kid."

"I love you too."

"I'll never, ever do that to you again, okay?" I said.

"Okay."

He pulled back, and I pushed him back into his chair. "This summer, I'm going to be living with my friends, but I'll visit you whenever you want, *and* my friend has a massive pool with a slide. I bet you could come over for some awesome pool parties."

"Yeah!" Gus yelped.

"I'm already on it." I stood up and kissed him

on his forehead. "Okay, go find the game and I'll buy it."

I spent a little bit of extra time with Gus, letting him show me the beginning of his game and making sure he felt extra loved, then I gave him a final kiss on the forehead and left, promising to be back soon. He saw me out with a smile, then I swung through the kitchen to give each of my parents a final kiss and goodbye. I returned to my car. It'd already been a long day, but I felt much better than I did at the beginning of the day. Ciara had been taken care of, my parents and Gus had forgiven me.

All that was left was The Royal Court—but for that, I'd need backup.

"Yello?" I smiled at the familiar sound of Sicily's voice. I might have liked to see him in person, but the day was running short, so a phone call would have to suffice to get his help.

"Hi."

"Hey!" Sicily squealed. "I haven't heard your voice in a whole week. You get your old friends back and suddenly you're too good for your old pal, Sicily?"

"You know that's not true," I replied. "I've mostly been sleeping."

"I'm just yankin' your chain. No one can quit ol' Sic," he responded.

Sicily had been my only friend through the past six months. Given that he and Deon became close in the time that Deon was at Postings Proper High before disappearing again, when Deon *did* go missing, Sicily was just as frustrated as I was. He too believed that Deon was still alive and out there, and we had been working together to try and find him. Though we'd had no luck, we developed quite the bond in the interim, and now I considered Sicily one of my closest friends.

"I just finished apologizing to my parents and Gus," I said. "It went *way* better than I thought it would."

"Glad to hear it. You headed to Nathan's now?" he asked.

"Yeah, and I was hoping you could meet me there? I know they were my friends before, but they've all changed so much in the past six months that it feels like I'm walking into a house of strangers. It'd be nice to have a familiar face there."

He snickered. "Aw man, you know I've got you covered. I've missed ya anyway, so let's take on The Royal Court together, girl!"

My smile grew, even if Sicily wasn't there with me. "Thanks, Sic."

"No problem. I'll leave here in the next five minutes here. See you soon."

"Yeah. Bye."

I hung up my phone and started up my car, but I waited a bit to leave. Postings Proper, where Sicily lived, was about fifteen minutes from Nathan's house, whereas I was only about five away. I spent a few minutes flipping through college offers that were still open to me, and a few internships who'd reached out due to my somehow stellar grades at the end of the year. Though I would never ask him about it and he would probably never tell me, I assumed Nathan paid to make sure I graduated. It was the kind of thing I felt like I should thank him for, but also the kind of thing that it seemed like he should have done considering what he put me through. Regardless, it was going to be one of those few things that was never spoken between us, especially because I had no idea what to do with it.

Even before Deon, I wasn't sure what I was going to do with my life post-grad. So many of my decisions were dictated by The Royal Court and what was best regarding my affiliation with them. I had no clue what I wanted to do now. Beyond finding Deon and ending things for good with Connor, I probably needed to set a personal goal to sort my own life out. To say that I was lost would be an understatement.

My self-loathing had killed enough time for the moment, so I put my phone away, started up my car, and headed out to Nathan's. I drove on memory, the trip being one I'd made a hundred times before, and it made me anxious the way it felt a little like settling into an old routine. Things would be very different now, though—for the better, hopefully.

I probably ran at Sicily for a hug a bit more eagerly than I should have, but it was really nice to see him. Not just because he had supported me through arguably the most difficult time of my life, but he also reminded me of Deon. Even once all of this madness was over, Sicily and I would remain close. I wouldn't have it any other way.

"Aw, hey there, gorgeous," Sicily said as he pulled me into a huge hug. "I didn't like not seein' ya for a whole week."

"Me either." I pulled away. "I have this thing where I recede in on myself when I'm sad. You may have noticed."

"Nah. No idea what you're talkin' about," Sicily replied. "Alright. You ready for this?"

"Yeah. Thanks for coming with me," I replied.

Sicily braced his hands on his hips and puffed

out his chest. "Not a problem, ma'am." He was wearing his signature newsboy hat, and his goatee was much fuller than it had been at the end of the year. The strangest, best superhero ever.

I grabbed my bag, which Sicily almost immediately pulled from my hands, and then we started towards Nathan's house. The stone facade of the main house was a little daunting given the myriad of awful experiences I'd had the last few times I'd been there, but ever since Nathan's mom was killed and his father went missing, he had the inside of the main house on his family's property renovated and now it was the official Royal Court clubhouse. He'd created a bedroom inside for all of the members, mostly by pairing, and he'd created a ton of entertainment spaces for enjoying ourselves over the summer. The story I'd told my parents and Ciara wasn't *entirely* untrue. We were planning to enjoy ourselves a little over the summer.

Whether or not we would succeed was yet to be seen. It mostly depended on if we found Deon, and exactly how much of our lives Connor was determined to ruin from wherever in Maine he was.

Once again, in spite of the key I had which would get me into the house I was in front of, I knocked. Just like with my parents' house, I felt like I had to earn the right to come and go as I pleased.

We waited a few moments in silence and then eventually, I could hear the door unlock.

It opened and the face I saw on the other side was so much more welcome than I could have possibly imagined.

"Cherri!" Avery yelped. She damn near jumped through the doorway to wrap her arms around me and pull me into a bear hug. I wrapped my arms around her and returned the hug. "I missed you!"

"I missed you," I replied.

Avery was my best friend. Through circumstances she had very little control over, I blamed her for losing Deon along with the rest of The Royal Court, when my anger should have been directed at people like Connor and anyone who helped him control Postings the way he did. I couldn't bring myself to entirely regret it—I'd lost so much of myself being in The Royal Court. Not only did stepping away allow me to get back to my more natural self, but it also led to me getting close to Sicily. That said, I ended up taking things to the extreme and hurting someone who'd only ever been like a sister to me.

She didn't deserve that.

We pulled apart a little, but I placed my hands on her face and looked into her eyes. "You're so beautiful. I'm so happy to see you."

She smiled wider and there were tears plucking at the corners of her eyes. "I'm happy to see you too. I missed you so much."

"I missed you too. I'm sorry for everything I did," I said. "I love you."

She snickered. "You've apologized to me about a thousand times this week and I already told you I forgive you."

"I know, but I was so mean to you and—"

Avery dragged me back into a hug. "It's *okay*, Cherri. We all had a tough time. If something happened to Ali, I can't say I wouldn't act the same. It's fine. Let's just put it behind us."

I squeezed onto her, loving the feeling of my best friend in my hands once again. "Okay. I'd like that."

We finally released, and Avery turned to Sicily with just as bright a smile. "Hi, Sicily."

"What's goin' on, Avery?" Sicily replied. "I forget. Are you one of the single ones?"

I backhanded his arm, frowning. "What is *wrong* with you?"

Sicily shrugged. "What? Your old pal Sicily's been working hard lately. It'd be nice to have a pretty face to come home to."

Avery didn't seem at all bothered by the question. "Well, as much as I think I'd enjoy being your pretty face, I am *not* single. I'm with Alistair."

"None of the girls in The Royal Court are single," I added on.

Sicily deflated. "Figures."

He shoved past Avery and walked into the house with his arms limply at his side, and though I knew he was mostly kidding, I also knew Sicily was an undercover romantic. Being in the house with all the couples was going to be hard on him.

I looked at Avery. "I don't suppose you know anyone we could set him up with?"

Avery shrugged. "No one that he doesn't already know. He'll find someone though, I'm sure. Sicily's awesome."

"He really is. It'd be nice if he could have someone great," I said. "Although, truth be told, I don't think anyone in The Royal Court is actually up to the task. He needs someone a little quirkier than we are."

"I'll keep an eye out," Avery said. "Well, come on in. Everyone's here."

"Oh." I hesitated in the doorway. "Really?"

Avery looped an arm around mine and pulled. "Come on, Cherri. Everyone here loves you and is very happy to see you. It'll be okay. We want to discuss what to do next about Connor and Deon."

I took a deep breath in and held it for a few seconds, then I slowly let it out. "Okay. I'm ready."

I hadn't seen The Royal Court since the day we defeated Connor's henchmen. I sat in Nathan's living room and sobbed until my eyes were sore, and then embarrassingly dragged myself out with Sicily and hadn't been back since. Apart from a few texts back and forth with Nathan to make my new living arrangements and several apologetic calls to Avery, I hadn't even spoken to them in the week since it all had happened. Why I was so nervous, I didn't know. They'd all been my friends before— maybe it was because they'd all changed so much, just like me.

Avery pulled, and I relented to her as she led us inside, shutting the door behind us. I could hear the quiet murmur of voices from the living room that got louder as we approached. Eventually, we rounded the corner to see that Sicily had already made himself comfortable on one of the plush couches and was chatting happily with Kyle. Nathan, Nikita, Jaxon, Colette and Alistair were also scattered around. As soon as we walked in, everyone looked up and smiled at me, and each gave me their own cheery greetings.

Colette, Alistair, Nathan and Kyle each stood up to hug me, while Jaxon nodded and smiled at me. Nikita just watched me. She and I still weren't on great terms, I imagined. If it wasn't the fact that I dated the man she was in love with for close to four years, then it was the fact that we'd gotten into a fight wherein she had swiftly kicked my ass. It was a blow to my ego, but it was also the beginning of my realization that I'd gotten so far beyond myself that I needed to re-evaluate what was going on in my life. She was still upset with me for punching Colette until she passed out, so her list of reasons to remain upset with me was long.

"Hey guys," I said, sitting down next to Sicily on the couch. "It's good to see you."

"I put your bag up in your room," Nathan said. "Sicily said you've already had a long day, so we don't have to do too much today, I was just hoping we could talk about what's next."

Right down to business—that was Nathan for you. "Yeah, that's fine with me."

"Sicily, how are the phones going?" Nathan asked.

Sicily let out an exhausted sigh. "It's goin', that's about all I can say. The unknown number that called you and the one that called Cherri definitely came from the same phone, but it was meant to be a burner. Now, Deon ain't some criminal mastermind despite the persona he puts on, so he didn't have a traditional, untraceable phone. From what I can gather, he was using an app to do it, but the app still scrambled the signal enough that I'm struggling to pinpoint where it came from or where it might be now. It gives me a massive list of possible pinged locations and I have to research them all individually and check them against places Deon *could* have been most likely. It's time consuming, but I ain't givin' up, I just need more time."

Nathan nodded. "Okay. Thank you for doing so much work on it. Take all the time you need."

"You say that," Nikita cut in, "but that's our only lead."

"Not the only one," Kyle replied. "We do have one other option. Brayden."

"We haven't been able to contact him," Nathan replied.

"*You* haven't," Kyle said, and there was a hint of arrogance in his voice. "He called me yesterday." I'd seen glimpses of it, but there was a new bond between Kyle and Brayden that I neither expected nor understood. Hopefully being around would give me a little more insight.

"Do you think you could get him to talk to us?" I asked. "I'd really love to talk to him."

Kyle nodded at me, and it was then that I

noticed how exhausted he seemed. "It'll take some doing, but I can get it done."

"Then while Sicily works on the phones, we'll go talk to Brayden," Nathan said.

"Not too many people," Kyle said. "I don't want to spook him."

"Just the three of us then," I said. "You, me, and Nathan."

Kyle nodded. "Yeah. I think that's the safest bet."

"Tomorrow, then?" Nathan asked.

Kyle and I locked eyes in silent agreement, and said the same thing in unison. "Tomorrow."

3
____

DEON

It felt weird not having my heart pounding out of control. For months, I'd constantly been on the run, constantly dodging the police, at the same time ducking the men my father had hunting me. I was trying to figure out exactly where my father was, all while being at large in the wake of violating my parole. Being stressed had become my new permanent state of mind.

Thanks to Venom, that was about to come to a stop, at least for a little bit. I stared out the window of my taxi at the large, three-story, green and white bungalow that he'd described to me. He wasn't able to give me much when I took the risk to go and visit him in prison, but he was able to potentially give me the most important thing—somewhere to stay with someone I could trust.

"You good, sir?" the cab driver asked.

I jumped a little bit, but turned and nodded at her. "Yeah, I'm good. Thanks."

I leaned over the seat and handed the driver the $500 that one of the prison guards had supplied me on Venom's behalf to pay the taxi with. A nearly two-hour drive from upstate Maine to the Japanese-inspired city of Ushuru near Maine's border was probably a little outside of the driver's purview, but whatever the guard who Venom had help me told him was enough to develop confidence or fear that the trip would be worth it. $500 for a single ride was probably a good trade off for the fares he lost shoveling me halfway across the state.

I opened the door, offered a final, "Bye," to the driver and then climbed out. Venom must have used intimidation to get me my ride, because the door had just barely met the frame before the driver was screeching away.

Whatever. That driver having a little pee in his pants was the last thing I needed to be worried about. Unkempt was an understated description for my appearance, but I did the best I could to comb my hair back with my fingers and smooth down my beard, though it was a far cry from my typical short goatee and much closer to a lumberjack goatee now. A shower would be needed for sure, and I'd have to start a new collection of clothes, but for now the mission was to just knock on the door.

With a deep breath, I walked up the sidewalk and up to the large white door. It had a giant "beware of dog" sign on it, but there were far scarier things in my life, so I knocked. Immediately, a dog's deep, bass-filled bark emanated from the other side of the door, followed by a woman yelling, "Concrete, hush!" Footsteps got closer and closer to the door until the door finally unlocked and opened. "Hello. You must be Deon."

The woman standing in the doorway was as beautiful as Venom had told me she would be. She had mocha skin, bright hazel eyes, and long, black braids held up on top of her head in a twisted bun. Even though it was mid-day, and she was dressed in a tank top and sweatpants, she had on a full face of makeup. She was curvaceous, slender and tall—there was no need to guess why Venom snatched her off the market. Behind her, there was a large, charcoal gray pitbull who was sitting, but had his eyes dead set for me.

"Yeah. Venom sent me," I said.

She smiled. "You've had a rough time I hear." She stood aside. "Come on in. Let's see if we can't get you in better shape." Even the tone of her voice was warm and inviting. It made me miss my mom.

There was something familiar about her that I couldn't quite pinpoint, but I was so happy to just be in a warm, inviting place again, I didn't care. "Thank you." I walked past her, into the house, and the pitbull quickly stepped up to me and started sniffing. I stood perfectly still and let him get a read. "Hello."

Behind me, the woman laughed. "I'm Felicity, and that's Concrete. He's a good boy. As long as you don't pose a threat to him, he won't pose a threat to you. He loves ear scratches."

In response to that, I crouched down a little and reached a hand out to start scratching behind Concrete's ear. Immediately, his tongue rolled forward out of his mouth and he flashed me an adorable dog smile, his tail wagging back and forth with vigor. "Ah, you're a good boy," I said, and he lunged forward a little to lick my face.

Felicity walked past us and down the long hallway that jutted out from her front door. Rooms to the left and right looked like a living room and dining room respectively, and the hallway led down into what appeared to be a kitchen. I stood up and followed her down, Concrete at my heels, into the large, open kitchen with a table of its own. Glass doors led out to the backyard and were a beautiful depiction of the wooded area that was nestled behind. It was a stunning home.

"Go ahead and sit down. Are you allergic to anything?" Felicity asked.

"Penicillin," I replied.

She chuckled. "I promise not to put any penicillin in your food."

"I'd appreciate it," I said, sitting down at one of the kitchen table's chairs. Concrete continued over to a water bowl against the wall and started to lap up scoops of water. "Thank you so much, by the way. It's been a long time since I've been somewhere comfortable."

"That's what Garrett tells me."

I tilted my head. "Garrett?"

She looked up and furrowed her brow, then unwrinkled her face as the realization hit her. "Sorry, Venom. I know him by his government name, Garrett."

I offered a small smile. "I never knew that was his real name."

"Yeah, well you know. He's got super tough appearances to keep up," she said with a laugh. "I'm surprised he didn't tell you, though."

"Why do you say that?" I asked.

"Because, Venom really cares about you. He'd

never send someone to see his wife unless he really trusted them," she replied. " He talks about you like you're his *actual* son. We've never had any kids of our own, but I don't know, every time he would call me and be like, 'I love this kid,'" she did a deep voice to imitate Venom, "I would think to myself, 'Sounds to me like I have a son I've never met before.'"

It was nice to know that Venom truly cared about me. I never understood why he took me under his wing so suddenly when I was locked up, or why he looked out for me as vigorously as he did, but even when I went to visit him, I was met with an intense desire to help me. He pulled all the strings he had, making sure the guards didn't violate me even though I was at large, and immediately gave me Felicity's address, telling me to come see her and stay with her. He was doing what an *actual* dad would do, and all from behind bars.

Connor Loche could go jump in a ditch for all I cared. I had a dad as far as I was concerned.

"He said it'd be easier to communicate with him if I was here," I said.

Felicity nodded as she pulled ingredients out of her fridge and started to mix them together. I had no idea what she was making, but it didn't take long before seasonings and spices filled the air and made my stomach grumble. "Yes. I'm also his lawyer, so it keeps all of our communications privileged."

"That's a neat trick," I responded.

Felicity snickered. "Well, to be fair, I was his lawyer first. He started asking me out, and even though I was strict about not mixing business with pleasure, there was just something about him. I knew he was the man for me. So I broke a few rules."

Silence filled the kitchen as Felicity worked on a particularly hearty brunch. She combined eggs, bacon and a variety of veggies into a delicious omelet and then made some hashbrowns with cheese and topped it all off with buttered toast. She poured me a glass of orange juice and then brought both the plate and the juice over to me and set them down in front of me. My stomach growled as I stared in awe at the best food I'd seen in close to nine months.

"Wow. Thank you so much," I said.

"Of course. There's more where that came from, so if you want another one, just let me know."

"After this, I'm going to fall asleep immediately," I said.

She laughed. "I've got a room all prepared for you, when you're ready."

I closed my eyes and breathed in a sigh of relief. "Good food and a nice place to sleep have been luxuries for me lately."

Felicity set a hand on my head. "Well, we're going to change that, aren't we?"

With that, she walked away and left me to my food. I ended up scarfing it down much quicker than I was planning on. It wasn't just that I hadn't had good food in a while, it was the fact that it was absolutely delicious. It was the best food I ever had, and apart from a few pieces of errant bacon that fell for Concrete to lick up, I ate every crumb on the plate.

Felicity happened to walk back through the kitchen at the exact moment I was finishing up, and laughed. "Wow. You weren't lying."

"You're an amazing cook," I said. "You should do this professionally."

"That's what Garrett tells me too. Unfortunately, his reputation follows me, so it's difficult to get a job at a notable restaurant."

"Start your own," I replied. "Open up a diner or food truck or something. With cooking like this, you'd clean house."

"Being a lawyer pays pretty good. Besides, I love cooking. I'd much prefer it to be a hobby than a job." She grabbed my plate and empty cup. "Do you want more?"

"I'm okay for now, thank you."

"Well then, come on, I'll show you to your bedroom."

She set my plate and cup on the counter near the sink, then started back down the hallway we walked in from. I stood up and followed her down, with Concrete sticking close. We walked through the doorway that was to the right of the front door, and there was a staircase on the other side of the wall leading up. She led up the stairs and down a subsequent hallway at the top of the stairs to the last door down the hallway to the left.

Setting a hand on the handle, she pointed back down the hallway to a door past the stairs leading down. "My bedroom's down there. You'll be in here."

She opened the door and I looked into a simple, but comfortable looking bedroom. There was a king-size sleigh bed centered in a recess against the back wall in front of large french windows. Matching bedside tables had plants sitting on top, and there was a dresser with a vanity against the western wall, right next to another door. A couple of chairs sat perpendicular to one another with a table in the southeastern corner of the room and an area rug sat center in the room. It made me sleepy just to look at.

Felicity pointed over to the door next to the dresser. "That door leads to your bathroom. There's fresh towels inside. I did buy a small supply of sweatpants, jeans, and plain t-shirts that are in the dresser there. Garrett told me about what size you were, so I made my best guess. Hopefully it fits, but if we have to go at some point and buy more stuff, we can do that no problem tomorrow."

"This…" My throat was actually knotting up a little at how kind Felicity and Venom were being to me. They really *were* treating me like I was their son. "Thank you for all of this."

"Of course." She stepped back out through the doorway, but Concrete ran further into the room and hopped up on the bed. "Looks like you have a roommate. That okay?"

"Yeah. I think it'll be comforting having him here," I said.

"He's got insane intuition, that one. He might be able to sense that you need a buddy. Just kick him out if he gets on your nerves. Sleep as long as you like. Garrett has a few people he wants to come by and lay eyes on ya just in case, but I told them to come slowly starting tomorrow so that you have some time to recoup. If you need anything, just let me know."

"I will. Thanks, Felicity," I replied.

She gave me one final smile, then left, pulling the door closed as she went.

I had no frame of reference for what time it was when I went to sleep other than the fact that the sun was up, which it was not when I woke up. Concrete was no longer in the room, so he must have gotten bored with me and barked or scratched until Felicity let him out. When my eyes finally adjusted to the dark, I could see there was a wrapped sandwich, bag of chips, and a bottle of water sitting on the dresser, and I smiled.

I was supposed to be looking for Connor, but I would enjoy being in a warm, comfortable home while I could.

Felicity had downplayed the number of people Venom wanted to meet me just a bit. Over the course of a few days, about ten different people came to meet me and assure me that, so long as I was at Felicity's house, Connor Loche wouldn't be able to touch me. Different rotations of the people stuck around the house at any given time, either watching the house from the outside, or sitting inside with us, enjoying a meal and conversation.

"Thank you for doing this," I told one of the last ones I saw before going to bed one night.

"No need to thank me," he said. "Venom's been good to me. I'd do anything for his kid."

His kid.

Hopefully I'd be able to look Connor in his eyes one day soon and tell him that someone was doing the job he was supposed to do, leagues better than he had done it.

And then I'd end his life.

4

CHERRI

There was a knock on my door followed by it opening and Sicily poking his head in. "Mornin'!"

"Good morning," I replied. "How'd you sleep?"

Sicily walked in, shutting the door behind him, and found a place to sit cross-legged on the floor despite the number of chairs around the room. "Are you kiddin' me? This place is like a hotel compared to my place. Don't get me wrong, I love my family, but a king-size bed all to myself in a sound-proof room is a massive step up from my brother's hand-me-down full with half the springs broken and no screaming kids running around. I'm in heaven."

"Well good. I'm glad I have you here. I'd feel uncomfortable otherwise."

"Why is that?" Sicily asked. "You've been friends with them much longer than you've been friends with me."

"I think it's because I'm not the person I was when I was with them. I put on a front, one I started to believe by the end of it, but that wasn't who I really am. When Deon showed up, I started to remember my old self and then this whole time I've been friends with you, it's been as myself. I mean, I know I lost it for a little bit there, but when we weren't at school and just hanging out, all of that was the real me. In a weird way, I feel like our friendship is built on something much more solid than my friendship with any of them was built on. Even Avery."

"Yeah, you're nuts about Avery though. I can see it," Sicily replied. "You just gotta show 'em more of *this* you, then. That's all. Avery's so over the moon that you're back that she wouldn't give a rip regardless. Hey, if Sicily can learn to love ya as you are, so can they."

"Hanging up hacking for psychology?" I joked.

He let out his gruff, raspy chuckle. "Nah, but I'll tell it like it is to a friend." He stood up and tapped my leg. "Come on. They're all downstairs havin' breakfast. Time to introduce them to the real Cherri."

With Sicily feeling so confident, I started to feel better myself and stood up off the bed. He led the way back out of the bedroom and down the stairs to where the entire Royal Court, apart from Brayden, was gathered eating from breakfast platters laid family-style in the middle of a kitchen island surrounded by stools that they were sitting on. There were a few remaining stools and Sicily and I walked in and sat down.

"Good morning," Avery said to me brightly. "How'd you sleep?"

"Not bad," I replied. "I don't sleep well in general, but it was really comfortable. I think I'll sleep better once we've found and talked to Brayden."

"I know where he is," Kyle said. "It's going to be a bit of an ambush, but as long as I can get in there and talk, I should be able to get to him."

"Okay, I trust you. When we get there, I'll leave it up to you," I said.

"Did you guys know that Cherri has a potty mouth?" Sicily said suddenly.

I looked over at him. "What are you doing?"

"And she *loves* trash talk. I'll tell you something, when you get a few drinks in this girl and wind her up, she'll tell you all the worst things about yourself and then laugh about it." He chuckled. "She nearly convinced me to shave my entire beard once."

"Please stop doing what you're doing," I said.

"You know, that's funny you say that, because whenever I wanted Cherri's honest opinion about something, I'd get her drunk first," Avery said. "That makes so much sense now."

"I noticed that potty mouth too over the course of the past six months," Alistair said.

"Not just the past six months," Colette said. "From when Deon first came back. She was throwing f-bombs like they were sprinkles."

Then everyone erupted into laughter. It was Nathan who noticed first how I was staring at the interaction in confused shock, and he smiled at me. "Cherri, relax. We know that you're not the same person you were when you were in The Royal Court before."

"Yeah." Avery wrapped an arm around my shoulder. "We want to get to know the real you, so don't hold back, okay?"

"Okay," I said. "I'll admit, I'm struggling with how to… I don't know, just fucking exist right now." Sicily did a knowing nod at me, and it was only then that I realized that I swore. I was about to apologize, but then realized that was the exact opposite of the point, so I didn't. "It's not like *no* parts of me from before were parts of who I am, but I was the more princessy version of myself."

"You were who you were when it was just you and Sicily, right?" Colette asked. "This isn't any different. Be with us how you are with him."

I snickered. "That seems like the quickest way to get you all to fucking hate me."

Kyle chuckled. "I am so here for Cherri dropping 'fuck' at seven in the morning."

After that, breakfast wasn't as uncomfortable as I expected it to be. We exchanged stories about how things were for all of us during the second semester of school, and heard the other side of the stories of my nasty fights with Colette and Nikita. Even though I easily could have come off looking like the shit-head I was, they told the stories in sympathetic ways that made me feel better, and it really changed the way I saw both women.

I didn't get much of an apology out before they stopped me. Everyone was desperate to put the last semester of our senior year behind us, which I was more than happy to do.

"So... how long before we can go talk to Brayden?" I asked. "I don't want to rush us or anything, but Deon's still out there and he could be in trouble."

"Whenever we're ready," Kyle said. "I told him I want to see him today, and he agreed, so we just need to decide where and when."

"Is… um…" I had a specific question I wanted to ask, but I wasn't sure how to ask it. "Will it be okay?" That wasn't quite what I was going for, but Kyle's lips flattened into a line as if he understood what I was trying to ask.

He nodded at me. "It'll be fine."

"Then, can we go soon? Within the next hour maybe?" I asked.

Instead of responding, Kyle simply pulled out his cell phone. He only needed to hit a couple of buttons, and then he brought the phone up to his ear. After a few minutes, he said, "Hey." There was a strain in his voice, but a warmth that was almost unfamiliar from the typically resolved, even-toned man. "How'd you sleep?" It almost felt awkward to just be listening to the conversation, but everyone sat there without saying anything, so I did the same. "Well, it'll get better, I promise. Hey, can we meet up soon? Maybe in like an hour?" He looked over at me and nodded then said, "Okay. Let's meet at the park by school. Okay. See you soon. Bye."

"Just a few of you are going, right?" Colette asked.

"That's best. It'll be good if Nathan's there, and then Cherri obviously, and me," Kyle replied.

Colette crossed her arms. "I feel like we're not helping enough. What should we do?"

Sicily slowly raised his hand. "Uh, I could use some help."

"Really?" Avery asked. "How?"

"Well, it's like I said yesterday, I have to manually check like a million pings to try and find which phone Deon called from. It's not hard to learn. If the rest of you were willing, I could show you and you guys could help me check pings."

"Oh wow! That sounds interesting," Avery said. "I'm in."

"Yeah… Interesting. Sure." Sicily let out a chuckle. "If that's what it takes for your help."

Jaxon looked over at Colette. "I am *not* sitting in front of a computer all day."

Colette giggled and petted the back of his head. "That's fine. You just keep me from going insane."

He let out a sigh and a nod. "I can do that."

"Alright, those are the teams then," Nathan said. "The three of us will go to Brayden, Nikki, Colette, Alistair, Avery and Jaxon, you all stay and help Sicily."

"Break!" Colette yelped, but no one moved. She

shrugged and popped a grape into her mouth. "Screw you guys. It felt like a 'break' moment."

After finishing up our breakfast, I said goodbye to Sicily, and then Nathan, Kyle and I piled into Kyle's truck. I relented the front seat to Nathan, because sitting in the front with Kyle seemed a little awkward, but being in the back didn't help much. The ride was totally silent, and there was a tension between Kyle and Nathan that I couldn't quite pinpoint. Part of me wanted to ask, but the other part thought that might shatter the stasis, so I didn't.

Eventually, we got to the park near Postings Proper High School, and Brayden's car was already parked in the lot. Kyle parked next to it and Nathan and I started to climb out, but Kyle didn't move. I managed to make it all the way out of the truck, but Nathan noticed me looking back at Kyle and climbed back into the front seat.

"You good?" he asked.

"He's gonna hate me," Kyle said. "He's gonna feel like we're ambushing him."

Nathan nodded with a snicker. "Yeah, well, after what he pulled he should be a little understanding." Kyle glared over at Nathan and I got nervous they were going to erupt, but Nathan seemed unphased. "Don't look at me like that. We babied him a *lot* during the last six months and he fucking sold us out."

"You promised me you weren't mad," Kyle said.

"I'm not, but I'm not going to tiptoe around him either. He owes us for what he did. The only reason I'm not beating it out of him is because you asked me not to."

"I'll kick your ass if you touch him," Kyle hissed.

"Okay," I interjected. "What the hell is going on?" Both Kyle and Nathan looked over at me with shock on their faces. "Last I checked, Kyle you didn't even fucking like Brayden, and he was Nathan's goddamn mini me. What did I miss?"

Nathan raised an eyebrow. "A lot." He looked back at Kyle. "I'm not gonna hurt him. I know my dad manipulated him too, but if I go walking out there he's not going to listen. We need you there, or this is useless. He'll forgive you because if he doesn't he's an ass." Kyle sat in silence, and all Nathan and I could do was sit there as well. Finally, Nathan put a hand on Kyle's shoulder. "We have to do something or he's going to drift so far away even *you* won't be able to bring him back. You don't want that. I know you don't."

Kyle shook his head. "No."

"Then let's go get him." That seemed to do the trick and Kyle finally unbuckled his seatbelt. As Nathan climbed out of the truck, he leaned in towards me. "This is gonna get weird, so just stand back."

"Since when does *he* care so much?" I whispered back.

Nathan flashed me an indignant expression. "Like I said… you missed a lot."

We walked around the car and followed Kyle further into the park. It was already shaping up to be a hot summer day, so the park was full of families enjoying the morning before it got too steamy. We stepped around everyone and made our way towards the picnic tables behind the initial playground, and Brayden was sitting on one of the tables facing away from us. Kyle did a stutter step when we first saw him, but kept going and when we were close enough, Nathan grabbed my arm to keep me from getting any closer.

Kyle walked up to the table and reached out to touch Brayden's shoulder. To my surprise, Brayden almost immediately climbed down and threw himself into a hug, one Kyle returned with passion.

"Nathan, what's going on?" I asked.

Before Nathan could answer, Brayden noticed

us over Kyle's shoulder and yanked himself back out of the hug.

"What are they doing here?" he asked. "You said it was just you."

"They need to talk to you," Kyle said. "They aren't angry."

"Bullshit. Nathan's fuming," Brayden barked.

Kyle looked over his shoulder and I looked over and saw Nathan *was* tense and glaring. I smacked his arm and he dropped a little out of it, relaxing his shoulders and attempting to calm his face.

"They just want to talk," Kyle said.

"No." Brayden turned around and started to walk away, but Kyle reached out and grabbed his arm and pulled him back. He snatched himself from Kyle's hold, but Kyle reached out again, attempting to grab Brayden again. "Stop it. Don't touch me."

"Brayden, don't do this," Kyle said. "Just—"

Before Kyle could get any additional words out, Brayden shot his fist out, making hard contact with Kyle's nose. When it happened, a look of horror flashed across Brayden's face before guilt settled in. He tried again to walk away, but Kyle reached out and grabbed Brayden's hand.

"Stop," Brayden said, and it was weak, like he was begging. "Just let me leave."

"You need to face this." Kyle pulled, but Brayden swung again. That time, Kyle ducked out of the way, but then Brayden swung back with his other fist, hitting Kyle's face again. I took a step forward, but Nathan pulled me back. "Brayden."

"Just let me go!" Brayden screamed. "I nearly killed you!"

"But you didn't," Kyle replied. He had a firm grip on Brayden's hand and refused to let go. Regardless of the hits he'd taken, he was standing tall, unphased. "I didn't die. None of us did. We know that you were backed into a corner."

All of the fight in Brayden deflated and tears filled the corners of his eyes. "I thought you were going to die. I thought I killed you. Just let me leave. I don't deserve—"

"Brayden!" Kyle snapped. "Look at me." Brayden slowly lifted his head and looked at Kyle. "Why am I still here?"

"I don't know," Brayden said.

"Yes you do," Kyle replied quickly. "Didn't I already tell you? I'm not going anywhere." My whole body covered with goosebumps as Kyle placed both of his hands on either side of Brayden's neck and looked directly into his eyes. Brayden's hands came up to rest on Kyle's wrists, and all at once I realized that 'a lot' hardly covered what

I'd missed. "They aren't mad. I mean, they're mad at the situation, but they aren't mad at *you*. They just want to talk. Will you talk to them please?"

"You won't leave?" Brayden asked.

Kyle flashed a small, warm smile. "Where would I go?"

Brayden nodded and Kyle pulled his hands away from Brayden, but stayed close to him as they turned to walk towards us. With each step, Brayden dwarfed more and more between his own shoulders, but once he was close enough, I charged forward. He winced, but I threw my arms around his shoulders in a hug.

"Um," Brayden said in my ear. "What?"

He never did hug me back, but I chalked it up to shock as I backed up and smiled at him. "Hey. I'm happy to see you."

"Really?" he asked.

"Yeah. I'm glad you're okay, and though I do want to hit you a little," I admitted, "I'm not going to. Right now, you're the best lead we have to finding Connor and Deon. If you're sorry for what happened, at all, you'll tell us everything you know."

Brayden gave Nathan a sideways glance. Nathan nodded, then he looked back at me. "Okay. I swear. I'll tell you everything."

5

DEON

It was a quiet morning at Felicity's when I finally woke up for the day. I'd gotten in the habit of sleeping until damn near noon, because each minute I spent awake, I hated that I wasn't doing something to track down Connor. Felicity had spoken with Venom and he was working on getting one of his contacts in line to meet with me. Felicity had this contact's info, but Venom insisted on talking to him first. While we were waiting, I'd settled into lounging around, which it turned out, I hated.

"Good morning," Felicity said as I entered the living room. Concrete was laying on the floor in front of her and looked up with a happy pant as I entered the room. "Or rather, good afternoon."

"Hey." I walked in and sat down in one of the arm chairs and Concrete walked over for some pets, which he got. "Did you sleep okay?"

"I did. How about you?" I nodded and she smiled. "Good. Do you want me to make you something for lunch?"

"Maybe in a little bit," I replied. "Have you heard from Venom?"

"Not yet," she said. "He's working on it, Deon. You just have to be patient."

"Connor could be trying to kill my brother or Cherri as we speak," I said. "I don't like just sitting around. I want to do something."

"Well, surely your brother has social media. Cherri too. Why don't you use my computer to check on them? You can't make contact with them, but you could see if any of them have updated recently so that you know they're safe. Or what about your mom?"

The idea of at least being able to see Nathan, or possibly even Cherri or my mom felt like doing more than nothing. "Yeah. Okay, that'd be good."

"Okay. Wait here." Felicity stood up and walked out of the living room and returned a few minutes later with her laptop in hand. She opened it, entering her password, then she handed it to me. "I'm already logged in on all the major socials, so just browse around as me, and even if someone happens to see it somehow, they'll think it's just some random woman."

"Thanks, Felicity."

I started with my mom. She was old school and just had the basic posts and pictures page that everyone had when social media became popular. It was easy enough to find her doing a search of her first and last name, and relief quickly settled in when I saw that she had posted just earlier that day. I scrolled through her posts, noticing that her statuses covered the same basic things—food, thoughts on her favorite shows, frustrations with work—but then I came across one that confused me a little.

From about two days prior, there was a post about her being sad to say goodbye to her room-mate. A few people had commented on it, mostly coworkers, but no one said *who* the roommate was. Had my mom been living with someone? The entire four years I was locked up, she never got a roommate, why all of a sudden after I disappeared? Grief?

I spent a little bit of time scrolling through her page, trying to find any information about who this roommate was, but though she alluded to the roommate a few additional times over the course of a handful of months, she never said the roommate's name or even mentioned a gender. It freaked me out a little to think that someone random had been living with my mom, but she didn't seem to be forced into anything, and was sad they were gone now.

I'd just have to add it to the list of many questions that needed answering.

Once I was confident that I had an understanding of what my mom was up to, I turned my attention to Nathan, and his results weren't nearly as inspiring. He, along with most of the members of The Royal Court, hadn't updated their social media much in the past six months. There was the odd passing selfie, mostly by Colette, and each of them had shared a memory or two of the year's prior summer season, but I anticipated they were sharing them mostly in the place of a lack of those happy feelings this year.

I did see a sweet selfie of Nathan and Nikita which led me to believe that they were maybe together, finally, but there was very little to tell me how any of them were doing *today*.

"Disappointing news?" Felicity said, walking back into the room yet again with a bowl of chili. She set it on the table next to me and walked around to stand behind me.

"Just no news," I said.

"No news is good news." She pointed at the picture of Nathan and Nikita I was looking at. "Who are they?"

"The guy is my brother, Nathan, and that woman is one of his best friends of all time, Nikita. They look pretty friendly though, they may actually be together now," I explained.

"Don't sound so happy for him."

"Well, I actually am happy for him, but he was supposed to be looking after Cherri for me, and I don't know how much attention Nikita would let him pay to her."

"How come?"

I thought of the one, brief interaction I'd seen Cherri and Nikita have and how contentious it was. "Not only do Nikita and Cherri not care for one another very much, but Nathan and Cherri dated for years."

"Your brother dated your girl?" Felicity asked. "Knowingly?"

"Yeah, but..." I shrugged. "Connor is such a fucked-up man, I have *no* idea how much of Nathan's bullshit was him and how much was Connor manipulating him. I don't even think I really know my brother."

"You wanna get to know him?" Felicity said.

"I'd like to. We had about a year together when we were preteens, but I didn't like being away from my mom. That's what set Connor off I think, the fact that I left. Nathan's apologized to me, and when we were kids we actually got along really well."

"If you can just get Connor out of the mix, you two will be much better off." She scoffed. "Hell, half the country will be much better off." Then she slapped my shoulder. "Show me this girl. *Cherri*. You've talked about her nonstop."

She wasn't telling any lies. Sometimes I felt like as long as I said Cherri's name from time to time it would keep her near me somehow. It was just like when I was behind bars, I did whatever I could to remind myself of the incredible woman that I once had. With any luck, she'd have moved on by now, but I'd always love her. Nothing would ever change that.

I navigated through Nathan's friends list to Cherri's page. There were no new pictures of her, and the most recent one was the selfie she took on the day of Nathan's birthday party first semester. Her signature, long blond hair and crystal blue eyes were just as perfect as I remembered, and I would have given up anything in order to just hold her and talk to her.

"Oh wow," Felicity said. "She's a knockout."

"Tell me about it," I replied.

"Oh my god," Felicity whined, then she pinched my cheek. "Look at you. Your expression got all soft and sweet. I didn't think you were capable."

"Shut up," I grumbled, but a small smile came to my face anyway. "You see her. How could I not?"

"I hope I get to meet this girl someday. I gotta give her my mom once-over. How does your *real* mom feel about her?" Felicity asked.

"Adores her. You would too. I know it sounds cheesy and cliche, but she's perfect." Felicity put her hands to her mouth and I closed the computer. "Alright, we're done with that." I missed Cherri too much to continue having that conversation anyway.

"Do you feel better at least?" Felicity asked. She walked from behind me and went and sat down on the couch, with Concrete following her in search of head scratches.

"I wish I could call Nathan," I said honestly. "The last time we spoke, Connor's goons grabbed me, and he probably thinks I'm dead." I looked at Felicity. "Nathan's careful. He has to be using an untraceable phone at this point. I won't share any information. Just call him from your phone and tell him I'm okay."

"It's not a good idea, D," Felicity said. "Even if one person immediately knows that we contacted them, if Connor has people watching them, which he no doubt does, if they change pace at all in a way that would suggest you're okay, they could snatch him, and then they're just a call log away from knowing where you are."

"We'll tell him to del—"

"You know as well as I do that anything is recoverable on a phone," Felicity said. "Unless you have a hyper hacker at your fingertips."

A friendly face immediately came to mind. Technically, Nathan *did* have a hyper hacker at his fingertips, but whether or not the two of them were even speaking to one another was a mystery to me. If he *was* working with Sicily, he'd probably already advised against answering unknown numbers, so it probably wasn't going to work to call from Felicity's phone regardless once I thought about it.

"Yeah," I settled for.

"I'm sorry," Felicity said, and her voice had true anguish in it. "Hopefully we'll be done with all this nastiness soon and you can get back to your family."

"Well, even if I can go back to Cherri and Nathan, I still won't have Venom. That sucks," I said. "I wish there was a way to get him out too."

Felicity went eerily quiet at that. She took a deep breath in, opened her mouth like she was going to say something, and then stopped short. "What?" I asked.

"Well… There *is* a way… technically, but…" She looked at me sadly.

"But what?"

"You… love Venom, right? Like a dad?" Felicity asked.

"Yeah," I said.

"Good, then hopefully what I'm about to tell you won't change your opinion of him."

I shook my head. "After everything he's done for me and my shit-for-brains sperm donor, that'd be pretty fucking difficult."

"I wouldn't be so sure." She lifted the remote from the couch and turned off the television which had been droning in the background. "Venom would kill me if he knew I was telling you this, but I think you deserve to know. You and his paths did not cross by chance."

"What do you mean?" I asked.

"There's a lot that you don't know about how you and Venom found one another, and I have a funny feeling you *aren't* going to like this story."

6

———

CHERRI

Once Brayden agreed to tell us what he knew, he asked for a few minutes to speak with Kyle alone. That was nearly an hour ago and Nathan and I were still standing far enough back to not be invasive, waiting for any sign of our ride being ready to go.

It was the first time I'd been alone with Nathan since his attack in the bathroom, and that must have been what was on his mind as well, because he was keeping his distance. For as awful as that was and as much as I wasn't about to give Nathan a total pass for raping me, I didn't really blame him for what happened. His father was as sociopathic as they come, and I knew firsthand the pressure he was under. Deon told me that Nathan had been under that level of stress since they were kids. He barely handled it as a teenager; how on earth he managed to survive up to that point was beyond me.

"Are you uncomfortable?" Nathan asked finally, breaking the silence between us. "Around me, I mean."

"I won't lie, it's a little weird, but I'm not afraid, if that's what you mean," I replied.

He tipped his head back and forth. "In a strange way, that's better than I thought." He turned to look at me properly. "Would it make you really uncomfortable to be alone with me for an hour or so?"

"You mean an additional one?" I asked.

He chuckled. "Yeah. By design."

"Um, I think that would be okay."

His eyes widened, but then softened. "Cool. Let's give these two some space and I can explain a little bit."

"That'd be good."

Nathan lifted a hand and called out towards Kyle and Brayden, "Hey, we're gonna Uber back. Just come along when you're ready."

Kyle stood up and shook his head. "No, sorry, here we come."

"Seriously," I interjected. "It's fine. Take your time."

Kyle looked at Brayden, then us, then Brayden, then us, then quickly shuffled over. He dragged his keys out of his pocket and handed them towards Nathan. "Take my truck at least." He looked at me and raised an eyebrow. "You good?"

"Yeah, I'm good." I set a hand on his arm. "Go. What's a few more hours?"

"Thanks, Cherri," Kyle said, then with one look back at Nathan, he ran off to return to Brayden, where the two easily fell back into conversation. At one point they smiled at each other, and my heart leapt.

"Okay, let's go fast, because I need to understand," I said.

Nathan and I turned our backs to Kyle and Brayden and made our way back to the parking lot of the park. We climbed into Kyle's car, this time with Nathan in the driver's seat and me in the passenger's, and then Nathan started up the car.

"Question. Why did you say we'd be alone for an hour? Your house is only like fifteen minutes from here," I asked.

Nathan looped his hand over the back of the passenger's seat in order to back up. "Yeah. I was hoping we could just cruise and talk for a bit? I won't put us in the disgustingly awkward situation of sitting in a room face to face or anything. This way the road can be a nice buffer."

"Oh. Sure."

Nathan pulled out of the parking lot, but instead of turning right, which was how we would get to the highway to head back to his house, he turned left. I recognized it as the direction one could go to take the backstreets towards North Postings. It was how I got home every day when I was still living with Ciara. The backstreets into North Postings instead of the highway were about a 20 minute trip, and then taking the highway from North to South Postings would be about 30 minutes, bringing us close to that hour.

Once we were well on our way, Nathan cleared his throat. "So… Thank you, for being willing to talk to me. I know there's some things that I have to say, I just haven't had the courage to say it."

"I know. I wanna say some stuff too," I replied.

"It's weird, right? It doesn't feel like we're exes, but all that nastiness is still there. Not hostility, just muck. I know that's mostly my fault, but you know, Cherri. I think you're pretty amazing. You're strong and smart and funny, and even in the midst of all this shit, you refused to break. I broke several times. I don't know how you do it." It shocked me to hear a stream of such positive, genuine compliments coming out of Nathan's mouth. He didn't even seem like the same man that I'd dated for four years. "Sorry. Did I start off too strong?" he asked when I didn't respond.

I shook my head. "No, I just… You're different. No offense, but the only time you used to compliment me like that was when you wanted something from me. You're so, I don't know, genuine and down to earth all of a sudden. I honestly think that's why being around you guys is making me so uncomfortable. You're totally different people."

"So're you," Nathan responded.

I watched the blur of colors pass outside the window. "Well yeah. It's this feeling, deep in my gut, that if you all were the people you are now and I was the person I am now, back when we all met, we wouldn't be friends at all. It's hard. Like I'm forcing it."

"I mean, you're probably right," Nathan said. "But I think that's true for all of us, not just you versus The Royal Court. I mean, you saw Kyle and Brayden back there. Part of the pull for me with Brayden was that he'd do whatever I wanted. He's a whole person now. I feel like I'm just now getting to know him."

"What is that about?" I asked. "Are they…?"

Nathan blew out a sigh. "Yeah. Kind of."

"Really?" I turned to look at Nathan, shocked. "Okay. I'm sorry if I go a little gossipy right now, but fuck, I did not see that coming. Who started it? What happened? How? I didn't even know either of them, ya know, swung that way."

"I think the general consensus at this point is that Kyle is pansexual and Brayden is gay, but not out. I actually couldn't say for sure who started what. I was going through all of my own shit with my mom dying and my dad cutting out, Deon disappearing. Plus I was trying to navigate this really weird relationship with Nikita. I didn't think we were even going to make it. While all that was going on, one day I show up and I notice they're giving each other these looks and Kyle is talking about how often the two of them talk and see each other. It was clear out of the blue. Then when prom came, Kyle asked Brayden to be his date."

My jaw dropped and I hated that I cost myself seeing that. "Seriously?!"

"Yeah. At first it seemed like it was just a joke. We were talking about going as a big group or as pairs, and Brayden got kind of snippy because, you know, Nikki and me. Alistair and Avery. Jaxon and Colette. All couples, so even if we went as a group, it'd be obvious what was going on. Kyle up and asks him to be his date. We kind of laughed it off at first, but Brayden didn't think it was a joke ever and got *really* upset about it. When he stormed away from the table we could all see it, Kyle was shattered, like he'd just been rejected. I asked him about it later that day, but he wouldn't say much. It was Avery who told me she thought Kyle was pan, but didn't think he liked Brayden. Kyle later told Nikki that wasn't true."

"Why would you guys think he didn't like him if he asked him to prom?" I asked.

Nathan's face got a little more sullen. "Turns out, Brayden was in love with me."

I went silent with shock as hundreds of tiny moments clicked into place. Random fits of what could only be described as jealousy, and any time Brayden would get all too excited to hang out with Nathan. It never clicked with me because I never even considered Brayden in that way, but once I thought about it, it occurred to me that I never once saw him date or even look at a girl.

"Wow," I murmured. "You know, that actually makes so much sense."

"Yeah. Nikki said the same thing. I had no clue. It wasn't until just last week that Nikita even told me that. I guess Kyle realized it and tried to serve as something of a distraction and ended up catching feelings."

"Aw. That's kind of cute actually."

"I think so. They're good for each other, but it seems like, whether out of guilt or something else, Brayden just won't put his wall down. I hope it works out for them though."

"Me too."

Silence filled the car for a few seconds before Nathan started up again. "Cherri, I'm sorry. I'm so sorry for… what happened. In that bathroom. I…" His hands strangled the steering wheel. "I have nightmares about it. Fuck, I shouldn't even be saying something like that to you. I'm not the victim, but I hate that I hurt you. Maybe I didn't have feelings for you like the way I did for Nikita, but you were there for me. Always." I was surprised when tears filled the corners of his eyes. "Losing you felt like losing a part of myself and I didn't know how to reconcile that with the fact that there *was* a woman I was really in love with, or the fact that I'd hurt you so badly, and never really treated you like a person."

There were tears in my eyes before I could stop them. "Nathan."

"Sometimes, I have these dreams, that Deon is back and the four of us do like brunches and shit."

He laughed as a few tears slid down his face. "I love you, Cherri. I really do. You're like family to me. Not being able to just talk to you last semester killed me so much more than I was even willing to accept myself. I just wanted to tell you that I was sorry and make it up to you somehow. Not that something like that can ever be made up. Even Nikki struggled with it. Knowing what I'd done to you. It was only after Sicily told her that you don't blame me that we made it. You're the reason I get to be with the woman that I love, because your depth for forgiveness is so much more than it should be." He took a quick moment to glance over at me. "Thank you." Then his eyes were right back on the road.

"Fuck!" I snapped. "You made me cry, you dick."

"I know, I'm sor—"

"No!" I smacked his arm. "Not then, right now. What Sicily told Nikita is absolutely true. I'm not going to tell you what you did was okay, because it's not, but I even told Deon that I didn't feel like that was you. The shit your dad put you through, no person should have to endure. You just snapped. The fact that you didn't snap sooner is amazing. I don't know how *you* do it. There were times when I saw glimpses of who you really are and I thought to myself, 'If I got *this* Nathan all the time, I'd be happy with him.'"

"You have to stop. Your blind compliments are making me feel more guilty."

"Sorry, but it's true. You said you aren't the victim, but you are, Nathan. I'm really sorry about your mom, by the way. Your dad, he did a number on all of us. As far as I'm concerned, it was Connor that did that to me."

We pulled up to a stop light and Nathan looked over at me. "Thanks."

"Yeah." Then I threw out a fist and clocked him across the face.

"Fuck!" he screamed. "Shit, that hurt!"

"Now we're even," I said.

Nathan blinked a few times to clear his vision. "It still feels like I'm being let off the hook a little too easy."

"I could hit you again if you want."

"No," Nathan replied quickly. "Please don't."

I smiled. "I'm sorry too. For the past six months. For what I did to Colette and for… allowing Nikita to kick my ass. I saw the look on her face when you covered for me. I'm sure that led to some unpleasant conversations."

"Yeah. We didn't talk for a little bit after that. I deserved it though. Because I wasn't being honest with myself about my complicated feelings towards you, it led to me hurting Nikita, which she didn't deserve either. It was… a trainwreck."

"I was so angry about losing Deon and about knowing he was out there and I couldn't get to him that I let that blind me to the fact that, regardless of the fact that we were all being kind of fake, we were friends and had been for years. You and me aside, Avery, Alistair, even Colette. They'd all been such amazing friends and I blamed them for something they couldn't control any more than I did. I hate the monster I was."

"Everything happens for a reason though," Nathan said. "If you hadn't been like that, I don't think we would have had the room to grow into the people we're supposed to be. Any of us, not us or you. We're all raw and new now. It's going to take some doing to gel again. It's been awkward for all of us. Don't worry."

"Good to know," I said. Nathan pulled onto the freeway to get from North Postings to South Postings where Nathan's house was located.

For the first time since reuniting with The Royal Court, I was actually comfortable. Despite the fact that Nathan and I had never been totally honest with one another about who we were, there was a closeness that was bound to develop with how much time we had spent together and how intimate we'd become. It felt like I'd finally gotten a piece of my old life back, and though I didn't have romantic feelings for Nathan by any means, it was nice to have him as a friend again.

If Nathan and I could make nice, the rest of The Royal Court should be a cakewalk.

We continued to catch up and laugh over the few good old times we had until we finally made it back to his house. Brayden's car was already parked in the driveway, and as soon as we pulled up, everyone came running out, led by Nikita, followed closely by Avery.

Nathan and I climbed out of the car, and Nikita threw herself into a hug with Nathan while Avery wrapped her arms around me. "Where were you?" Avery yelped. "Kyle said you left the park before they did. We were terrified. You weren't answering your phones."

At the same time, Nathan and I pulled out phones out of our pockets, and I assumed he had the same collection of missed calls that I did. "I didn't even hear my phone ring," I said with a chuckle.

Nathan shook his head. "Me either." He put a hand on Nikita's face. "I'm sorry."

Nikita had a look of judgment on her face. "What were you doing?"

"We were just talking," Nathan replied, then he leaned in and kissed Nikita. "Easing the last of my guilt."

Nikita shot a sideways glance at me and I was nervous that she would misconstrue the situation, but I nodded regardless. "Just two guilty souls not trying to irritate the shit out of our friends anymore."

To my surprise, Nikita nodded and smiled. "Good."

I must have gasped out loud because Avery linked one of her arms through mine and squeezed. "Yeah. Nikki's a little different too. You'll see."

"Let's head inside," Kyle said from the back of the group. "Brayden's ready to talk now."

Brayden was standing behind Kyle and nodded. "I hope I can be of some help."

We all walked back inside and took various seats around the living room space. Brayden sat next to Kyle on one of the couches, and Kyle made no attempt to be discreet as he slid so close the two were touching. "Just like we talked about," he said. "Just be honest, and it'll be fine."

Brayden nodded. "Yeah, okay."

Nathan let out a sigh. "I hate to start with such a broad question, but Brayden… what happened?"

Brayden fidgeted a little in place. "I guess it started right at the beginning of the semester. A couple of men approached me, those two guys who attacked you, and they told me that you were in trouble and your dad needed my help. He told me that Deon was dangerous and looking for you, and all I really had to base anything off of was how much you seemed to hate him. It seemed plausible to me."

"That makes sense," Nathan assured.

"When I got to him, the story changed a little. He said that he was trying to get you away from Deon and the entire Royal Court because they didn't have your best interest at heart. He told me that if I helped him, he'd…" Brayden's voice trailed off and he stopped talking. After a few seconds, he turned and looked at Kyle and Kyle nodded to reassure him, then he looked back at Nathan and continued. "He said I could stay near you. That he'd make sure we could spend lots of time together. As much as I wanted. He said he'd make sure to remove anyone from the picture that I wanted. Cherri, Nikita… anyone."

Nathan's jaw clenched as his anger grew. "He knew exactly how to manipulate you."

"Connor's not a stupid man," Kyle growled with the same level of aggression.

"Then things changed even more and Connor started talking more about trying to hurt The Royal Court, but he told me if I didn't continue to do what I was doing, he'd kill me. At first, I didn't care. I knew you guys didn't really like me all that much, but then you all started treating me so much better, and..." He looked over at Kyle again. "Things changed." His head drooped and his eyes fell to the floor. "I didn't want to do it. Any of it, but there was nothing I could do. I tried to get some information on where to find Connor, but that was when he snatched me. He kept me locked up for... I don't even know how long."

"Where?" I asked. "Where were you?"

He shook his head. "I don't know. Whenever I was brought to interact with Connor, I was blind-folded. The two guys that attacked you always covered my eyes and ears and then handed me over to someone else."

"How long did the trips take?" Nathan asked. "Thirty minutes? An hour?"

"It varied. I don't think they were bringing me to the same place every time," Brayden said.

"Shit," Nathan replied.

"Why didn't you just say something?" Avery said. "We would have helped you."

Brayden started to chuckle, but it was drenched in self-loathing. "You guys *just* started to like me. If I'd told you I was working with Connor, that would have ended in a snap. I didn't..." He looked up at Kyle again. "I didn't want to lose you."

No one responded to that sentiment. It was likely because they all knew he was telling the truth. We could pretend that we'd be better people and forgive Brayden regardless, but the truth was, none of us were that great of people, at least not back then. If I'd caught wind of that, I probably would have beaten Brayden black and blue. Everyone else had similar looks on their faces.

"Well, that's behind us now," Kyle said. "All that's left is to look forward."

"Towards what?" Colette asked. "No offense Brayden, but this hasn't been very helpful."

"Maybe not yet," Nikita said, "but there's another strand we can maybe tie with this one. Jaxon and I found Brayden. Together, we just might be able to find where Connor was hiding."

7
———

DEON

Felicity had been nervously shifting her gaze all over the room, but at me. She was flicking the frayed edges of one of her pillows and her breathing had hastened. I didn't want to press her to start speaking until she was ready, but I was growing impatient with how much time she was just sitting there saying nothing.

"If we need to talk about this later, we can," I said.

Felicity shook her head. "No, it's just, you like me so much and you care about Venom so much. I don't want to ruin it just yet."

"You couldn't," I said. "Not after everything you've done for me."

"Reserve judgement until the end of my story,"

she responded. "It's like I said, your path crossing with Garrett's was not serendipitous. He used to work for your father. He was one of the men who Connor frequently charged with taking care of anyone who posed a threat to him or his family. Garrett actually liked Connor quite a bit. He knew he was cutthroat, he knew he was ruthless, but Venom's got a mean streak as I'm sure you've noticed."

I had flashes of images of Venom beating the dog shit out of anyone who messed with me behind bars, threatening guards into doing what he wanted, causing even the warden to fear him. Venom was kind to me, but I knew what happened to people he *didn't* like. He was probably pretty similar to Connor in that regard, but there was one difference.

He knew how to tell the difference between those he loved and those he didn't.

"Yeah. When I first got to the adult prison, a few guys tried to punk me around. One of them never walked again," I explained.

Felicity smiled. "Yeah. I remember Garrett telling me about that. He didn't like that those guys hurt you like that. Not after everything you'd already been through."

I furrowed my brow. "What do you mean? I

never even spoke to Venom until after that. How did he know what I'd been through."

"He didn't just know," she said. "He played an active role in what happened to you."

My heart started to beat a little faster. "An active role? How?"

"Well, like I said, Garrett did a lot of Connor's dirty work. A lot of it was questionable, but Garrett did a good job of separating himself from Connor's shit. It was normally all just guys exactly like Connor, and Garrett didn't mind thinning the 1%, but then one day about four years ago, Connor came to him and said he needed him to kill someone completely innocent with no criminal background at all, and then drop the body at a specific time and place, to be provided after the kill. Garrett didn't want to do that, obviously. Why kill someone innocent? He refused, even after Connor offered him half a million dollars to get the job done."

"He turned down half a mil?" I said, shocked. As good of a person as I may have considered myself to be, I didn't know if I was that strong.

"Garrett's hard, but he's not evil. He wouldn't do it for any amount of money. Unfortunately for us, Connor had an ace up his sleeve that neither of us was aware of until it was too late." Felicity took a deep breath. "Me."

Just like that, it hit me—rather, it smashed into me like a speeding semi-truck. I realized why Felicity looked so familiar to me when I first met her.

I'd seen her once before.

"You've slept with Connor," I said. "My mom has a picture of you."

Felicity's eyes widened. "What?"

"When Connor tried to fight for custody to take me from my mom, she had one thing that made him back down, and that was evidence of all the affairs he'd had. Pictures that he'd taken or screen-shots from videos. She found them while she was cleaning his house and saved them in a box just in case. You looked familiar to me when I first met you; that's why, because your picture is in that box."

"Well then your mom did what the rest of us couldn't do," Felicity replied. "Yes. I'd had an affair with Connor while Garrett was locked up once. It was still back when Garrett liked him, and he and I have this arrangement that if he's locked up, he doesn't expect me to just go without. My heart will always be his, but… I'm only human. Turned out, being human in that situation tanked us. Connor had all sorts of videos and pictures, and he'd made it worse by discussing some of Garrett's criminal activity with me too. If he released those videos, I wouldn't just be shamed as a woman, but Garrett would have been locked up for life and I would have been barred. It left us no choice, Garrett had to do what Connor asked."

"He killed an innocent person?" I asked.

Felicity nodded as she took a few deep breaths. "Garrett tried to make as discretionary a decision as possible and kill someone who was bad and just hadn't been caught, but it didn't make him feel much better. Then Connor gave him the order to drop him in Postings Proper park at sundown. He said he'd see two kids there, and he was to make sure the body dropped right in front of them."

Slowly the realization hit me. Four years ago. Two kids in Postings Proper Park. Sundown. A body dropping from the sky.

"Our first date," I said, more to myself than anything.

"Apparently, Connor wanted to frame his own son to give his other kid a leg up. Things didn't go quite according to plan. The kid turned himself in and took all the blame on himself. It never went to trial and stayed pretty hush, despite what he wanted. When Garrett realized what you'd done just to protect Cherri, he was racked with guilt. Not just because he played a role in ruining your life, but because he felt like he should have done that too. Whatever it took to protect the woman he loved."

"I don't get it. If he did what Connor told him to, how did he end up in prison?" I asked.

"Garrett was technically on parole. Even though Connor assured us that he'd leave us alone if we did the job, he violated Garrett's parole to make sure no one who knew the truth was on the outside. Then he gave me the half mil as hush money, telling me that as long as I took the money and kept my mouth shut, there wouldn't be any other problems. So here we are."

I looked down at the chair I was sitting in. "Am I sitting in a hush money chair?"

"God no," Felicity yelped. "All of this is built through my and Garrett's Connor-free hard work. I immediately turned around and donated the half mil to the NAACP. Made it in Connor's name too." A smile crossed her face. "*That* pissed him off pretty bad, but he didn't retaliate. It was just money to him regardless."

"He's a monster." I bit the inside of my lip. "I can't believe it."

"But he loves you, Deon. Like a son."

I looked up at Felicity. "What?"

"Garrett cares about you. *So* much. When he took you under his wing, it was to make up for what he did, but he grew to adore you. He talked about you every time we spoke. He still does."

"I'm not talking about Venom," I said. "Connor. He's a monster. I told you already, I could never hate either you or Venom. You're just more of his victims. More people that he's hurt. If anything, I have even more reasons to take him down now. As far as I'm concerned, Venom's my dad, and Connor hurt my dad, he hurt my brother, he hurt the woman I love, he hurt you." My hands balled into fists. "I want him dead, Felicity."

Felicity nodded, a look of relief flashing before determination fell in its place. "You and me both, kid."

"There's one thing I don't get. By the time I got out, Nathan was on top of the world regardless. There had to be a ton of ways to boost him that wouldn't have ever had to involve me. Why go to such lengths?"

"Garrett has often said that he thinks there was more to the story than just what we got. The little bit that Connor tried to tell us never made much sense, and it's like you said. Half a million dollars, killing an innocent man, all to frame a middle schooler, it just didn't add up. Connor was up to something else, but what, I couldn't tell you."

I couldn't even get angry any more, I was just astounded. How long had Connor been manipulating every facet of my life? How much longer was he going to? "If we can take Connor down, would there be a way to get Venom out?"

"That's the hope," Felicity said. "If we can get enough evidence, we can maybe file an appeal. If we fail, that's it. Venom's locked up for life." Her voice cracked right at the end of the statement, and all I'd seen from Felicity was nothing but strength. But under the pressure of potentially losing Venom for good, she was cracking.

I owed it to her and Venom to find a way to fix things.

"I *will* find my father and I *will* take him down. I'm going to undo all the wrong he's done in all of our lives, Felicity. I promise."

Imagining wrapping my hands around Connor's throat and squeezing the life out of him used to terrify me, but now it was all I could dream of. I'd ruin the man who ruined me, even if it was the very last thing I did.

8

CHERRI

I jolted upright, holding my throat and gasping for air. My chest felt like it was about to cave in on itself, and sweat was pouring down my forehead. Connor's evil smile loomed at the front of my brain, having been the last thing I saw in my dream as he braced his hands on my throat, slowly squeezing the life out of me. My heart pounded like it was trying to escape from my chest, and for a few minutes, I really struggled to convince myself that I wasn't being drained of my life.

"Cherri?" My bedroom door flew open, and Nathan came running in with Nikita right behind him. He was shirtless and looked as if he had just jumped out of bed, while Nikita was wearing Nathan's missing shirt, and looked like she was somewhere between terrified and irritated. "What's wrong?" Nathan asked.

"What?" I asked.

"You were screaming," Nikita said.

My jaw dropped a little. "I was? I'm sorry. I had a nightmare."

"About Connor?" Nikita asked. "I have them too."

Nathan ran a hand through his dark brown hair. "I think we've all had them at this point."

"I've been having them almost every night lately. I don't sleep much," I admitted.

Nathan waved a hand at me. "Come on. Come sleep on our couch. It's really comfortable."

"Um," I stammered. "Wow, there is not much on the planet that sounds more goddamn awkward than that."

"I'm with you," Nikita said, "but I think it would help."

The thought of going to stay in my ex-boyfriend's bedroom with both him and his new girlfriend seemed odd to be sure, but it also seemed better than staying in my room all by myself. "Okay. Thanks."

I grabbed my cell phone and one of the pillows from my bed and followed Nathan and Nikita out of my room. They led me down the hallway to the room that I recognized as Nathan's old room. It had been completely rearranged and all of the furniture had been replaced with newer stuff. Nathan and Nikita's bed was a big, four-poster bed, and in one corner of the room, there was a seating area with a couch and a couple of chairs. The couch had a high back and looked particularly plushy, so I walked over to it and laid down. Nikita disappeared into the closet and came back out with a spare comforter and unfolded it over me.

"Let's not just think about how weird this is," Nikita joked, then she winked at me and went and climbed back in bed with Nathan.

"Thanks guys," I said.

"No problem. Goodnight," Nathan said.

Weird though it was, I felt infinitely more comfortable in a room with other people, and the couch was pretty damn comfortable, and in no time at all, I'd settled into a deep and thankfully dreamless sleep.

By the time I woke up the next morning, Nathan and Nikita were no longer in the room. I took my time waking up, took a few minutes to text Ciara, my parents, and Gus that I loved and missed them, then I dragged myself off the couch and down to my bedroom. I changed into a pair of plain blue jeans and a black t-shirt to match a pair of my favorite combat boots, then I fluffed up my hair, starting at the brown roots and dragging my fingers down to the blond tips at my shoulders, then I left the room.

A murmur of voices got louder as I made my way downstairs, and just like the day before, everyone was sitting around the kitchen island, helping themselves to a new collection of breakfast foods, this time pastries and fruits. I took a seat next to Avery and dropped my head to her shoulder.

"Good morning," she said, kissing my forehead. "How'd you sleep?"

I looked across at Nathan and Nikita. "Much better with a couple friends close by. Thanks."

They didn't respond, but each gave me warm smiles, and I was happy some of the discomfort was shaking loose and I was feeling better being around my friends. Sicily had gone home the night before, but just before I had a chance to ask if he was planning on coming back, he came wandering into the kitchen.

"Hey!" he called out.

"Hey!" everyone called back like we were on the set of a sitcom.

His jaw dropped. "Oh wow. I didn't think that would work." He looked across the kitchen at me and pointed. "There's my girl."

"Hey, Sic," I greeted with a warm smile.

Sicily sat down at an open stool and helped himself to a few fruits and pastries.

"How did ping checking go yesterday?" Nathan asked.

"Really good," Sicily said. "We still got a couple thousand left to go, but we can get it done in a week, maybe, with everyone's help."

"That's good," Nathan said. "Brayden was helpful, but we didn't get a whole bunch of information to trace since he was always blindfolded when he traveled to meet with my dad. Nikita had an idea though."

"Well, Jaxon and I found Brayden walking out in North Postings. If we work with him, we may be able to find where he was before he got to where we found him. Maybe if we just drive back there, a sound, a pothole he might have felt, anything that could steer us in the right direction," Nikita explained.

"Ooh, ooh, yeah! Like that sense memory thing," Sicily said.

Everyone went silent and stared at him, so I said, "Explain."

"Sometimes when people get robbed or raped or assaulted from behind, cops will use sense memory to try and help someone remember details they don't think they have. There was a point at which you *weren't* blindfolded, right?" Sicily asked Brayden.

"I'd meet the two guys, usually outside of school, and then they'd put the blindfolds on me and take me to whatever car and hand me over. I'd have the blindfold on then until they took it off of me in Connor's office or wherever he was," Brayden explained.

"When you were walking out where Jaxon and Nikita found you, were you blindfolded until you got there?" Sicily asked.

"Uh…" Brayden screwed his face as he tried to think backwards. "Yes."

"Did you walk or did they drive you there?"

"Walked," Brayden said, "Well, they dragged me there. They didn't even take the blindfold off, just stood me there and unbound my hands. Eventually, I pulled the blindfold off myself and then a few minutes later, Nikita and Jaxon found me."

Sicily put a hand on Brayden's shoulder, and it seemed to bolster Brayden's confidence. "That's awesome. So all you guys have to do is take Brayden to about where he started, blindfold him again, and see if you can remember which directions you turned in and stuff. Like Nikita said. Try and feel a pothole, remember if you heard anything. You'd be surprised what your brain took note of."

"Okay," Brayden replied immediately. "I'll give it a try." He looked over at Kyle. "Will you come?"

"Yeah," Kyle said with a smile. "I'll be by your side every step of the way."

"Well, it can't be a whole lot of people this time either," I said. "I'd like to go, and Nikita and Jaxon should go, since they found Brayden."

"Can I go?" Avery asked. "No offense, Sicily, but the ping checking stuff was super boring. I just don't wanna do that two days in a row."

Sicily waved a hand. "Nah. I get it."

"My truck seats six, so with me and Brayden, Jaxon and Nikita, Cherri and Avery, that maxes us out," Kyle said. "Does that work for you?" Kyle asked Brayden.

Brayden nodded. "Yeah, that's fine with me."

"Okay," Kyle said. "Let's finish up breakfast then, and head out."

Conversation was light and enjoyable over breakfast, then we separated into our two new groups for the day and then Team Drive Brayden piled into Kyle's truck, and we left for Postings Proper High. Avery and I were in the third row of seats way in the back, and not long into the ride, Avery reached over and grabbed my hand and held it. I looked down at her hand in mine and smiled.

What was I doing? Avery was my best friend. Her telling me to go for it with Deon, or protecting me during Nathan's outbursts flashed across my mind. She jumped between me and a gun. *I* was the one making things weird. She just wanted to be friends again.

That was what I wanted too.

"I missed you," I said. "So much."

Avery turned and looked at me and must have been able to hear the desperation in my voice, because her smile was less sympathetic than others, and more genuinely happy. "I missed you."

I leaned in closer to her, hoping that no one else would hear me, but knowing they might and not caring. "We never got to talk about it, but before he left, Deon and I…" I fluttered my eyebrows up and down. "Twice actually."

"Oh my god, seriously?" She repositioned herself in her seat so that she was facing me. "How was it?"

I rolled my eyes clear into the back of my skull remembering the feeling of Deon all around me. "Like *nothing* I've ever experienced before. We just *fit* together, you know?" I frowned then. "I miss him."

"Aw, honey." Avery pet the side of my head. "I

know you do. I don't know *what* I'm going to do while I'm dorming at Yale."

My eyes went saucer wide. "You got accepted?"

Avery flashed me a cocky grin. "Of course. Who do you think you're talking to?"

I pulled her into a hug. "I'm so proud of you, Avery. They aren't gonna know what fucking hit 'em!"

Avery giggled as we released. "That's the hope. Thanks, Cherri. When I got my letter, all I wanted to do was call you."

"Yeah, and thanks to your dick friend you couldn't," I grumbled. "Fuck."

Avery started chuckling again. "It's gonna take some getting used to hearing you swear all the time."

"Shit. Sorry," I said, then I yelped. "No, shit. I mean shoot! Damn it. No. Ugh!"

"Just stop," Avery said. "I like potty-mouth Cherri."

I smiled. "Good."

We made it to school and parked just outside the walls. Brayden walked to where he usually met with Connor's goons. "Okay, I usually met them here. They would blindfold me, and I assume they were putting me in the back."

"Okay. Avery and I will be Connor's thugs.

Kyle, since you're driving, you, Nikita, and Jaxon will be the hand-offs. Put him in the back, Jaxon and Nikita, you ride in the far back, and Avery and I will get in the passenger's side front and second row seats," I explained.

"Okay." Kyle put a hand on Brayden's shoulder. "You good?"

"Yeah, I got this. Thanks."

With that, Kyle, Nikita, and Jaxon walked back over to his car and started it up. Avery pulled the scarf she'd grabbed out of her pocket and then walked up to Brayden and started to wrap it around his eyes. I noticed Brayden's entire body tense up, so I reached out and stopped Avery.

"Are you okay?" I asked.

Brayden took a deep breath and then nodded. "Yeah. I'm okay. You can keep going."

"Okay. We're right here. If you need me to, just say the word and the blindfold comes off," I said.

"Thanks, Cherri," Brayden replied. Avery resumed putting the scarf around Brayden's eyes and then stepped back. "Oh shoot," Brayden said, lifting his wrists. "My hands were usually zip tied. The only time they weren't was that one time Nikita and Jaxon found me."

"Uh, okay. We'll use my hair tie," Avery pulled the rubber band out of her hair and her perfect brown curls fell down in front of her cocoa skin. "It's not as tight as a zip tie."

Brayden scoffed. "That's just fine."

I held Brayden's wrists together and Avery laced her hair tie around them. Once again, I noticed his body tense up, but that time I just gave his hand a little rub to assure him that we were there, and then pulled back.

"Okay. Where did they normally grab you?" I asked.

"My arms. My left one, typically, because they were usually dragging me across the street," Brayden said.

Avery grabbed Brayden's arm and dragged him across the street, and Kyle picked up on the hint and did a U-turn to pull up next to us. We loaded Brayden into the seat he was normally in, and then I climbed in the front passenger's seat with Kyle, while Avery climbed into the second row passenger's seat across from Brayden.

"Okay, I'm gonna go. If we get somewhere where you feel like you remember a turn, just let me know," Kyle said.

"Okay," Brayden replied. There was a shake to his voice, and I could see in the way Kyle looked back over his shoulder that he noticed it too, but then he just looked at me, and pulled away from the curb.

We started going straight for a few blocks until Brayden weakly said, "H-here."

"Where?" Kyle asked. "Left or right?"

"Um. I don't know." Out of the corner of my eye, I could see Brayden shifting awkwardly. "Left ma—" He took a sudden deep breath. "No, right?"

"Brayden?" I said. "You okay?"

Kyle's eyes shot up into the rearview mirror.

"Brayden," Avery said. She reached over, and it was as if we all saw it in slow motion, Brayden started to shake. "Um…"

"Kyle, pull over," I said.

There was no hesitation. Kyle immediately pulled to the side of the road, causing a car behind us to honk in irritation, but it didn't break Kyle's stride a bit. He jumped out of the driver's seat, and I jumped out as well, just in case he needed extra hands. I ran around just as Kyle was pulling Brayden out of the car. He was convulsing, bordering on a seizure, and there was sweat pouring down his brow.

"Brayden!" Kyle yelped.

"Take the restraints off," I said.

Kyle quickly ripped Avery's hair tie from around Brayden's wrists and the scarf from around his eyes. They were red, swollen, and teary and they were glassed over like he was far from where we were standing.

"He's having a panic attack," I murmured.

"Brayden," Kyle said. "Brayden, look at me." He put his hands on Brayden's face. "Bray, calm down. Just breathe." It wasn't working. "I don't know what to do!"

"Anything that will ground him!" I called back.

Nikita was climbing over the seat and out of the car just as she said, "Kyle. Kiss him. A quick one to not make it harder to breathe."

Kyle charged forward and pressed his lips to Brayden's, and I watched as the rising and falling in Brayden's chest started to slow. Kyle pulled back and gently petted the sides of Brayden's face. "Hey. I'm here. Just look at me." Brayden's eyes regained some of their focus, centering on Kyle, and then the color started to come back to his face as he slowly evened out. "There you go," Kyle comforted.

Brayden craned his head again and Kyle met him with another kiss, longer and more passionate. When they parted, Kyle muttered something quietly that I couldn't hear and Brayden nodded, then Kyle took a few steps back. At that point, Brayden seemed to realize that Nikita and I were watching, and after a few seconds, Avery came to stand next to me.

"Kyle, take a few seconds," Avery said.

With a nod, Kyle dragged Brayden away from the car and hugged him to continue to help him calm down.

"They're so good together," Avery said. "I wish they could just pull the trigger."

"I still can't believe it," I said.

"None of us could," Nikita said. "It threw us all for a loop, but I agree with Avery. I wish they could just commit to it. I think it's Brayden keeping them from locking in."

Kyle walked back towards the truck, holding Brayden at his side. "Hey, can we maybe do this another day. This sort of unexpectedly triggered him."

"Of course," Avery, Nikita and I all said at the exact same time.

"It doesn't make sense to break ourselves trying to put ourselves back together," I said.

Brayden shook his head. "I don't know what did it. I'm sorry."

"Don't apologize for something that triggered you, Brayden," Nikita said.

I put my hand on Brayden's arm. "I've had tons of panic attacks over things I didn't expect these past six months. This shit we're going through is fucked. It's bound to happen. We'll try again some other time."

"Let's head home," Kyle said. "So you can get some rest," he said to Brayden.

We piled back into the car, swapping around so that Brayden was back in the front with me in the middle row of seats with Avery. The ride was a quiet one home, and Kyle left us all behind in the interest of getting Brayden inside immediately once we got back.

"I of course don't mind waiting until Brayden is more comfortable, but that was pretty much my plan for the day," I said to Avery as we walked with Jaxon and Nikita towards the house.

"Yeah, I was thinking that too. How about we do a girl's night instead? Dinner and drinks?" Avery said.

"Oh, sure. Will we invite Colette too?" I asked.

Avery smiled. "Yeah," then she reached out for Nikita. "You'll come too, right Nikki?"

I was surprised she even asked. In all the time I was in The Royal Court, Nikita dealt mostly with Nathan and Jaxon, occasionally Kyle, and that was it. She never came out with Avery, Colette and I. I got the sense she didn't really like us all that much.

"Oh, you know I'm there," Nikita replied. "So

long as we go to Colette's mom's place. Her sushi is my favorite."

I stopped in place, staring at Avery and Nikita as they walked and laughed side-by-side. It seemed the new romantic relationships weren't the only thing I was going to need to get used to in the revamped Royal Court.

9

CHERRI

Avery flipped through the clothes hanging in my closet. Back before I cut Avery and the rest of The Royal Court off, Avery and I used to love picking out one another's outfits and dressing one another up whenever we'd go out. In the wake of deciding that we'd spend the day we lost going out for a girl's night instead, Avery came up to my room and immediately went to my closet. I didn't stop her. It was nice to have her getting comfortable around me again.

"Wow. Even your style has changed so much. Move over chiffon, leather is in the house," she joked.

"Yeah, well, I had one of Deon's jackets that I hung onto, and I realized that it felt more comfortable," I explained. "I didn't wanna go *full* Nikita, but my wardrobe got generally darker and yeah, I had to invest in a few leather and jean jackets."

"Well, I wanna be Cherri for a day, so you'll definitely have to pick out some of this stuff for me, but I'd like to see you in…" She came walking out of the closet with a pair of tight fitting black jeans, a light blue t-shirt, and a sleeveless black jean jacket. "This." She threw them on the bed. "Don't think I haven't noticed your lack of heels lately, either. I'll respect the comfort, but I'm putting you in a pair of my shiny black pumps because they'd be…" She finished the statement by doing a chef's kiss with her free hand.

I held up my hands. "Fair enough."

She walked over and fluffed her fingers through my hair. "I never really got to tell you that I love the new haircut. Don't get me wrong, I loved your hair before, but this just feels like it fits you so much better. The short shows off your gorgeous angles, and the brown color makes your eyes shine." She squealed. "Ugh. My best friend is so beautiful."

Tears filled my eyes before I could stop them and I reached out and wrapped my hands around Avery's waist and buried my face in her stomach. "I don't know why I thought I could survive without you. You're gonna leave for school in three months and I wasted six of my last nine months with you being angry." I really did hate myself for it. "I love you."

"I love you too. Yes, I leave in a few months, but it's not like I'm never going to visit you, and it's not like you're never going to visit me. I can't wait to show all those people in New Haven how wonderful and cool you are. Hopefully they're okay with swearing," Avery said.

I leaned away, but still kept my arms wrapped around her and looked up at her. "Hopefully, because I did enough prim and proper shit for The Royal Court."

"There she is," Avery said with a bright smile. "Okay, come on. Pick something out for me."

I knew exactly what to pick. Disengaging from Avery, I walked into my closet and sifted through the clothes until I found the few things I had in mind. A pair of form-fitting leather pants and a gray bustier top were two of my favorite things that I owned, and I knew they would look amazing on her. Even though it was pretty warm outside, I convinced her to lace up a pair of my knee-high combat boots, and the way the colors looked against her brown skin was amazing. It was definitely the right way to go. I got dressed in the outfit she picked out for me, and we of course took a copious amount of selfies to mark the occasion.

"Okay. Time for the true test," she said. She took my hand and led me out of the room and we walked down the hallway to where her and Alistair's room was located. She knocked a couple of times on the closed door before opening it. "Babe?"

Alistair was laying on the bed flipping through a graphic novel. "Hey."

"Hey. How do we look?" Avery asked.

Alistair peeked up from his novel, and then suddenly sat straight up. His eyes nearly bugged out of his skull and he smiled. His eyes flicked up and down Avery's form and I felt a tinge of pride over how excited he looked. He gave me a once-over, though much more respectfully, and smiled. "Damn." He started to laugh. "Baby, you look smokin' hot."

Avery beamed, elbowing me. "Nice pick, Cherri."

"You look good too, Cherri. You two are gonna knock 'em dead out there tonight. I damn near don't want to let you go," he said.

I snickered and Avery waved her hand. "You know you're the only one for me, Ali."

"Still, maybe I should just tag along. I'll sit a

couple tables away with fake glasses and a mustache. It'll be fine," he replied.

"Nice try." Avery hooked one of her arms through mine. "Don't wait up. It's our first girl's night reunited, so we're partying til we drop."

"Well I *will* be waiting up, but only because I'm not letting that sexy-ass outfit go to waste," Alistair said, then he leaned back on the bed.

I nodded. "Glad to see the love is still very alive here."

Avery chuckled. "Let's leave before you get caught in the crossfire."

We turned around and left the room, closing the door behind us, and made our way downstairs. I couldn't shake the empty pit in my stomach that I felt from watching Avery and Alistair interact.

I wanted that.

My brain immediately started to paint a picture of showing Deon my outfit and him descending into playful overprotectiveness. Looking at me with wide eyes and telling me he was going to wait up. I missed him so much it made my stomach hurt, and all of a sudden, I didn't feel much like going out. I should be looking for Deon.

"Cherri?" Avery asked. We'd made our way clear into the living room while I was lost in thought and Avery pulled me down onto the couch. "Are you okay?"

"Yeah. Just that interaction between you and Ali made me miss Deon more than I was expecting," I explained. "I feel like I'm not doing enough to find him. He could be in trouble and I'm about to go out for a fucking drink with my girls."

"There's only so much we can do." Avery pet my head gently. "And honestly, I think we're doing more than most teenagers would be able to do in this situation. Yeah, we have a ton of money to throw around, not to mention our own personal technical genius, but at the end of the day, we're just a bunch of kids, even if Nathan has the brain and maturity of like a thirty-year-old."

"I guess…"

"For two days, we've made strides, or we've tried to at least. All we're doing is what it takes to survive as kids in this world. We already lost our entire second senior semester, we can't throw away our summer too. Deon's a strong, capable guy, and we're doing the best we can. We shouldn't just be miserable while we're waiting for the other shoe to drop."

I nodded. She wasn't wrong, and I knew that, but it didn't mean I missed Deon any less. "You're right. I'm sorry."

"You don't have to apologize. I know you miss him, but I believe, and I know you do too, that Deon is out there, alive. We'll find him or he'll find us. We just have to be patient and in the meantime, you said so yourself, we have to make the most of the time we have left." Avery pulled me into a hug. "I'll try to be less coupley with Ali."

"No, no, I don't want that. Thank you for being willing, though," I said.

After a while, Colette and Nikita came down to the living room, then we all piled into Avery's car and left for Colette's mom's sushi restaurant. The dynamic was different, but in a good way. Avery, Colette, and Nikita were all so comfortable with each other, especially Nikita and Colette. The shroud hanging over Nikita before I left The Royal Court that seemed to be lifted, and though she was still dressed in dark colors and jeans with chains hanging from them, her jeans were a little more form-fitting, and her t-shirt/vest combo showed a little more skin. There was an added femininity there that was different, but nice to see on her.

We were seated at a private table near the back of the restaurant. We'd been there many times before, but it felt extra comforting for me—like coming home after being gone for a long time. A bottle of wine had already been corked and was waiting open in a chiller for us. Thanks to Colette's family owning the place, we were allowed to skate on some controlled underage drinking. An edamame appetizer had been placed in the middle of the table as well. Waiters came over quickly enough to take our orders, and then we were left to ourselves.

Surprisingly enough, it was Nikita who bubbled up the conversation. She looked across at me and gave me a coy grin. "You were shocked I agreed to come, huh?"

"You got me," I replied. "I remember you avoiding us at all costs."

"I'll admit, before, I wasn't really interested in bonding, least of all with you. I mean, you were with Nathan, and everyone loved you..." She looked at Avery and Colette. "These two adored you, so it wasn't like I could bond with them without you."

"I'm just gonna say it," Colette said. "Cherri, I am *so* happy that you're back, but you leaving The Royal Court..." She cast nervous glances at Avery and Nikita before settling on me. "It was *kinda* the best thing that's ever happened to us."

"Ouch," I said. "I deserve that."

"It's not meant to be insulting, like I said, I'm so glad you're back, but The Royal Court was toxic, and a lot of it was centered around you and your relationship with Nathan. You didn't make us toxic, in fact, you were the only thing that was still kind of good about us, but it was all kind of self-serving, and that always came back around to the fact that you were the queen. I knew I was never gonna be *better* than you, so I just worried about myself."

"Yeah!" Avery yelped, then she looked at me with wide-eyes. "I love you, Cherri, so much. It broke my heart when you left, but I get what they're saying. You and your relationship with Nathan was like this crazy benchmark I was never going to hit. You're so perfect."

"Then we saw that you weren't," Nikita said with a smile. "We saw you deteriorate and change, and when you were gone we fucking fell apart. I'm not lying, it was like you were the pin in the grenade. Once it was pulled, things went to shit fast."

Colette started to chuckle. "Oh my god. We used to just sit at the lunch table in complete silence. Seriously. I'd try my hardest to start a conversation, but it was like I was talking to a wall. Nathan was guilty, Nikki and Avery were heartbroken, I was delusional, Brayden was planning our imminent demise, and poor Kyle, Jax, and Ali, they were *exhausted* just trying to hold us together."

Avery and Nikita joined in the laughter. "It was touch and go for a while," Avery said. "Nathan dressed up like Santa in, what was it, January or February? I can't remember. Time is a blur."

"Yeah, and Colette trying to give Cherri that box." Nikita had tears in her eyes. "Remember when Cherri completely ignored her and then she turned around and told everyone she'd talked to Cherri and things were going to get better?"

Colette shivered. "It makes me cringe just thinking about it."

Nikita shook her head. "I was like, oh man, this girl has really lost it."

I couldn't tell if I was warmed or uncomfortable by the conversation, so I just sat and let them toss the ball around. Finally, Avery looked across at me and smiled. "Yeah. Turns out we were all *way* more attached to you than we realized." It made me think of Nathan's confession that he thinks of me like family and it killed him when I was gone. "Ali didn't want to forgive Nathan for a long time. Nikki either actually."

"We struggled," Colette said, "but that struggle led to some pretty astounding changes. We got closer. We became *actual* friends. Even you, Cherri. You grew and changed so much and now you're so much more of the person you want to be. That sucked. God, it sucked so much. I think I cried every day for months and got no sleep, but I can't bring myself to say it wasn't worth it."

"Yeah," Nikita said, "And not just because I'm finally with Nathan, but because it took the blinders off for me." She smiled at Colette and Avery. "I can't believe I spent so much time not letting myself get close with these two." She side-eyed me. "Or you."

"Wow," I said. "I guess I've been so apologetic this whole time that I didn't realize the good it did. I'm glad. I'm angry at myself for being such a fucking brat and hurting you guys." I looked at Nikita. "Or in your case, getting my ass handed to me." Everyone laughed. "But I'm glad that it made us all stronger." I lifted my wine glass. "To aging like ten fucking years in six months."

"Here here!" Colette said, and she, Avery, and Nikita lifted their glasses to meet mine. "Oh! Cherri! Did you see how Nikita looked at prom?"

My eyes widened as I remembered the shimmery ensemble with the first time I'd ever seen Nikita's hair down or her wearing makeup. "Yes! Oh my god, you were smokin'!"

Nikita smiled. "Thanks."

"I'm serious, I even told Sicily how amazing you looked, you can ask him. I was seriously like,

I'm so angry at them, but damn she looks good. You all did, but Nikita was like…" I whistled. "How did that happen? One of you did it?"

"Well, we convinced her to get dressed up, but you'll never guess who picked it out," Avery said.

I tilted my head. "Not Nathan?"

Nikita nearly choked on her drink. "God no. I've spent the last six months making his wardrobe less douchey."

"Jaxon," Colette said proudly.

"No way."

She nodded. "Yup. Avery and I kept picking out these poofy dresses, and they looked good on her too, but fortunately Nikita dragged Jaxon along—It was back when we were still navigating our new friendship—and he picked it out. The only thing we added was the headband."

"I'm impressed," I said. "Didn't know he had it in him."

Colette shrugged. "That's generally true of Jaxon."

"Well, you would know. You two are like the real deal now," I said. "I will never forgive myself for missing that."

"You know, it occurs to me that we've never really talked about it," Avery said. "How *did* it happen?"

My eyes widened. "Wait. You don't know?"

"I know a little bit, but not the full story," Nikita said. "She's right, it was just a thing one day."

We paused the story for a minute while our food was delivered, then Colette perched one of her maki rolls between her chopsticks as she started to speak. "I guess it mostly started during winter break."

"Bullshit," I said immediately.

"Yeah. Cherri and I saw you with hickies back in like October," Avery said.

"Okay," Colette whined before popping her sushi roll in her mouth. She chewed and swallowed then wrinkled her nose. "I'm telling the story of how we got to *official.*"

I held my hands up in retreat. "Fine. Sorry."

"You're right, we would like makeout and stuff before winter break," Colette explained, "but that was actually really rare, and usually we would just sort of trip and fall into it."

"He would trip and his lips would fall onto your neck?" Nikita said.

Colette chuckled. "Damn near. Literally, it was like we would get together to study in a perfectly public place and it would just happen. I swear to god, the first time we kissed I asked to borrow a ruler he had, he reached across the table to hand me the ruler and he kissed me. I was confused, but not unhappy. Then there was this other time we were standing by my locker and I leaned past him to reach into my locker and I brushed a little too close to him, all of a sudden we were kissing. I don't even know how we got there. He says I started it."

"That's amazing," Avery said. "I love the idea that you're just all of a sudden like kissing and have no idea how you got there."

"*Then*," Colette said with overdramatic pronunci-ation, "It all started around winter break. Those couple of weeks after Deon went missing were so tense and I just couldn't sleep well. I was texting Jaxon and mentioned that I couldn't sleep, and eventually he came over and we would just talk, and I was finally able to get some sleep. It wasn't much, but enough. We didn't do anything over winter break. No kissing or sex, just spent a ton of time together and slept a lot."

"That's what he told me too, so I can confirm," Nikita said.

"That's so cute," Avery said.

"He was so worried about you," Nikita said. "I've never seen him like that before."

"Then, like right after I had the issue with Cherri and the box, when I got home I just broke down. I mean, like full on ugly crying, and he just held me and told me everything was going to be okay and that he'd be there for me."

"Jaxon?" I said. "He doesn't speak."

"You'd be surprised," Nikita said. "When it comes to the people he loves, he's surprisingly sweet and passionate."

"That was when I first realized we were more than just hooking up as one of the last remaining single people in the group. That time when we kissed, it was on purpose, and naturally, everything else followed. Then it was hard to be apart from him."

"That was obvious based on the fact that you two became inseparable," Avery said.

"Avery, when Colette clocked that guy with the pan at Nathan's, Jaxon looked at me and said, 'Shit, Nikki, I think I fucked around and fell in love.'" Nikita laughed. "I honestly never thought I'd see the day."

Avery looked across at me. "You okay?"

I tilted my head. "Yeah? Why wouldn't I be? I'm having fun. It's nice hearing about this stuff that I missed."

"You just have this really sad look on your face," Colette said.

"Is it more guilt over Deon?" Avery asked.

I shrugged. "Maybe. Hopefully he'll forgive me for having a little bit of fun."

"Why shouldn't you have fun?" Nikita asked. "I learned this really important lesson with Nathan, especially after seeing how much I loved getting to know Avery and Colette better, I realized I was living my entire life *for* Nathan. All the decisions I was making were based on my feelings for him and it caused me to miss out on a lot. Deon's a grown man just as much as you're a grown woman. He may need help, and we're trying, but I also feel like you've just created an identity around Deon. I did the same thing, and it'll lead to frustration every time. It's okay to live your life. The Deon stuff will work itself out."

I'd made an identity *around* Deon. "Yeah?"

"Yeah," Nikita said. "It's okay to live your life *with* him, so long as you aren't living your life *for* him. Who are you when he's not here? That's what you have time to figure out now. Let us carry some of the weight while you put the pieces together."

It was remarkably good advice and incredibly comforting. "Okay. Thanks, Nikita."

"Nikki," Nikita replied. "It's pretty much what people call me these days."

"Nikki," I repeated. "Got it."

Colette chuckled. "She's not lying about that

either. Sometimes Nikita just shuts Nathan down when he gets very Nathan-y. It's awesome."

"It's because we're the only ones who have any sense," Nikita said.

Avery lifted her wine glass. "A toast. To being the ones with sense!"

Colette, Nikita, and I lifted our glasses and tapped them against hers. Even if I didn't think we really had any idea what we were doing, it was nice to pretend that we did, just for a while.

10

DEON

"Well, you're up early," Felicity said. I'd just walked down from my bedroom and Felicity was sitting over a bowl of cereal at the kitchen table, flipping through her phone. "How'd you sleep? Has it gotten any better?"

It had been about a week since Felicity told me the truth about how Venom and I came to cross paths, and it had definitely messed with my sleep. If it wasn't just me laying awake ruminating about all of the pain and damage my father had caused so many people in my life, it was nightmares of him making a valiant return to kill all of the people I cared about, from my mom and Cherri to Nathan and Venom.

"Not really, unfortunately," I replied, sliding into the chair opposite Felicity.

"I went with something simple because I didn't think you'd be up, but I can cook something for you. What would you like?" she asked.

"No, it's okay. I'm fine with cereal." I replied, but Felicity still stood up from her chair. "Why?"

"I'm gonna get you a bowl at least. Do you want toast?" she asked.

"Why are you like this?" I asked.

She looked back at me and stabbed a finger out in my direction. "Listen. Acts of service are my love language, okay. Just let me take care of you. I like it."

I sighed, but nodded. "Fine. Yes please to the toast."

She gave me a victory nod, then turned around and made her way to the toaster. She popped a couple of pieces of bread in the toaster and then grabbed a bowl and spoon. "What to drink?"

"Orange juice, please," I replied.

She set the bowl and spoon down for a moment and then grabbed a glass from the cabinet and set it down as well. She opened the fridge and grabbed the milk and orange juice, then filled the glass with orange juice, and carried the bowl, spoon, glass of orange juice, and jug of milk over to the table, balancing them all with precision.

She set them down in front of the table and then I started pouring myself a bowl of cereal from the box on the table. "Thank you."

"Of course. I've got good news by the way," she said. "No more sitting around for either of us today."

I looked up at her as she twirled back to the counter to retrieve my toast. "Yeah?"

"Yep. Garrett set up a meeting with one of his guys, Nico. Originally, I was going to go, but I have to go meet with a client, so…" She pulled my toast out, slid pads of butter onto each slice, and carried the plate over to me. "I'm going to let you go, and you're not going to tell your father that I did that."

I snickered. "As long as you don't tell him, I won't."

Felicity let out a little squeak. "It sounds good coming out of me, doesn't it? The whole mom secret, don't tell your dad, thing?"

"It really does." I gave her a smile. "You're a good mom."

"Maybe if we can get Garrett out, we can look into getting you a little brother or sister," she said. "Which would you prefer?"

For a moment, I thought about having a younger sibling. A little girl or boy to spoil and snuggle, and it made the pit of my stomach burn with anticipation. "Either. I'd love that."

What I'd learned in the time since I'd come to stay with Felicity was that she really did want to have a family with Venom. After she realized that I had committed myself to calling *him* my dad, as opposed to the man who was supposed to be my dad, she was happy to play along as the loving step-mom and I was fine to let her. She really would make a wonderful mother, just like Venom was a wonderful dad. I wanted more than anything to absolve Venom and Felicity of the fate Connor had set out for him so that maybe one day they could have a kid of their own.

"Oh my god, I just imagined trying to convince a little boy that being a brooding, super tough guy isn't all it's cracked up to be," she said, rolling her eyes. "*But Deon does it,*" she said in a nasally voice. "I've got my work cut out for me."

"I'm not brooding," I growled.

"No... I was talking about a different Deon," she responded and then quickly returned to her chair. "Anyway, you're going to keep it a secret, and I'm going to send you with one of my cars to see him. So long as you mention Garrett as soon as you get there, you should be okay."

I was overcome with relief. Not only was I finally going to get to leave the house and make an active effort to find and stop Connor, but I was going to see people other than Felicity and drive around like a normal person. Part of me wanted to stop at a fast food place or something to mark the occasion. It didn't even occur to me how much my current life had in common with when I was locked up. Yes, I had access to much better food, and a roommate like Felicity was significantly better than some of the guys I was behind bars with, but the restrictiveness and not being able to go anywhere I wanted was the same.

Connor Loche had made my entire life a prison.

Felicity furrowed her brow when I hadn't said anything in a while. "Is that okay? I'm sorry. I guess I just assumed—"

"I'm thrilled," I replied. "I know that I don't have the best 'thrilled' face, but I'm excited. I actually get to do something and not just be a sitting duck, plus I will actually get to see the outside world. What is this guy going to be able to do to help?"

"Like I said, his name is Nico, and he's kind of

that guy who can dig up just about anyone on the East Coast. His resources stretch far and wide, and though he's not a 'boots on the ground' kind of guy, he's good at finding people. The biggest issue is that he doesn't typically accept payment in the form of money. He just doesn't need it, so Garrett had to negotiate a different payment with him. What that was, I don't know, I don't ask. You shouldn't either," Felicity explained.

"Trust me, I learned not to ask questions when I was locked up," I said.

She nodded. "Right. Nico's good people, and he has a lot of respect for Garrett. Just tell him what you know about Connor and the last time you saw him. Any helpful information you can think of, share it with him, and hopefully he'll be able to track him down. I've seen him work before, he's good."

Felicity and I finished our breakfast, then for the first time ever, she led me into the garage. It was a long, four-car garage, and three of the four spots had cars in them. One spot had a big, army green Hummer in it that appeared to have collected a good amount of dust, and I assumed that was probably Venom's car. The other two were smaller and sleeker, one sports car, and another more typical family car, though it was clearly the brand new model. Felicity grabbed two sets of keys off the wall and handed one to me, surprisingly, the one with the luxury car key on the ring. After dropping it in my hand, she opened the door to the luxe car and programmed an address into the GPS, then she leaned back out and poked a finger into my chest.

"Okay, Nico's address has been programmed in, just follow it, and then if you activate the GPS when you get back in, there's a shortcut for home. Deon, I swear to god if you crash my baby, you won't have to worry about Connor, because *I'll* kill you," Felicity said.

I snickered. "I thought you were sticking me in the soccer mom car for sure."

"I figured you could use some fun," she replied with a wink. "This key is for the house if you get home before me." She pointed out one of the plain silver keys and then she walked over to the other car and started to get in.

I climbed into the luxury car and a few seconds later, the garage door started to open, likely from a button pressed by Felicity from inside her car. It did feel nice to be inside such a beautiful car and left to my own devices. Felicity backed out first, then I followed suit and the garage door started to close. Even though it was a hot day and the AC might have been better, I opted to roll the windows down and enjoy the fresh air. The address I was driving to was about thirty minutes outside of town, an old storage container turned house near the coast. To protect Felicity's car, I parked a couple blocks away and walked to the house. I felt a little too vulnerable walking up with no weapon to protect myself, but Felicity was confident Nico wouldn't hurt me, so I had to take the risk.

I knocked on the door, and in no time at all, I heard the click of several guns. Two men walked around from either side of the house with rifles pointed at my head, and then the front door opened and a woman shoved her hand out with a pistol in it, setting the barrel damn near on my nose.

"Whoa." I held my hands up.

"Who the fuck are you?" the woman growled.

Beyond her, I could see a few additional people inside, one in particular was watching me from the shadows at the far back of the container. "I'm Deon. Venom sent me here to talk to Nico."

The woman kept her gun pointed out at me, but looked back over her shoulder. "Is that what you were told."

"Nah," the man said from the back.

"I know that his wife, Felicity, was supposed to come. She had a client so she sent me instead. I've been staying with her while Venom has been trying to help me find Connor Loche," I explained. Both Nico and the woman were staring at me like they weren't entirely sure I was telling the truth, so I decided to take a calculated risk. Felicity said I should mention 'Garrett' as soon as I got there. I assumed she just meant what I knew him by, but maybe she was being specific. "Trust me. Garrett sent me here."

Nico jumped up immediately and ran over to the woman, shoving her arm down to remove the gun from my face. He reached out and waved his hands at the other guys to wave them down. "Jesus Christ, kid. Say that shit from the beginning. Do you have any idea how much Venom would kick my ass if he knew I had guns pointed at his kid?" He was a short, muscular man, with faded hair and a clean-cut goatee.

"Sorry," I said. "I won't mention it if you don't."

"Cool. Come on in. Can I get you a beer or something?" Nico asked.

The woman scoffed. "You can't get him a beer. He's not 21."

"Relax, KT. His own father's hunting him down and trying to kill him, for god's sake. The man can have a beer," Nico said.

"I appreciate it, but I'm okay," I replied.

Nico motioned to a chair. "Well, come sit. I've got a busy schedule today, but I'd like to get boots on the ground for you as soon as possible."

I sat where Nico told me to, and he returned to the seat he was in when I first arrived. He crossed his arms and looked across at me. Even though he was shorter and less bulky than I was, his aura was intimidating, like I wouldn't survive just thinking about doing something to him.

"So, Deon, tell me about this man you need me to find. Don't get me wrong, I know who Connor Loche is, I don't think there's a person in the world who doesn't, but I'm assuming your experience with him is different from the facade he projects to the world," Nico said.

"That's an understatement," I said. "What's considered helpful? Do I tell you that he's a murderous, womanizing, abusive asshole, or does that not help?"

He chuckled. "I mean, it's good to know where his mindset is. There are other things that might be more helpful though. Any places that are important to him?"

I couldn't help but wish that I could reach out to Nathan and put *him* in touch with Nico instead. He was probably a wealth of knowledge. Then again, I did like that he wasn't getting any more sucked into that world than he already was.

"Well, when he kidnapped my brother, he took him to a cabin about an hour north of Postings. I don't know the exact address, but we took highway 10 all the way until it ended, and then took the first right. There was a cabin all the way at the end of a winding road and that's where they were. His company is in downtown Postings of course, the address is publicly listed. He's not at his home, at least not the one where he lived with his family. My brother is still there, at least he was last time we spoke." I racked my brain for anything else that would be helpful. "The only other thing I can think is that he's probably still within reach of Postings. I know that's not hard to do in Maine, but he was tormenting them. Through his men, but I imagine he wasn't far. I've learned he's a hands-on kind of guy."

"Okay," Nico said. "This brother you keep talkin' about. That's Nathan Loche, yeah?"

"Yeah," I said. "He's a good guy. Our dad fucked him up pretty bad, but he's working on himself. You don't have to worry about him."

Nico nodded. "Right. I may still send a guy or two just to suss him out, but he won't be harmed, I promise."

"Thank you."

He let out a whistle. "I didn't even realize Connor Loche had another kid. Kinda makes you wonder if there are any more of you out there."

"I've had nightmares about that," I explained. "But I'm inclined to think no, or at least the woman was smart enough not to tell him. Connor's possessive. He feels like anything that has anything to do with him belongs to him. That's how it is with me and my brother. If there was another kid, at least one that he knew about, he'd have dragged that kid into this shit too."

"Anything else you can think of?" he said.

"I mean, he's got Postings bugged to high hell. Postings Proper High School, any major corporation, for sure everything in the building his company is in. I was only there for a couple of months between getting out and having to go on the run again, but there wasn't a place I could go to where he didn't hold influence. Anywhere you'd go in Postings, there's someone, somewhere, who has helped him."

Nico nodded. "That's good to know. We'll be exploring that avenue for sure."

"How long will it take to hunt him down?" I said. "It's not just for me, it's for Venom, Felicity, my brother. He's tormenting my whole family. I want him down."

A smile crooked up Nico's cheek. "Well, you really are Venom's kid. Don't you worry. These things take time, but for every contact in Maine that Connor has, your boy Nico's got two. I'll dig him up. It's only a matter of time."

11

———

CHERRI

"**O**kay, go!"

I held my phone up as Gus barreled into the swirling slide that splashed down into the main pool of Nathan's house. Water went everywhere, spraying over Kyle and Colette who were standing closest to the bottom, and Kyle quickly wrapped his arms around Gus and lifted him out of the water, tossing him away. Gus' cheery laughter filled the afternoon air, and I smiled.

It felt good to just be happy for once.

"Cherri!" Gus popped up from the water at the edge of the pool. "Did you get it?"

"Yeah, bud, I got it. I'll send it to your phone," I said, stopping the recording. "That makes about twelve videos you've had me record."

The hot sun felt good against my exposed skin, and I was excited for the tan I'd be getting. Avery was sitting next to me, her legs dipped into the pool, with her head knocked back, soaking in the rays. Nathan, Nikita, and Jaxon were sitting at the bar, drinking and laughing, each in their own swimsuits and Alistair was camping at the table that Nathan had stacked high with food. As soon as I mentioned that Gus wanted to come over for a pool party, The Royal Court went all out. They decorated, Nathan bought a bunch of brightly colored pool floats, and food and drinks of all sorts were brought in. When I asked Gus if he wanted to invite some friends, he funnily enough said no—he wanted all the spotlight on himself.

"What are you going to use all the videos for, Gus?" Avery asked.

Gus' face lit up. "My YouTube channel!"

My eyes widened. "Your what?"

"I want to become a YouTuber! This kind of stuff, like playing in a rich, fancy pool, gets like millions of views," Gus said.

Nathan looked over from the bar. "You should do a tour of the whole house, even the back one," he pointed to his smaller house towards the back of the property. "Title it 'Connor Loche's decommissioned house'."

Colette snickered. "That's clickbait."

Nathan shrugged. "It's not. It's true."

"Will you give me a tour?" Gus asked.

Nathan nodded. "Of course."

Gus clapped. "Yes! I'm gonna be famous."

He swam away, over to where Kyle and Colette were wading, and started to play with them. I looked over at Avery, with my brow furrowed. "Is… is my baby brother gonna become a douchebag?"

Avery giggled a little. "He's certainly on his way."

"Great," I replied flatly, making a note to myself to talk more with Gus about his new venture later. YouTube had been blowing up with kids lately, and he had what it took to be a successful one, but being in the limelight that much could kill a kid. I at least wanted to make sure he knew what he was getting into. "Here," I said, handing my phone to Avery. "You're on camera duty while I pee."

Sitting up straight, she took the phone from me and pointed it out at the pool. "Mission accepted."

I dragged my legs out of the pool and stood up, grabbing one of the towels off a nearby lounge chair to dry off as I walked, and made my way into the house. There were a dozen bathrooms inside, but the closest one was just on the other side of the kitchen. I walked through to get to the bathroom and noticed Brayden sitting at the kitchen island. He had a plate of food, and it was only then that I realized he'd gone in claiming to be going to the bathroom, but never came back out.

"Hey," I said.

Brayden looked up. "H-hey."

Instead of continuing on to the bathroom, I slid down onto one of the stools across from him. "You doing okay?"

He nodded. "Yeah, I'm okay. Just needed a few minutes. I feel… bad, out there."

"I know what you mean," I said. "I was the biggest bitch in the world to these people, and it doesn't feel fair that now I get to just have a pool party with them and have fun."

Brayden popped a chip from his plate into his mouth. "Exactly."

"We miss you out there, though. We're supposed to be spending time together, all of us. We've all done shit wrong. I think we've committed ourselves to just pretending none of that shit ever happened. Looking forward, you know?"

"Yeah." Something else hung on the end of Brayden's voice. He kept shifting his eyes up to me, then away again, before finally bringing them up to land on me. "Hey… can I ask you a question? More of a favor?"

"Of course. Anything," I replied.

"Can you not tell Nathan about…" His voice trailed off and his gaze slipped from mine. "The, uh, the kiss?"

"Oh." I furrowed my brow, but nodded regardless. "Yeah. It's not really my place to talk about."

He lifted his brown eyes back to me. "Cool. Thanks."

"Since we're on the topic though, and I can use the fact that I have no fucking clue how to define my friendship with you as an excuse, can I ask. What's up with you two? You and Kyle, I mean?"

Brayden got fidgety again immediately. "Um."

"I mean, I don't want to overstep, but you two seem so perfect for each other. And you know we'd all accept you, right? If you guys want to be more than—"

"We're just friends," Brayden said suddenly, and there was a shake in his voice that broke my heart. "He's… Kyle is… I mean he…" He stammered a few more times trying to form a sentence, but then eventually just dropped it. "Yeah. We're just friends."

I got the sense that Brayden was very uncomfortable with the topic, and whether it was because he didn't understand his own feelings, or was afraid of how others might take it, I wasn't sure. "Okay. I'll leave it there then."

"Don't tell him that I said that," Brayden said. "The friends thing."

Poor guy. He was in a house of mirrors and couldn't get out. I knew that feeling all too well. "Let's just say anything you and I discuss stays between us."

He offered me a little smile then. "Thanks, Cherri."

"Yeah," and I stood up. "Well, I actually *do* have to pee, so I'm gonna go do that, but you should come back out. I want all my friends out there. Gus deserves to see the excellent people I get to call friends. Every single one of you."

"I'll go back out. I promise," he replied.

"Cool."

I turned to walk away, but then Brayden cleared his throat. "Hey, Cherri?"

"Yeah?" I looked back over my shoulder.

"Tomorrow, can we try again to find Connor using the driving blindfold method?" he asked.

At that question, I turned back around. "Listen, Brayden. We can find another way to do this. There's no guarantee that we'd even figure anything out that way, and I'm not gonna fuck you up more in the brain for that. I appreciate that you're willing, but we'll do it another way."

He shook his head, and I saw some determination flash into his eyes. "No! I want to do it. After we talked about it, I realized that Connor must have known… everything. He knew exactly what to tell me and he used me to hurt the one person who has always been there for me. Then he used me to hurt all of you guys. I don't want him to get away with that. I want to fight back."

I smiled. "That's awesome, Brayden. You deserve that. If you aren't comfortable, we'll figure something else out, but if that's what you wanna do, then we'll do it."

"Tomorrow," he said with a nod. "Let's do it."

My smile grew. "Yeah. Let's do it."

Instead of the arrangement from the first time, we decided to leave Nikita and Jaxon behind for the second attempt. Everyone slept in after the pool party, and then I had to take Gus home, but not long after lunch, we met up to try the blindfold method again. We opted to take two different cars, so Kyle and Brayden rode in his car, while I rode with Avery in hers. We started at Postings Proper High School, and did the same thing we did the first time.

Avery wrapped Brayden up in a blindfold and

put a hair tie around his wrists, then we led him over to Kyle's truck the same way we did the first time, and put him in the back seat. We had a feeling Brayden would feel less pressured and more comfortable if it was just Kyle in the truck, so we left the two of them and climbed back in Avery's car to follow behind.

After a few minutes, Kyle pulled away from the curb and Avery kept a close tail on them. Brayden must have felt something solid the first time we did the experiment, because around the same place that Brayden wanted to turn at the first time, was where Kyle turned right. Avery followed and every now and again, Kyle would turn, and eventually, we ended up on the highway that was taking us to North Postings.

"This is good, right?" Avery said. "Nikita and Jaxon found Brayden wandering around North Postings."

"Yeah?" I said. "If that's the case, then we could be on the right track for sure."

At one point, Kyle got off the highway, and the turns got more erratic and uncertain. A few times, Kyle put on a blinker to turn, before turning it off and continuing straight. "What's going on?" Avery asked.

Finally, Kyle's car pulled over and stopped. We

could see him looking over the backseat, talking to Brayden. About five minutes passed, and I was just about to climb out and walk over to the truck, when Kyle climbed out and walked back to Avery's car.

Avery rolled down her window and Kyle leaned in. "Hey."

"Is he panicking again?" I asked. "We can stop."

"No, he's fine. He's doing great, but we think he may have screwed up on the exit, he said he felt like it might have been too soon. I asked if he wanted to start over, but he said he thinks if we go back to the Postings Proper exit and get back on the highway, that he can get it right the second time. I'm gonna take Millworth back to the Postings Proper exit, and then get back on the highway and try again," Kyle explained.

"Okay," Avery said. "We're behind you."

"Cool." He tapped the side of Avery's car and then pulled back from the window and walked back to his truck.

"Hopefully, the third time's the charm," Avery said.

"Hopefully," I agreed.

Exactly as Kyle had said, he took Millworth, a street that ran all the way from South Postings, through Postings Proper, and into North Postings, back to the highway exit we'd started on. He hesitated for a moment, likely allowing Brayden to reset and focus, and then eventually he got back on the highway. We drove down the highway following Kyle, but that second run, he got in the left lane. We passed the exit we got off on, along with a couple more, and we were fast approaching the final exit for North Postings—a left exit—but then Kyle got off.

We followed and the car slowed significantly, and then it started to turn left and right at certain intervals and then finally, Kyle's car pulled over and stopped. Avery and I watched as Kyle got out of the front seat of the truck and opened Brayden's door.

"They're getting out," Avery said.

I opened my door to get out and Avery followed suit, just as Kyle was pulling Brayden out.

"We would walk straight for a while," Brayden said. "And we'd cross the street. I know because sometimes we'd stop at the light, then we'd immediately turn right."

"Okay. Let's go," Kyle said. He looked over his shoulder at Avery and I, and we both nodded and followed behind him.

We moved exactly as Brayden had expressed, and he was more confident, likely because he was on foot as opposed to in the car. We crossed the street and then turned right, and Brayden stopped. "Is there a door near here that is glass with a metal frame?"

Kyle, Avery and I looked around, and two doors up in a row of buildings from where we were, was a door matching what Brayden described. "Yeah," Kyle said.

"Don't tell me where. I'm gonna walk straight and then stop, and you tell me if I'm in front of it." Without confirmation, Brayden walked forward and then came to a stop directly in front of the glass door we'd seen. He turned to his left so he was facing it and said, "Is this it?"

"Yeah, Brayden," Kyle said with a smile. "Is this the place."

"This is definitely one of the entrances I took," Brayden said. Avery and I walked up and looked at the building, but the door was grated shut, and the building itself had boarded windows and seemed totally abandoned. Kyle took the initiative and took the blindfold and wrist tie off of Brayden, and when he saw the door locked up, he deflated. "Shit."

"How did you know about the glass door with a metal frame without seeing it?" Avery asked.

"The sound," Brayden said. "It's that very

distinct sound of the door jam chain rattling against it. That kind you hear when you walk into any of those high end stores in South Postings."

"Being rich strikes again," Kyle said.

"Well, I think we found where they'd bring you, but it doesn't seem like Connor's here anymore," I said.

"But maybe there are clues if we can get in," Avery said.

"We can't break in," Kyle said.

"No, but there's another option," Brayden said. "This is where they brought me in, but it's not where they brought me out. I have a feeling that when I was dragged out and dumped after Connor kept me, that they brought me out the back way, so maybe there's more hope that way of getting in. The only thing is, I was totally out of it when Nikita and Jaxon found me. That's going to be harder."

"So, we'll just take it one step at a time," I said. "The next step is to bring Nikita and Jaxon here and see if they can help us work backwards to somewhere that could still be connected to this building. It's like Nikita said, if we work together, we'll be able to find our way forward."

"Sorry," Brayden said.

I looked at him and then turned him to face

me. "What are you sorry for? Look at what you did? I don't think I'd be able to do this." I pulled him into a hug. "We're one step closer to Connor because of you. Brayden…" I pulled back. "Thank you."

12

DEON

To say that I got slightly irresponsible in driving around town in Felicity's car would be an understatement. It was so refreshing to be out in the world temporarily without the fear of being snatched, or killed, or having a body drop from the sky in front of me. I did go to a fast food restaurant, drive along the coast, and take in the fresh summer air.

The last of my stops was a pier that hung out over the ocean. The sun was cresting over the sky and starting to set, and for some reason Cherri came into my brain. Maybe just because the sunset was beautiful and so was she, but I couldn't get her out of my mind. I wished beyond anything that she could be there next to me, looking at the amazing colors against the waves. Maybe I'd get lucky enough and one day I'd be able to bring her and we could just sit for hours.

Us having sex in her car blossomed into my mind then. I hadn't thought once about how starved for her skin I was until that moment. Finding and taking down Connor was more important than ever because I wanted to get back to the love of my life. I wanted to hold her and make love to her again, and I wanted to be the one who could protect her from anything trying to hurt her.

The sound of a car pulling up near where I was sitting on the pier made me jump, but when I turned around, Felicity was pulling up in her other car. She got out and walked down the pier and sat down next to me.

"You scared me," she said. "I thought something happened. Thank god I have the locator activated on my car."

"Sorry," I replied. "I got out of prison last July, and then I went on the run again in October. I was bouncing from place to place until Connor's guys snatched me in like March or April. I don't even fucking remember. I haven't been able to just…" I took a breath in and then let one out. "Sit. When I came to stay with you, I finally was eating good food, sleeping in a comfortable bed but—"

"It still feels like prison?" Felicity finished.

"I love living with you," I said. "But I don't remember the last time I was able to just sit and not feel like I was running. Even after I got out of prison, I saw Nathan and Connor almost right away, and then it felt like I was dodging them again. I haven't had a normal life since the 8th grade."

"I hate that," Felicity said. "We're gonna get you back to a normal life, but when you just disappear…"

"I know," I cut her off. "I'm sorry for scaring you."

Felicity put her hand on my back and started to rub it. "You're safest at home. I know it sucks, but all it takes is for one wrong person to see you. I just need you to hang on a little bit longer. We're gonna get you back home, back to your family, back to your woman. We're close, probably closer than it feels like. Just be a little more patient."

I nodded, knowing she was right. "Yeah."

"How did the meeting go?" she asked.

"Good. I told Nico everything I knew. Nathan probably would have been more helpful, but I'm glad he's not this deeply mixed up in all this shit. Nico was pleased with the information I was able to provide. He seemed confident that he'd be able to dig something up."

Felicity let out a sigh of relief. "Excellent. I'll be sure to brief Garrett when I see him next week."

"You're seeing Venom next week?" I asked.

"Yeah, to go over his appeal," Felicity said. "It's been filed, but I keep filing extensions on the court date because I want to make sure we have everything we need to be successful in the case. We only get one shot locally, then we'd have to take it federal, and that's gonna be much harder with judges who don't understand the influence Connor has. I think I'm going to set the court date for later this month. If we can file while Connor isn't around to testify, then the main thing that caused the violation of Garrett's parole won't be there. We stand a good chance."

"But what if Connor *does* show up?" I said.

"Well, it wouldn't look good for Garrett, but then we'd have him at least," Felicity said.

"I'm not willing to wager Garrett's freedom like that," I said. "We have to wait."

That seemed to suck all the air out of Felicity. "I don't want to wait. This is so important. This might be the only shot we get."

"It's too risky. It will be better if we can get rid of Connor for good and ensure that Garret gets out. We can't rush it," I said. "It's like you just said, we have to be a little more patient. If we can sort

Connor out, there's more than one problem we're going to be able to solve."

A smile came across Felicity's face. "Okay," she said. "We're in it together, so we wait it out together?" Felicity said.

I nodded. "Exactly."

"Okay. I'll file for another extension. The judge respects me a lot, but hopefully we can bring this to an end soon. Their patience with me has got to be running out."

"Nico's on the case now, and if I know my brother at all, and oddly enough, I think I do, he's not just sitting around either. The other shoe is going to drop, we just have to wait."

Felicity started to laugh. "Wait, when did it flip from me convincing you to you convincing me?"

I joined her, chuckling myself. "I think we may both be much better at giving advice than we are at receiving it."

"You know, that's not the first time I've heard that," Felicity said, then she stood up. "Come on, let's get home. I'm sure Concrete is chomping at the bit to see you."

"Yeah, let's go."

Over the course of the next few days, Felicity made an intentional effort to make me feel more comfortable and less locked up. She frequently suggested I run errands with her, so long as they were going to be short and get me back home soon. She also allowed me to start taking Concrete on his walks around the neighborhood, even though a car that was one of Garrett's people keeping an eye on me, always stayed close behind. I chose to ignore it and pretended that I was just some guy walking his dog around his neighborhood. It was my favorite of my new activities. The morning walks turned into runs, which reminded me how much I liked to work out. After mentioning that to Felicity, she brought me into the garage to present me with a surprise.

"Ta da!"

She opened the garage door, and I saw that in the fourth spot in the garage, where there was no car, had been converted into a workout center. She'd purchased a bench press, treadmill, exercise ball, and weights, and had laid them out in a way I could use them. A dog bed was in the corner of the garage, no doubt for Concrete to hang out on while I worked out.

"This is way too much," I said. "This is so nice."

"You said you like working out. Honestly, I've been waiting for you to mention *any* hobby or interest, so that I could create an abundance of it for you. I know it's no fun being cooped up, so I want there to be things that interest you here. You haven't even touched the new gaming system I bought," she said.

I laughed. "I've never been much of a gamer honestly. Although, I did see a cooking game."

"Yeah! The co-op one! I want to try it. We need to play it together," Felicity said.

"That sounds amazing. Let's do it tonight," Deon said.

"Cool. Thinking spaghetti for dinner tonight?" Felicity said.

"Yeah. Actually, can I help?" I asked. "I want to learn more about cooking."

She smiled. "Sure."

"I feel bad, like I shouldn't be enjoying myself so much, but if I have to be locked up, this is a pretty damn good way to do it," I said.

She gave me a hug. "I know I'm not your first choice, but if there's anything that can make waiting it out more comfortable, please tell me."

"I will," I said. "Thank you. What would honestly really help, is for you to let me help you out around here." Felicity pulled away and I smiled. "Make me clean and shit. Let me cook for you sometimes. I just want to try and feel reasonably normal. I feel like I should be doing more to stop

Connor or get back to Nathan and Cherri, but since I can't, I want to just feel normal here."

"I can do that," Felicity said. "I'll go full mom."

I smiled at her. "I can't wait."

"I'll leave you to your workout equipment," Felicity said, walking away, but as she passed a few bags of cement she pointed down at them. "Can you bring these to the backyard when you're done? They need to be poured for the new back patio."

"Yes ma'am," I replied and Felicity chuckled as she walked in through the garage door that led into the house.

Hopefully Nathan and Cherri would forgive me for being okay with my new normal. I wanted my life to cross back over with theirs eventually, but I wasn't done being Felicity and Venom's weird, hybrid son just yet, and while Nico hunted for Connor, I was going to lean all the way into it. I wanted to make up for the childhood I'd lost.

13

CHERRI

After sorting things out with Brayden and following his trail to the end, we decided to let things cool down for a little bit. Brayden had strained himself much more than he let on to get to where we got, given he fell asleep on the way home and slept for the next six hours once we got back home. We knew that we wanted to compare notes with Nikita and Jaxon and try and find another way into the building, but I also didn't want to push Brayden past his limit. He'd already done so much, and the last thing I wanted was to break him.

"Good morning," Avery said.

She was walking into the kitchen with Alistair right behind her. They were both still in their pajamas, and Alistair was yawning. Avery slipped by my stool to give me a hug around my back, and then sat down next to me and Alistair across from her. The morning's breakfast selection was a variety of meats, crackers, and cheeses, along with a basket of sweet breads, and the typical selection of fruits.

"Morning," I said. "Hey, Ali."

Alistair smiled at me. "Hey, Cherri. How'd you sleep?"

"I've been sleeping better these past few days. I don't know if it's because we actually took a huge step forward, but it's been a little easier," I replied.

"That's good," he said. "I really think we're getting somewhere with Sicily and these pings. We're really whittling down the list. Maybe we'll strike gold and track down Connor and Deon at the same time."

I rolled my eyes at the thought. "That sounds so overstimulating, I don't know that I'd even be able to handle it."

"Same," Avery agreed. "Either one or the other. Not both."

"Which would you prefer first?" Alistair asked with a sly smile on his face.

If it was his idea of a funny joke, I didn't appreciate it, but I chose to ignore the jab and just answer the question. "Well... I really do want to find Deon as soon as possible because I miss him so much, but I think it would be better if we could find him *after* Connor, so that he can come back and be comfortable and get back to a normal life. I don't want him to have to come home to a fucking fight."

"That's true, but I think Deon's kind of our missing secret weapon," Avery said. "Both you and Nathan are so much stronger when he's around, and I think he's got some pieces of the whole Connor puzzle that we're missing."

"I totally agree," Alistair said. "I can't shake the feeling that things would go better if Deon were here."

"Hey, don't get me wrong. If we came across Deon first, I wouldn't complain. We got so little time together, that I don't want to waste any more time. I just imagine things have already been so stressful for him, that it would be nice if he could just come home and not have to worry about any of that, you know?"

Avery nodded her head as she munched on a piece of cinnamon bread. "That makes sense."

Still, what they said was a logical response as well. We still didn't entirely know how wrapped up Deon was in Connor's world, wherever he was, and he probably did have an entire safe of good information that we could use to track down Connor and hopefully stop him for good. If we did manage to find Deon first it'd be good, not just because I'd be over the moon to see him again, but because then he could help.

The kitchen slowly started to fill with the rest of The Royal Court, starting with Jaxon and Colette, then Nikita, Brayden and Kyle, and last, but not least, Nathan. The kitchen island over breakfast was fast becoming our official Royal Court meeting place. Once Nathan had gathered his plate, he looked over at Kyle and nodded.

"Your sleeping in is causing delays," Kyle joked.

Nathan shrugged as he chuckled. "What do you want from me? I'm taking advantage of not having my kingly duties right now."

"Wait," I said. "What?"

Everyone turned to look at me, furrowing their brows in confusion, and it was Brayden out of everyone who seemed to get it first. "Oh, right, Cherri wasn't there." He set his hand on Kyle's shoulder. "Kyle is king right now."

I dropped my jaw. "What?"

"Yeah," Nathan replied. "I was sort of losing my mind there for a while, and I wasn't doing the best job leading. I handed King to Kyle and became Prince in Line."

"I just automatically assumed that you were still

King and Nikita had moved up to Queen," I responded.

"Actually," Colette said. "Nikki hasn't moved up. Not officially anyway. She's still a Knight. In fact, if we're being the *most* technical, you're still Queen, Cherri."

For whatever reason, that made me really uncomfortable. I didn't feel like I should have the weight of The Royal Court on my shoulders anymore. It wasn't just because of all the things that I'd put them through, but they'd all changed and grown so much that it wasn't fair for me to lead them anymore.

"I don't think I should have that title anymore," I said.

"You know, I don't disagree," Kyle said. "Honestly, I think there are many changes that have to take place. Maybe now's as good a time as any to do it."

"We're still missing someone though," Nathan said.

Almost as if he'd been summoned by the mention of his name, we heard the front door open and a few moments later, Sicily rounded the corner into the kitchen. "Hey hey!"

"Good morning, Sicily," Colette greeted.

"There she is!" He held out his arms towards

Colette. "You have *no* idea how much of a whiz this chick is." He walked over and stood behind her and put his hands on her shoulders. "She figured out a way to check four times as many pings a day as we were checking. At this rate, we could get through the list *way* faster than we were planning on."

Across from Colette, Jaxon silently picked up a butter knife off the island and held it out in Sicily's direction. "Move."

Sicily held up his hands and backed away. "Right. Sorry."

"Knock it off," Colette snipped at Jaxon, but he ignored her apart from setting the knife down on the counter and resuming his breakfast.

"I forget, I'm the lost, lonely single in this group." Then he put his arms around Kyle and Brayden. "Well, I have these two at least. Just three single guys doing what we do, right?" Everyone went silent, and I actually had to fight back a laugh, but then I looked across the island and saw Brayden biting his lip to keep from laughing. Finally, Kyle broke and started snickering, which sucked in Brayden, and soon we all erupted with laughter. Sicily raised an eyebrow. "Ah, I missed something."

"No, it's fine," I said.

Sicily smiled over at me. "My best friend!" He walked around the island and I stood up to meet him in a hug. "I've missed you. I feel like we haven't seen much of each other lately."

"I expected you to be hanging around here more," I responded.

"To be fair, we've been working him to the bone," Alistair said. "When he's here, we lock him up in his dungeon and make him work like Cinderella."

"I think we're circling the drain on backtracking to Connor through Brayden, so hopefully I'll be able to join the tech side soon," I said.

Sicily rubbed my back. "Aw, I'd love that. Just like old times."

Back before I reconciled with The Royal Court, when we were still in high school, Sicily and I would hole up for entire weekends sometimes just grinding through the internet for any clue regarding Deon's whereabouts. Though we didn't find much, we would often catch streaks of information and would get excited following the trail to its end. Even if we were disappointed at the end of it when we didn't find anything, there was something about plugging in and chasing a ghost together that was fun and exciting. Our friendship was built on that.

"Okay, well, grab a seat, Sicily, we have some things to go over this morning," Kyle said.

"Oh. Okay." Sicily took a seat on the stool that was empty next to me and started loading some of the breakfast food onto a plate. "Are you guys breaking up with me?"

Kyle and Nathan exchanged a look and then Kyle smiled at Sicily. "Quite the opposite, actually. I'm offering you an official role in The Royal Court. Baron."

Sicily's jaw dropped to the floor. He looked over at me and I nodded with a smile, then he looked back at Kyle. "Yeah? I get to be official?"

"If you accept," Kyle said. "I'm not going to muscle you like Nathan did us."

"Okay," Nathan grumbled.

"Yeah, hell yeah! I get to be part of The Royal Court?" He looked at Jaxon and Nikita. "Does that mean these two won't bully me anymore."

"Oh calm down, you baby. We haven't done that since first semester senior year," Nikita hissed.

Sicily held out a hand towards Jaxon. "He *just* pointed a knife at me like five minutes ago."

I giggled and shook my head. "Well, we can only do so much. Maybe just don't touch Colette."

"Hey," Colette said. "He can do what he wants, and Jaxon will be fine." Jaxon looked up and glared at her, and she glared back, totally unfazed. "Trust me," she said directly to him, "He'll be fine."

A flash of excitement crossed through Jaxon's eyes, then he smiled and returned to his food. They were such a unique couple. I was excited to see more of them together over the course of the summer.

"Is that a yes?" Kyle asked Sicily.

Sicily snapped his fingers and threw up finger guns. "Hell yeah that's a yes."

Kyle frowned. "Did you just throw finger guns at me?" He looked at Brayden. "Did he just throw finger guns at me?"

Brayden chuckled and looked at Sicily. "Don't do that."

Sicily put his hands down. "Right. The Royal Court is finger-gun-free. Got it."

"Well then, with that matter sorted, I'm requesting to move Cherri down from Queen to Princess," Kyle said. "Does anyone have any objections?"

No one said anything, least of all me, but then Colette raised her hand. "Who will be Queen?"

"Well, I suppose that goes part and parcel with my next request, which is that Nathan moves back up to King, and Nikita moves up to Queen with him, and I'll of course move back down to Prince in Line for now." Kyle explained. "No offense, you guys are fun, and I love you more than anything, but you stress me out. I'm going to relax, enjoy spending time with," he gave Brayden a quick glance, "everyone, and bask in the glory of *not* having all the responsibility."

"Aw, but I like being retired," Nathan whined.

"That's too damn bad," Kyle replied.

"I'm in," Avery said.

Alistair nodded. "Yep. Me too."

Everyone else gave their own messages of affirmation and then Kyle picked up an unpeeled banana and banged it on the island like a gavel. "So ordered, and thank god."

"Well, then what's next, your highness?" Colette asked Nathan.

He looked back at me. "What'd you guys learn from driving blindfolded?"

"Brayden did amazing," I said. "He was able to get us to a place that we're relatively certain Connor was meeting him in, but it's all locked up. He's pretty sure that there's a back entrance that they pulled him out of when Nikki and Jaxon eventually found him, so the next step is to have Jaxon and Nikki take us back to where they found Brayden and see if he can walk us back to the back entrance, and hopefully it'll be an easier one to get into."

"Oh good. We're adding breaking and entering to our list of leisure activities," Alistair said.

"Well, only a few people have to go," I said. "I'm pretty certain he's not in there anymore, so we'd mostly be looking for any new leads or clues. I'll go, obviously. Brayden will have to be there, so Kyle will be there. Nathan, you should probably go because you know the most about your dad, and then we'd just need Nikki and Jaxon."

"Yeah, and breaking and entering is already on our repertoire," Jaxon said, and Nikita chuckled.

"I'm going," Avery said. "I've seen this thing through this far."

Alistair put a hand on Avery's. "Baby, I don't think that's a good idea. If you guys got caught and got arrested or something, Yale could pull your scholarship."

Avery opened her mouth to protest, but I cut her off before she could. "Avery, I agree. The rest of us don't even know what we're fucking doing yet, but you have so much at stake. You've been awesome up to this point. Let us take over from here."

Avery eyed me, and I could see in her gaze that she was upset, but she took a breath and then nodded. "Fine."

The relief on Alistair's face was easy to read,

and he looked at me as if to say 'thank you,' but allowed the words to remain unspoken. It was one thing I just wasn't going to do: ruin anything else for my friends while trying to make things right. They didn't even have to fight, but they were because they loved Nathan and they loved me. The least I could do was not drag them into situations they had no business being in.

"We shouldn't waste any time then," Nathan said. "Let's finish up, and those of us who are going can ship out."

We divided into two cars again, Kyle, Brayden, and me in Kyle's car and Nikita, Nathan, and Jaxon in Nikita's. Kyle led the way back to the spot that Brayden had led us to and then pulled his car over so that Nikita could pass him. She took the lead and drove a couple of blocks away, down a block that ran between the backs of two sets of abandoned stores, and parked.

We all got out and followed Nikita and Jaxon about halfway down the block where Nikita said, "This is where we found Brayden wandering."

"You said you ripped your blindfold off at some point, right Brayden?" I asked. "Is there *any* chance it's still around here?"

"It's not like Postings is shelling out all their taxpayers' dollars on keeping this area clean, so it's possible," Kyle said. As someone who lived in North Postings and would see the same pieces of litter hanging around in the streets for months at a time, I knew that to be true.

Brayden did a couple of circles with a look of determination on his face, and then he started walking up the block. Nathan noticed first and started following, and the rest of us eventually fell in line. Both expectedly and not, he stopped in a spot and bent down and picked up a black bandana that was laying on the ground and he handed it over to Nathan.

Nathan ran his thumbs over the fabric and then nodded. "Yeah. This is my dad's handiwork."

My stomach bottomed out. "You… recognize it?"

Nikita was next to Nathan in a second, rubbing his back. "Let's not talk about that right now. If it's confirmation that it was Connor's, then we're on the right track."

"Bray, do you think if we blindfolded you again that you could walk backwards like you did last time?" Kyle asked.

Brayden was totally unresponsive. He had a look of horror mixed with sadness on his face as he watched Nikita console Nathan. It only took Kyle a few minutes to take notice of the situation and he looked away, his expression breaking as he did. It was heartbreaking.

Someone exhaled next to me, and I jumped a little before realizing it was just Jaxon. He was watching the scene before us with a pensive look that was befitting his more observant nature.

"Things are pretty fucked aren't they?" I whispered to him.

Jaxon shook his head. "You have no idea."

"So maybe we don't do the blindfold," I said, louder. "Maybe just close your eyes?" I was less concerned with finding the place, and more with breaking up the unexpectedly tense situation we'd found ourselves in.

"I can do that," Brayden said.

He closed his eyes, his chest raising and lowering a little more dramatically as he did so, then he turned around a couple of times again and started off. Kyle trudged behind, and I rushed up to stay between Nathan and Kyle. It wasn't that I thought Kyle would hurt his best friend for any reason, but they needed some space. We followed Brayden down the block and across the street, and then he started to hesitate. He started to go left, then backtracked and tried to go straight. His movements got uncertain, and every time it seemed like he was off, he'd stop and turn around.

"Lost?" I asked.

He opened his eyes and blinked a couple of times. "I hadn't slept or eaten in like two days." He looked at me. "I can't really remember. I'm sorry."

"That's okay," I replied.

"I mean, we can just do some spatial deduction from this point anyway," Kyle said. "Although we're a little far from the original building."

"Oh!" I yelped, then turned around and ran back to where we found Brayden's blindfold. "Brayden," I called. "It's not that you don't remember. You went too far."

Everyone came back to where I was as Brayden asked, "How do you know that?"

"You said before that they just sort of dropped you and eventually you pulled your own blindfold off, right? You didn't walk for that long blindfolded." I pointed at the doors nearby. "The first building he led us to is over there, but maybe there's an underground tunnel or something that led here."

"That would be very like my dad," Nathan said.

"He walked pretty confidently up to the end of the block," Kyle said, and then put his hand on a door right near the corner. "Here maybe?"

Brayden looked down the brick wall and then his eyes widened. "Yeah! It's that door! It opened to the right. I remember bumping against the open door frame on the left side."

"He's right," Nikita said. "The rest of these doors look like they open the other way around."

Jaxon walked over to the door Kyle was standing near and started to fiddle with it. Kyle and Brayden watched over his shoulder, and I did a quick cursory glance for any onlookers or cameras. Security was low in a place like North Postings, I knew all too well, but I still wanted to be able to see if someone was coming.

Eventually, Jaxon managed to get the door free and opened it. Brayden stepped inside and then back out. "This is it. I remember going upstairs. Two flights." Jaxon pulled a gun out of his waistband and held it up as he led the way in, and we all filed in behind. Nikita propped the door open so we wouldn't somehow get locked in, and then we followed Jaxon and Brayden down two flights of stairs. "There were lots of hallways," Brayden said. "Twists and turns, but there will be a door first."

We got to the bottom of the stairs and all stopped dead in our tracks. All at once, each one of us deflated entirely. It wasn't that there were no twists and turns.

There was nothing at all. It was a big, empty

room that stretched in all directions for probably two blocks.

"Do we have the wrong place?" I asked.

Nathan shook his head. "No. We're in the right place. My dad just made sure it was totally cleaned out before he moved on. Even had the walls torn down. That's just like him."

"He tore the walls down?" I asked. "That's excessive even for him. Are you sure?"

Kyle walked a little further into the room and pointed down. There were bright lines cutting through the floor, dividing it into halls and rooms like some sort of blueprint. "Here's where the walls used to be. The dirt and grime is significantly less here."

Nathan looked at me. "You shouldn't underestimate my father. We wouldn't be in this position if he wasn't a lunatic."

"So what do we do next?" Brayden asked.

"Nothing," I replied. "We just hit another dead end."

14

DEON

"You have to go get the fire extinguisher!" I screamed at Felicity. "Hurry up! Everything is burning to the ground!"

"I don't know where it is," Felicity barked back.

"On the counter over there! Hurry!"

"Oh my god, oh my god, oh my god."

"Felicity!" I screeched.

"Shut the fuck up! I've got it! Move so you don't catch on fire."

On the screen, big, bright red letters that said 'mission failed' appeared. I turned and looked at Felicity, who was still flicking the button on her controller that operated the fire extinguisher as if we hadn't already lost.

"I think you can stop," I growled.

She held her hand up in my face. "Don't look at me like that, you brat. The kitchen caught on fire because of *you*."

My jaw dropped. "How was it me? You were supposed to be watching the fries!"

Felicity was sitting in her favorite spot on the couch, while I was sitting in the comfortable armchair. Concrete was curled up in a ball next to Felicity on the couch, and his ears flicked every time we yelled back and forth at one another, like he was irritated we were disrupting his nap.

"*You* were supposed to be watching the fries," Felicity whined back at me. "I was doing the pizzas."

"The ovens for the pizzas aren't even on your side," I argued. "That doesn't make any sense."

All the playful frustration left Felicity's face as she stared at the course layout on the television. "Oh… Yeah, you're right."

"Okay. I'm going to try again. Please don't let the fries set the whole kitchen on fire."

She side-eyed me. "Don't get lippy with me." Just as I was about to hit the button to restart the level of the co-op cooking game we were playing, Felicity's phone rang. She glanced over at it on the table next to the couch, and then sat up a little straighter. "Oh. Hang on. It's Nico." I sat up at attention too as she brought her phone up to her ear. "Hello? Hey."

She stood up and walked out of the room and though I was tempted to follow her, I let her go. She preferred to have conversations isolated, I'd noticed. It was less about keeping information from me, because she always told me everything, but more about being able to focus her thoughts. All I could do was hope that his call was a sign that he'd found something.

"Concrete." I tapped my leg. "Come here, boy." Concrete turned his head in my direction and looked at me, but didn't move. "Come here." He offered a couple of blinks, but stayed in place and I snickered. "Fine. I guess I'll come to you." I stood up and his tail immediately started to flap, growing more excited as I closed in and sat down where Felicity had been moments before. I sat down and he did move then, but only enough to scootch forward and set his head in my lap and bear his belly. "Brat."

I started to scratch his stomach, and in no time at all his tongue rolled out of his mouth and to the side and his eyes drifted shut again. As I laughed at him, I realized how difficult it would be to leave him when the time eventually came. I'd have to get a dog of my own as soon as I could, probably one very close to Concrete. I smiled, imagining moving into a small, modest place with Cherri and getting a dog. Maybe Venom and Felicity could come and visit and bring Concrete and our dog could bond with him. Was it dangerous to dream of such a delightful life? I had very little faith that I'd ever have that kind of life, but it didn't keep me from wishing for it.

"Hey," Felicity said, walking back into the room.

"Hi," I said. "Any news?" She frowned, and that was enough of an answer. "No luck, huh?"

"Connor's proving slipperier than he thought," she said. "He's coming up short, but he's going to keep trying."

"I know we agreed that we'd leave Nathan out of this, but the information he has could be really useful. Maybe we should reach out to him," I said.

"That's a last resort option," Felicity replied. "Let's give Nico a little more time and then if it really feels like he's not getting anywhere, we can consider it."

"Fine," I said.

"There is something though," Felicity said.

"Something else I'm hoping you'll keep a secret from your dad."

"Okay?"

"There was a place he used to go. A trade show of sorts. It's masked to look like a car show, but it was something of an underground black market. They use these flashy cars and all their money to hide just about any illegal business. Nasty stuff. Trafficking. Drugs. Embezzling. Blackmail. Murder for hire. If it would be considered a felony, you can find someone there who will do it," Felicity said.

"Connor has to have used a place like that," I said.

Felicity nodded. "That's what I'm thinking too. Garret wouldn't tell me where to find it, but Nico did."

"Wait... You're gonna go? That's gotta be insanely dangerous," I said.

She punched my arm lightly. "Maybe, but I can take care of myself. Plus, it would be worth it if it meant we could get a solid lead on Connor."

"Let me come with you then," I said.

She glared at me. "We agreed—"

"I know, but we also agreed we were going to work together," I retorted. "If Venom knew I let you go somewhere he didn't want you to go, alone, he'd break my legs. I'm not letting you go alone. Either we both go, or neither of us."

She watched me quietly for a few minutes, and her jaw flexed and relaxed in a pattern while she considered it. Finally, she blew air out of her nose and nodded. "Okay. We'll go together."

My stomach actually lurched a little at the thought. It'd been a little while since either of us had mentioned Connor or looking for him, and July was officially underway. I'd very nearly tricked myself into thinking that this was just the life I was living. I was just a normal kid living with his mom and adorable pit bull, doing chores around the house, and getting a little too into co-op video games.

But no.

Reality came crashing back into me and it made me anxious, but also reminded me of what I was doing in the first place. I had a family to get back to, a real one. My mother, my brother, my best friend, and the love of my life. They were waiting for me and this was an active effort to move in that direction. I was glad for the opportunity. We turned off the video game and each spent a little bit of time showering and getting ready, then we fed Concrete and left in Felicity's hot rod.

Not surprisingly, the car show took place at

night, and instead of being at a convention center like a regular show might be, this one was outside in something akin to a warehouse district close to the coast. Like a scene out of a movie, everyone filing into the show was receiving a mask to wear, likely to protect identities. I was shocked when I saw some police officers standing around, but the booze most of them were working on and scantily clad women dancing around them led me to believe they were dirty cops paid by some powerful men to keep things orderly.

I was slightly nervous that getting in would be difficult, but Felicity knew the right things to say to the guy guarding the entrance, and then we received our masks and were allowed inside. It was helpful that, despite being 18, my muscular stature and overgrown facial hair made me look older, and I kept close to Felicity as she led me further in.

"Okay," she whispered to me when we were safely inside. "It would probably be best for you to not be seen asking about Connor, even if your face is covered. I'll ask about him, I just need you to stay back and stay discreet."

"I don't want to do nothing," I said. "I'll ask around too, I just won't ask about Connor."

"Deon, that's not a good idea. He could have people here. If you even ask about something related, you could end up getting caught," Felicity said.

"The same is true for you. It's not like Connor doesn't know who you are." I put a hand on her shoulder. "I don't want to just be passive in my own fate anymore. I want to do something." There was more hesitation in her expression than I'd seen up to that point, and I could tell she really didn't want me to do it. "We spend less time here if we divide and conquer. We each hit up a few places, ask a few questions, and then get the hell out of here before any dust kicks up."

She took a deep breath in, held it, and then let it out. "Okay, but Deon, you have to swear to me that if anything seems suspicious, even a little bit, that you find me so we can get out of here. I mean, if someone lingers on you for more than a few seconds, you need to tell me."

"I will. I promise," I said. "Same goes for you."

Felicity did a little side-step, like she wasn't certain she wanted to leave, but eventually she walked away, and I did the same. The entire yard was arranged like a car show with beautiful, luxurious cars spaced all around. Display boards were set up with stats for each of the cars, but no one was looking at them. Everyone was mingling and talking to one another, and the people that seemed to be informants for the cars were at the center of all the attention. No one was in the market for a car, so it was just a matter of figuring out which industries were which.

Thinking about Connor, there was one aspect of his life I'd had more than my fair share of experience with, and that was the number of women that he used to his personal gain. I wasn't an idiot—Connor was a good-looking man—but word spreads fast in a small town like Postings. Not only that, but Felicity was a woman from well outside of Postings, and just so happened to be a woman in a very specific, very useful capacity. The same was true for my mom, Connor's former wife Alicia, and Miss Abrams at Postings Proper High School. Somehow, Connor was digging up women who were of use to him in very specific ways.

So I was looking for a trafficker of some sort, potentially someone who trafficked specific women's information without them knowing, as opposed to the women themselves.

I wandered around for a bit, standing near the back of different conversations and listening for anything that sounded like what I was looking for. The different things I heard made my stomach turn. More than anything, I just wanted to leave and get away from all of those deplorable people before I ended up punching someone in the face, but I kept my family in the back of my mind, both the one I had currently and the one that was waiting for me back home, and resolved myself so that I could find the information I needed.

Finally, I came across a man in a rather high-scale suit, standing near a brand new Mercedes. Unlike a vast majority of the other cars, there were *only* men situated around this one, and very few of them were discreet about watching the women walking around. I was surprised more of them weren't salivating.

I approached the collection of people and got close enough to stand near the back of the current conversation taking place.

"So, you're sure she's the right one?" One man asked the suited man.

"Sir, trust me on this. Not only is she beautiful, but she's got a sick mother. Once you've spent enough time, she'll do just about anything to get the money she needs for her care," the suited man said.

The guy talking to him smiled. "Perfect."

He reached into his pocket and pulled out a wad of cash and peeled about ten, one-hundred dollar bills off the wad and handed them over. In exchange he received a manila envelope and the suited man gave him a knowing nod. "Best of luck."

The man took his envelope and walked away and then the suited man turned his attention to me. "Why hello."

"Hi." Even though I didn't see anyone who I thought would recognize me, I wanted to use as few words as possible, just in case."

"Are you in the market for a beautiful car today?" he said.

"Possibly," I replied. "I'm browsing."

The man took a step back and raised an eyebrow. "Browsing?"

"Yes." I looked over my shoulder to make sure no one was looking at me and then turned back to face the suited man. "A teacher possibly."

He crossed his arms and I got the funny feeling I'd done or said something wrong, though I wasn't sure what. "I'm not in the business of teachers anymore. Not since all of that mess in Postings."

My heart started to beat a little faster. I was in the right place at least. If I could just get the guy to relax a bit, I'd be in a better spot. "That's a shame. I'd pay well for one."

The man looked over my shoulder and nodded his head. I glanced back in the direction he was looking and saw two masked people staring back at me. In a slow-motion, heart pounding moment, one of them reached up and lifted the mask on his face up, revealing that he was one of the two who'd captured and tortured me before I managed to escape.

Shit.

I turned and looked back at the suited man and raised an eyebrow. "I guess you don't want my business."

He smiled. "You're right. I don't."

With that, I slid away from the area and started to scan the crowd for Felicity. It was harder with everyone masked, so I simply kept an eye out for her signature braids and the dark blue dress she'd worn. As I turned a corner, I risked a look to my right and saw that the two people, including one of my former captors, was still following me. I didn't know what I'd done wrong, but maybe Felicity was right, it was a bad idea to ask around.

Eventually, I came to a bustling corner of the show and saw Felicity standing amongst the fray. I tried not to raise any eyebrows as I slid and pushed my way towards her, and instead of reaching out to grab her, I just moved and stood at her side.

"Felicity?" I asked.

She turned and looked at me. "Hey. You good?"

"Um, not really," I replied. "Remember when you told me to come find you if I ran into any trouble?"

"Yeah," she said, nervousness in her voice.

I looked over her. "Well this is me finding you."

15

CHERRI

No one mentioned the dead end we found for a handful of days. Though none of us were willing to say it, I think the same one thing was true for all of us.

We weren't expecting to still be searching for answers a month later.

Sicily was still trying to work his way through the muddle of information he ran into from the unknown number that had called Nathan and I, which turned out to be how Deon was communicating with Nathan, but the information he was getting was hard to stick to anything. The only thing he'd learned was that a majority of the pings from the number were in and around Maine, which meant Deon was likely still in the state, but he had no idea where. Just being *in* Maine was useless to us.

The road we'd followed with Brayden trying to find Connor had hit the same brick wall. Wherever Connor *had* been meeting with Brayden, it had been totally cleaned out. Apparently Connor was a man who liked to cover his bases.

Who knew?

Brayden had mentioned that there were a few different places he'd been brought to, but none of them sat as clearly in his mind as the one we'd found and now knew was of no use to us. We had made a couple of attempts that same day we hit the first dead end to find something else—it was Brayden's way of trying to keep us all from getting too down in the dumps—but nothing led anywhere near as concrete.

Suddenly, it felt like we had *nothing*.

Stalemate.

A knock on my door pulled my attention over, and I looked up to see Nathan walking into the room. "Hey."

"Hi."

Nathan walked in and sat down in the chair sitting at the desk and spun it to face me. "How you doing?"

"I'm okay. I just feel… out of options," I said.

"I feel like we're no closer to finding Connor or Deon than we were a month ago." Nathan slid his hands into his dark brown hair. It'd gotten much longer since we were dating. "You taking a stand against haircuts?" I asked.

He chuckled. "Nah. My therapist and I talked about it. I've always liked my hair longer, and Nikki likes it long, but it's more of a control thing. It's one thing I have control over, whether or not I cut my hair." He laughed. "I know that sounds dumb."

"No." I smiled at him. "Are you really seeing a therapist?"

He nodded. "Yeah. It's been great. I mean… I needed it."

"I'd say so," I responded.

"My dad used to do strange shit," he said suddenly. "He'd blindfold me, or bind my hands, and I usually had to pass some test or recall specific information before he'd let me out. He said that if I had pressure to get the information right, I always would. He wasn't wrong, but I didn't even realize until I started going to therapy how much I'd repressed that stuff. I'd forgotten."

"That's probably why you always felt like the best way to communicate was to trap who you were talking to," I said.

He nodded. "So I've discovered. Not doing that

is hard. It's scary not being able to control every-thing in my world, but I know now how unhealthy that is."

"Why are you telling me this?" I asked.

"I saw how disturbed you got when I said some-thing about the blindfold," Nathan replied. "I… want us to be close again, Cherri. Not romantically, but you're important to me. I want to be open and honest with you." He shrugged. "I mean, you'll probably be my sister-in-law… someday I think."

"Oh god. I will have dated my children's—"

"Nope," Nathan cut me off. "We're not going to talk about that… ever."

I laughed. "Fair."

He stood up from the chair and tapped me. "Come on. I've set up a dinner meeting for all of us. Hopefully it'll help you not to feel so lost."

"Okay." I stood up and Nathan started to walk away, but I grabbed his arm and pulled him back. My heart started to pound a bit faster, but I closed in on Nathan and wrapped my arms around him in a hug. He hugged me back, and I could feel in the way he squeezed that it was just as needed for him as it was for me. I stepped away and laughed. "Sorry.

"No," he said. "Don't be. Our first real hug. That was awesome."

"Agreed."

Bit by bit, all the tension that I'd built up was easing. I missed Deon and couldn't wait to have him home, but I was happy to be getting close with my "royal" family while I waited.

We met up with the rest of The Royal Court and we split up into a few different cars to drive to one of our favorite pasta restaurants in downtown Postings. A table had been reserved, and we were ushered to it in a back, private room as soon as we arrived. We sat around the table starting with Nathan, then Nikita, Jaxon, Colette, Kyle, Brayden, Alistair, Avery, me, and Sicily, and then there were two open chairs between Nathan and Sicily. Water in crystal goblets were at each seat, and there was a large basket of a few different types of bread at the table.

"Surprise guests?" Alistair said.

Nathan nodded. "Hopefully they can help us glean a little more information."

We made idle chatter and enjoyed the bread and butter until, eventually, two more people were brought back to the private room. The woman was medium-height, with shoulder-length light brown hair, and a dark blue cocktail dress showing off a fit, toned body. She was beautiful, no question, but the most unique feature about her were her eyes, which were a sparkling green. The left moved around naturally, taking in the different people at the table, but the right, though realistic-looking, wasn't moving at all.

The man was tall. The only person in our group that maybe stood taller was all six feet, four inches of Kyle. His arms and legs were built like tree trunks, forcing the fabric of his button-up and slacks to do the work of keeping them contained. He kept a hand situated low on the woman's back, making me feel like they were romantically involved.

"There's my boy!" The woman yelped.

Nathan jumped up out of his seat, and the smile he got was blinding and bright. "Anisa!" He damn near threw himself into a hug and the woman squeezed him close, reminding me of a mother holding her son. The man slid over and put his hand on Nathan's shoulder, and Nathan unfurled from the woman he'd called Anisa, and clasped into a hug with the man. "Cobalt."

"Man, you've gotten tall. It's been too long," he said.

Colette balanced her head in her hands and smiled at the interaction. "The parents he deserves," she whispered to herself, and it actually brought a tear to my eyes. There were people out there who loved Nathan the way he deserved. That made me happier than words could express.

"My god, is that Nikki?" Anisa said, and Nikita nodded. "Oh my god. You look beautiful! Look, Cobalt." Then her eyes scanned further. "And Kyle!"

Kyle's jaw dropped. "Wow! Oh my god. Anisa. Cobalt. It's been… *years.*"

Nikita and Kyle were the two people that Nathan knew even from before starting The Royal Court, so it made sense that they'd know them as well.

Anisa and Cobalt settled down into the two empty chairs and Nathan returned to his seat. "Guys, this beauty here is Anisa, and this titan of a man is Cobalt. They *used* to work for my dad, but they left his employ after seeing how he treated me."

"Nathan was just this cute, innocent little thing, and that man was destroying him," Anisa said. "I couldn't stand by and watch it. I would have done anything to take him with me."

"He turned out okay though," Cobalt said. "I'll admit, when you called us, we lost our minds. I don't think Anisa stopped crying for two days."

"Well, I have these people to thank for that."

He set his hand on Nikita's. "You guys know Nikki, and we're together now."

"Seriously?!" Anisa yelped. "Yay!"

"Next to her is her best friend Jaxon, his girl and my friend Colette next to him. You remember Kyle, and that's my friend Brayden next to him. Then my friend Alistair and his girlfriend Avery." He pointed at me. "That ray of sunshine there is like a sister to me, Cherri." Both Anisa and Cobalt shifted a little at my name, but continued to smile and nodded at me. "And then next to her is my friend Sicily."

"That's right. I'm his friend. Me. Sicily," Sicily said.

"That can still change," Nathan joked.

Sicily held up his hands. "Sorry."

"Anisa is a military war hero who took shrapnel in the eye defending her platoon. She's the strongest person I know, and when my father was trying to torture me, she was taking care of me. She'd sneak me candy and toys. I loved it," Nathan explained. "Cobalt... well, no one really knows what he did, but I did manage to get out of him once that he *may* have been in the Secret Service."

"I can neither confirm nor deny," Cobalt said, and then winked.

"About five years ago, they left my dad's employ,

right before I started The Royal Court. Anisa tried to keep up with me, but my dad wouldn't let her. Then when we trapped those two goons a couple of months ago, I called her for help," Nathan explained.

"Ah, so *that's* where they went," Avery said.

Nathan crossed his hands. "It was a quick, darkened exchange, so I didn't get to really see or say hi to them, and they've been keeping them for me, but I figured it was finally time to come together and compare notes, given that all of our trails seem to be running cold."

Anisa frowned. "I tried to tell you we don't have much. Those guys are pretty tight-lipped."

"I know, but I wanted to see you, and I figured it couldn't hurt to all toss some stuff around. Who knows, you guys could have a single piece of information that would answer a question we have." He smiled at Anisa. "Plus I wanted to see you," he repeated, earning himself a kiss on the cheek. "I hope it's okay, but I didn't want anyone just wandering back while we're talking and hearing something they shouldn't, so I just ordered large portions of their four main dishes to share. I said they could start them once the last two guests arrived, so they should be out soon."

Over the course of the next hour, Anisa and

Cobalt explained all of the information they'd managed to gather from the two men that had attacked us, whom they'd been keeping under lock and key. A lot of what they knew was already stuff that we'd managed to discern ourselves, and mostly it sounded like the men were being very tight-lipped.

"That doesn't surprise me, knowing my dad," Nathan said, but he seemed more frustrated than he did at first. He looked around the table, letting his eyes eventually land on me. "I'm sorry, Cherri. I really thought there would be more."

"There is one thing that's pretty obvious. Connor is still operating in and around Postings," I said. "That's better than nothing."

"No wait," Sicily said. "It really *is* better than nothing." All eyes fell on him. "Connor had Deon snatched too, right? Would that suggest that he's here too?"

Silence enveloped the table as we all pondered that thought. How had that never occurred to us before?

"Deon, wow. A blast from the past," Anisa said. "You still haven't found him?"

"No," Nathan said. "We've had a few leads, but we're coming up empty."

"If only we could get into those guys' phones.

I'm sure they've been communicating with Connor, or at least other contacts of his. They get pretty regular phone calls, but the phones are so protected, you have to know the password just to answer a phone call," Cobalt explained.

"You have their phones?" Nathan said, and then his eyes shot over to Sicily.

Sicily leaned back in his chair and a sly smile crossed his face. He interlocked his fingers and stretched them out away from his body. "Once again, it's time for Sicily to save the day."

"Once again?" Colette said. "We're still grinding our way through the fifty thousand pings you dug up."

"Hey!" Sicily snapped. "We are all learning a marketable skill, and we're doing it together. Trade and friendship. That's invaluable."

I just shook my head and chuckled at him. Be it comic relief or just his pure inability to be anything other than laid back, Sicily was a much-needed light in the dark halls of The Royal Court.

"I can bring you their phones," Anisa said. "Do you think you can get in?"

A voice we rarely heard croaked up. "He can do it," Jaxon said, bringing everyone's attention to him. "What? I can recognize talent."

Sicily's hands flew to his face. "Did… Did

Jaxon just compliment me?" He picked up a napkin and dabbed it at the corners of his eyes. "I wasn't prepared for this. I'd like to start by thanking my parents, and my best friends, Deon and Cherri."

"You mean Cherri and Deon?" I said.

"Stop," Jaxon growled.

Sicily nodded. "Stopping."

Cobalt chuckled. "I like this one. He's weird."

Nathan rolled his eyes. "Yeah, he is, but Jaxon is right. If you can get us those phones, Sicily can get in."

Anisa smiled. "I'll bring them by tomorrow."

Just like that, the trail that was running cold was blazing again. This was different from my and Nathan's phones that only contained a single, designed-to-be-untraceable phone number. These guys worked for Connor and could have even communicated with the people who were after Deon. It was a huge development.

The rest of dinner with our renewed hope was enjoyable and delicious, so much so that the restaurant had to kick us out when it was time to close. We spilled into the parking lot laughing and chatting, and Nathan gave Anisa and Cobalt each huge hugs, promising to see them again soon. I watched them and my stomach burned thinking of my own parents. I'd apologized, but it still felt like there was a huge wall between us.

One only I could break down.

"Cherri?" Avery said. "You ready? I know you rode with Jaxon and Colette but…" She glanced over in their direction and I followed her gaze to where the two were embroiled in a massive make-out. "You probably aren't going to want to ride back with them."

"Yeah, uh, actually… Do you think you can bring me to my parents'?" I asked. "I just… I never told them the whole truth about everything, and I think I'm ready. Nathan and Deon both had these fractured families and I have two parents who love me that I'm lying to. It's time to come clean."

"Wow," Avery said. "Sure, if that's what you really want."

"It is," I replied. "My parents deserve to know everything."

16

DEON

Felicity was fidgeting back and forth, while I kept trying to keep a clock on the people who were following me, a tough enough task on its own given that everyone was in masks.

"How did this happen?" Felicity said. "Was it immediate? We haven't been here that long."

"I'm not quite sure. I found a man who I think was the guy who put Connor in contact with a bunch of the women he slept with for the purposes of using them for his own gain. All of the women that my mom discovered he was sleeping with, including you and her, are women who had some sort of second use for him. His wife Alicia may have just been a trophy, but my mom cleaned his house, including some shady areas most likely, you have pull over Venom, this teacher at my school was blackmailing my brother. Every woman he used, he used for a reason, and I think he found the right ones here," I explained. "I found the guy, but when I started inquiring about a woman, almost immediately, he flagged these people down."

"What people?" she asked.

I looked over my shoulder again, and the people still had their eyes on me, but weren't advancing, at least not at the moment. "About 8 o'clock. Don't look though, I don't think they realize I'm with you."

Felicity didn't listen, which I might have expected. She turned to her left first and pretended as if she was looking for something, then she turned to the right and did the same, then got back to facing forward. "I see them."

"One of them is one of the guys who snatched me on Connor's behalf a few months ago. I don't know if the other one is his partner or not, but if it is, I'm more afraid of her. She's vicious."

"Well, it's like you said, Connor knows some unique women," Felicity replied. "Shoot. I have a hot lead too. I'll have to find a new way to follow it."

"No," I said. "If you have a lead, we need to follow it. We're struggling enough as it is. I'll lead them away and keep them busy while you do what you need to do. When you're ready to go, go stand by the bright pink Caddi near the front, then I'll know you're ready to go."

She didn't immediately respond, but then sighed and said, "Okay. Deon… please be careful."

"I will. You too."

At that, I flipped around and left the group of people and headed straight for the center of the car show that was the most congested. Peeking behind me, I could see the two were following, which was good, because I just wanted them as far away from Felicity as I could get them. Once I'd done that, then I could worry about giving them the slip.

In the congested center of the show where there were several booths set up selling food and drinks, I weaved in and out of the crowd in no particular order. The last thing I wanted to do was draw more attention to myself, so I'd move a little, pretend to be assessing a menu, and then move again. The two that were following me, however, were doing a pretty good job of keeping an eye on me, so I had to come up with another plan.

Finally, I looked over and saw a woman in an extravagant white dress drinking a beer. There were several people standing around her, and whether it was because she was someone of importance or just because she was stunning, I wasn't sure, but she was the center of attention. Keeping the people chasing me in the corner of my eye, I slid closer and closer to her, and then I pretended as if I tripped. I knocked into someone standing closer to her and he bumped into her, sending her beer spilling all over her. She let out a loud screech as her beer dripped down her dress and drenched her hair, and the people encircling her created an uproar. They were tripping over themselves offering her napkins or their jackets to hide the spill, and the congested crowd started to close in on where she was.

Letting the crowd push me inwards for a bit, when I was right in the midst of a sea of people, I ducked down, crouching, and kept myself low in the crowd. A bunch of people were running back and forth between the nearest booth to get napkins to help the victim of the beer spill, so I crept my way along the side of them until I was able to successfully duck behind the booth. Fortunately, a car was not far from the back of the booth, giving me a little nook to crawl into and hopefully stay hidden. I looked in all directions to see if the two were still following me, but no one was looking in my direction and I let out a sigh of relief.

I waited longer than felt comfortable before I stood up and looked around the booth to see if my pursuers were still nearby. The crowd that had converged on the woman had mostly dissipated as she'd chosen a specific person to help her, but the center was still thick with people eating and drinking. I scanned the group until I finally managed to catch a glimpse of the two people against one of the booths opposite the one I was hiding behind. Their eyes were flicking in all directions, and I could tell they had lost track of me. As long as I could stay hidden where I was, I would be able to stay out of trouble and meet up with Felicity when it was time.

At least that was the plan, until the two chasing me started to move.

I furrowed my brow and watched them closely. Were they giving up? Did they see someone else that they think was me?

Against my better judgement, I crept out from behind the booth and side-stepped my way back into the crowd. My height had me at a disadvantage as I was looking over the heads of most of the people around me, but at least I was able to keep an eye on the two goons. The tables were turned and it was now me who was stalking them, but what they were up to, I still wasn't sure. Connor would have told them not to leave without me. There was no way they'd give up so quickly. Were they baiting me out? If so, it was working.

They had their attention focused on something in the distance, but it was difficult to see what until one person broke away from a group they were looking at. As soon as that person walked out of the group, their eyes followed and they changed direction to keep up. I stopped watching them long enough to get a glimpse of the new person they were tracking.

It was Felicity.

"Shit," I growled to myself.

I thought I'd successfully kept them from figuring out that we were together, but maybe I didn't do as well as I thought. That was proving to be the theme of the day. I wanted to believe that I was fully prepared to hunt Connor down and stop him from tormenting me and my family, but I was quickly learning that it was not the case. My confidence was shaken, but now was no time to worry about that. I had to protect Felicity.

Keeping a safe distance for the moment, I stayed on the trail of the two who'd been chasing after me, as they turned their attention on Felicity. They seemed to just be keeping tabs on her, maybe assuming that I'd show back up at her side at some point, but then she came to a stop near the front, at the car we'd designated as our meetup spot. She stood still, keeping her eyes out on the crowd, and eventually her eyes landed on our pursuers.

Slowly, they lifted their masks off their faces and revealed themselves to Felicity outright. Everyone around stopped and turned to look at them, and then backed away, giving them a ton of space. The man was the one who'd revealed himself to me earlier, and the other was, in fact, the woman who was the other torturer who'd captured me. She was the truly sadistic one of the pair, and I didn't want her seeing Felicity's face and knowing she was helping me out.

Leaving to come to the car show with her had been a mistake.

Then both of them reached for their waist-bands. Peeling back the jackets of the suits they had on, they each reached for a gun they had hidden, but their eyes were on Felicity, not me. I panicked, thinking that things were going to get worse for Felicity or they were going to figure her out, so I did the only thing I could think to do.

The dumbest thing, for sure.

I stepped out into the clearing that the crowd had created and screamed out, "Hey!" Both of them turned to look at me and smiles curled across their faces. If it had been their plan to coax me out by threatening Felicity, it had worked. "I'm what you wanna see, right? Make good with your boss? Come get me."

Felicity took a step forward. "Deon!"

"I'll meet you near Concrete!" I screeched, then I turned around and bolted back into the fray of the car show.

A couple of gunshots cracked against the music playing in the background of the show, and all of the attendees started to duck and run for cover. There was no longer anywhere to hide, only do the one thing I'd mastered in the past year.

Run.

I leapt over anyone that got in my way, including shoving people aside to get around them. The good news was, they weren't openly shooting at me, at least not while I was around everyone. As long as I could keep a few people between them and me, I could keep from getting shot in the back.

The car show was surrounded on all sides by barrels turned into a fence with the use of white poles that had been bolted to connect them. Some of the dirty cops that were on guard were standing near the perimeter, and I was hoping that maybe getting closer to them would turn my pursuers around. I ran straight in their direction, even after they locked eyes on me, but then they pulled their guns too.

"Stop!" One screamed.

"That's the one," the woman who had captured me screamed from behind me. "Grab him!"

I should have expected that they were all in on it together. Connor had more influence than anyone anticipated. Looking to the left and right, I considered turning around and dodging back into the show, but there were more people stepping away from the screaming, running people, all set for me. The longer I stayed in the show, the worse things were going to get.

I had to get out.

So I continued to run straight at the police officers. They had their guns drawn and were screaming at me to stop, but I didn't slow. Similarly to the man and woman behind me, the cops weren't shooting, so the public was working to my advantage. Once I was on the other side of that fence, that protection would be gone, so hopefully my limberness wouldn't fail me now.

I shoved between the two cops that were looking at me, and braced my hands on the top pole of the fence and vaulted myself over. I immediately threw myself into a serpentine movement, and not a moment too soon, as bullets immediately started to fly at me. Outside of the show, the warehouse district was nothing but shadows and shipping containers. Plenty of places to hide.

"Deon," the woman who snatched me sang from behind me. "Don't make me chase you. It's only going to make things worse.

I could hide behind any one of the shipping containers, but there was only so much I could do before they found me again. However, the coast was directly in front of me. Thank god I didn't have any electronic devices on me. I continued to charge forward, despite the people behind me screaming after me not to do what they could see I was doing, and a bullet pierced the silence.

And then I felt a burning pain in my leg.

My face hit the dirt before I even realized I was falling. The coast was about ten feet in front of me, but I could feel blood pouring down my shin and the stinging searing my skin. The gunshot wound I'd taken to the stomach courtesy of Connor still throbbed in the middle of the night sometimes. Now I was back to point zero.

But I refused to go back.

I crawled up to my feet and continued to charge towards the coast and out onto the dock that was hanging over the water.

"Deon, don't!"

I held up my hand with my middle finger stabbed up, and rushed right off the front of the dock and crashed into the waves below. The forceful tide was attempting to suck me out to sea, but I fought against it to swim backwards, underneath the dock instead. A few pieces of cord were hanging from the dock, so I grabbed onto one and twisted it several times around my arm, and then let my body flow with the rush of the waves, hopefully keeping me from sticking out of the water too much. My leg was screaming in pain and I knew that the chances my fresh wound would end up infected were high, but that was a concern for later.

Above me, the man and woman who were chasing me charged out onto the dock. Their feet pounding against the wood were so loud and close, but I could barely hear them over the waves and blasting of my own heart. Even though the water was loud, I still held my breath, praying that they didn't look down.

"Fuck," the woman said. "I can't believe his crazy ass jumped."

The man scoffed. "If I was threatening to drag you to Connor Loche what would you do?"

It didn't make sense. If they knew how dangerous he was, how could they bring me back there?

"Well, whatever, there's nothing we can do. We're just going to tell him we never saw him," the woman said.

"Fine by me," the man replied. "Let's go. It's cold by this fucking water."

With that, they turned around and walked back down the docks and retreated until I eventually couldn't hear them anymore. Even long after they were gone, long after my leg had gone numb from pain, and my arm had gone numb from pain, and my vision and hearing were waning, I stayed there treading water. I tried counting the minutes to myself to keep track of how long I stayed down there, but then I started to shake and lose breath, and I knew I was probably close to giving myself hypothermia.

It was a struggle, but I managed to drag myself back out of the water. The car show was no longer lit up, and either because it ended or because of the pursuit, it had been shut down. The warehouse district was abandoned and quiet, so I limped my way along the edge of the shipping containers until I could cross back through the warehouse district and eventually to the main road. I had no phone or way to get a hold of someone, but finally, I saw a few people walking near the edge of the road. They kept their distance from me, which was fair, so I held up my hands.

"Please. Can you just call me a cab?"

None of them responded to me, but one did press a few buttons on their phone and lifted it to their ear. I was briefly afraid they were calling the cops, but then I heard him say, "Hey, can I get a cab? Right outside the warehouse district on Melcost Lane. I'm a big guy with red hair and I'm soaking wet. You can't miss me. Cool, thanks."

I nodded. "Thanks." Then I dropped and sat on the edge of the road and waited. The people, though they never got closer or spoke to me, stood nearby until the cab came, and then waited as I climbed inside. "There's a $200 dollar tip if you can get me home. I fell in the ocean and lost my wallet."

The man looked at me through the rearview mirror at me. "I will call the police if you don't pay."

"I swear. Just get me home, and my mom will pay you."

He nodded, so I provided Felicity's address, and we started off. I nearly faded from consciousness a few times and I was shaking violently, but eventually the cab did get me back to Felicity's house. I kept looking around, afraid that I'd been followed, but for the time being, no one had come. As soon as the cab pulled up, those of Venom's men who had been watching the house surrounded it with their guns drawn, but I quickly climbed out and called them off.

"Can someone please give this guy $200? I'll give it back to you," I asked.

"Don't worry, D," one of the guys, Max, said. "He reached into his wallet and pulled out a few hundred dollar bills and handed them to the driver. "More money for your trouble and to keep your mouth shut, huh?"

The cab driver nodded his head dramatically. "I was never here."

"Good man," Max replied.

The cab screeched away and I limped my way up the walk to Felicity's front door. I knocked and it opened almost immediately, a teary Felicity appearing on the other side. "Oh thank god," she whined and pulled me into a hug.

"You were right. I shouldn't have gone," I said.

"Yeah," she replied. "Let's not worry about that right now. Come inside before you catch death."

All I could do was laugh at her phrasing. Little did she know how close I'd come.

17

CHERRI

listair and Avery both got out of the car in order to walk me up to the door. Because I hadn't spoken to my parents in six months, neither had any of my friends. Avery and Alistair were the two people I considered my 'real friends' from The Royal Court before everything changed, so my parents had gotten used to seeing them around. When I asked Avery to drive me back to their house so that we could have a chance to talk, both her and Alistair got excited about the idea of being able to say hi for the first time in half a year.

I lifted my hand to the door and went to knock, but then stopped. My keys were in my pocket, and my parents didn't take them away from me. Even though it felt awkward, I used them and let myself, Avery, and Alistair into the house.

It was a little after eight at night, but I could hear the quiet drone of the television coming from the living room. I led the way towards it and walked in to where my parents were sitting on the couch, my dad totally passed out, and Gus was sitting on the floor, also half-asleep.

"Cherri," my mom said, and then she smiled. "And look who else you brought."

Avery lifted her hand with a smile. "Hey, Rebeccah."

The voices stirred my dad and Gus, who awoke and looked over. "Cherri!" Gus yelped, jumping up and running over. He slammed into me in a big hug and I squeezed him back as tightly as I could. "I missed you."

"I just saw you a few days ago," I replied, but Gus squeezed tighter.

"I know. I always miss you." He was such a sweet kid, and I had to imagine still traumatized by my sudden disappearance, so I took this statement with the weight it held and kissed him on top of his head.

My mom stood up and walked over, offering both Alistair and Avery hugs, then she turned to me for one. "Hi, baby."

I hugged her back. "Hey, mama."

"To what do we owe this unexpected visit?" my dad asked, sitting up on the couch and stretching.

"Uh, I actually have to talk to you guys about some stuff, but Avery and Ali just wanted to say hi," I explained.

Alistair put his arm behind my mom's back and pulled her into another side-hug. "I'm hoping we can have a homemade Rebeccah dinner sometime soon."

That lit my mom up. "Of course! I'd love it! You just say the word and it'll be done!"

"We'll have to do it soon because Ali and I are leaving for New Haven in a couple of months," Avery said as she beamed. "I got accepted to Yale. Full ride!"

My mom and dad gasped loudly, then my mom threw her arms around Avery. "Oh sweetheart! Congratulations! I always knew you'd knock 'em dead." There was probably a part of them that was sad they were missing out on the college experience with me. It wasn't like I *wasn't* going to college. It wasn't like I definitely was either.

I had no idea what my plan was. I was just focused on finding Deon.

"Thank you," Avery said, then pulled away. "So, yes. I'd love dinner soon. To celebrate!"

My mom nodded. "I'll make whatever you want. You just tell Cherri what and when and it'll be done."

"Okay!"

Alistair put his hand on my head and ruffled my hair like I was some little sister. "Well, we won't take up any more of your time. I know you have things to discuss. If you need us to come back for you, just let me know."

"Thanks, Ali," I replied.

Avery and Alistair offered a final round of hugs to my mom, Gus, and my dad who finally wandered over, then they offered me warm smiles and good lucks, and left.

"Are you hungry, honey? There are leftovers if you'd like. Dad made his fresh fried rice," my mom said, already charting a course for the kitchen.

"I'd love that," I replied.

I wasn't hungry at all. In fact, I'd gorged myself on pasta at the restaurant, but the idea of getting a mouthful of my dad's home cooking was too good to deny. Looking back over my shoulder, I smiled at my dad. "You comin', daddy? I got some stuff I wanna talk to you guys about."

My dad had his hand on Gus's back, and Gus was already starting to drift again even though he was standing straight up. "Yeah. Let me just get this kid to bed. He can barely stand up."

"No," Gus whimpered. "I wanna stay with Cherri."

"You know what?" I said, walking up to him and putting my hands on his face. "I'll stay over tonight. Once I'm done talking to mom and dad, I'll come up and snuggle with you just like we used to do, okay?"

Gus nodded. "Yeah. Okay."

I released him and my dad led him off towards the stairs and I turned into the kitchen instead. My mom was just setting a bowl of the heated fried rice down on the kitchen, and the smell of the spices was comforting. I sat down at the island stool behind the bowl and dug in immediately. The taste was even better than the smell and it simply reminded me of home. Not necessarily the large home we were in currently, or the smaller one we used to live in in North Postings, but just being around my family and loving one another regard-less of the circumstances.

"Okay," my dad said, walking into the kitchen. "That was easier than I thought it'd be."

"Really?" I said. "He was damn near asleep standing up."

He chuckled. "I guess that's true."

"So, what did you want to talk to us about, sweetheart?" my mom asked.

I set my fork down and slid the bowl aside. "Well, it occurred to me that there is still a lot you guys don't know about what's going on with me right now. Not just now either, but why all that stuff happened during my spring semester."

My mom tilted her head. "I thought you said it was because your friend died."

"Kind of, but it's more complicated than that… way more." My parents exchanged a brief side-eye and there was something in it that was mysterious, but I didn't ask. There was already too much in my brain to worry about for the moment. "Well, in the interest of making a long story short, but also kind of long, Deon isn't dead. He's alive, although we don't know where he is."

"He's alive?" my mother asked. "Why would you lie about something like that?"

"It wasn't a complete lie," I replied. "I *did* think that Deon had died, that's what Nathan told me, but I had a feeling he wasn't, and then Nathan finally came clean about a month ago that he's still alive and out there somewhere. I was so angry with him for lying to me, and for dragging me away from Deon in a situation when he almost died that I cut off the entire Royal Court and turned into a demon. I'm so sorry."

My dad crossed his arms. "I don't understand. What do Nathan and Deon have to do with one another."

"Right, yeah. I'm sort of starting in the middle of the story and I probably should be starting at the beginning." I reeled my brain backwards trying to find a good starting point, and landed on the most important fact. "Well, I suppose it needs to be said right away, my friend Deon from our old neighborhood is Connor's son."

Both my parents' jaws dropped and eyes nearly came out of their heads. They seemed so much more shocked than I expected them to be. "What do you mean?" my dad asked. "What about Nathan?"

"Nathan is his son as well. They're half-brothers, sharing Connor as a father. Deon's mom is Ciara, who he lived with back in our old neighborhood, and Nathan's mom was Alicia," I explained.

My mom took a nervous breath. "*Was?*"

"Yeah," I said. "Alicia is dead. Connor killed her."

I could see the gears of fear turning in my parents head as the words left my lips, but it was my father who managed to speak first. "Why would he kill his own wife?"

"The same reason he'd try to kill his own children, because they're threatening his power and existence," I said. "Also, and please don't freak out, but… he's trying to kill us too."

My mom crossed her arms. "What?"

"Who's 'us?'" my dad asked.

"The entire Royal Court, but specifically Nikita and me, because we mean so much to Nathan and Deon." I shook my head, annoyed. The words I was saying weren't coming out in a way that made sense. "Let me back up." I took a deep breath. "When we lived in the old neighborhood, I met Deon and… I fell in love with him. The day that we went for our first date, this body literally dropped from the sky in front of us. We just naturally assumed that it was a jumper, but the cop thought we'd killed him for some reason. Deon said we should run, so we did, and I didn't find out until the beginning of senior year that Deon ended up confessing to it, but he didn't do it, I swear. He confessed just to protect me."Again, my parents side-glanced each other and my father in particular looked very nervous. "Okay. What is that?"

My dad looked back at me. "Well, you finish first, then I'll tell you."

That freaked me out, but I believed he would explain when the time came. "Well, not long after Deon went to prison, you got promoted and then I was introduced to The Royal Court. It sounds like Connor orchestrated my meeting Nathan. When Nathan and I started to drift apart last year, specifically because Deon came home, Connor started to melt down about it. He flipped out, killed Alicia, tried to kill Nathan, and framed Deon for that teacher that killed herself."

My dad's head dropped into his hands and my mom rubbed his back. "Chris. It's not your fault."

"It *is* my fault. You told me not to accept that promotion and I did anyway," my dad replied.

"Daddy, moving us to South Postings had nothing to do with this. Connor was going to do what he wanted regardless, that was just the avenue he chose," I said.

"No," my dad shook his head. "Not that promotion. The one that brought us to Maine to begin with."

"W-what?" I said. "What do you mean?"

"Connor promoted me rather suddenly, saying that the transfer from our original office to the one in Postings was necessary. How ironic that you would end up near Deon," my dad said.

"Cherri, you know that we think you are so

much more than just how beautiful you are, but think of Alicia. You share similar qualities. You're as pretty as a model and would look good on anyone's arm. I'm beginning to think Connor handpicked you for his son," my mom explained.

My dad looked up, weary-eyed. "And for some reason, when things didn't work with you and Deon, he promoted me again, and suddenly you ended up with Nathan."

"Deon told me that he went to live with Connor for a year, but he refused to stay and eventually came home. Ciara, Deon's mom, had a bunch of information about all of the affairs that Connor had been having, and was able to use it to get him to back off of trying to take Deon from her. Shortly after that, we came here and I met Deon. Then this thing happened with this weird body and Deon getting framed for it, and then you got promoted and we moved," I said. "That means…"

"Yeah," my mom said. "Connor had to have had something to do with Deon getting framed."

"He came to me," my dad said, and then my mom looked at him confused. "He told me about Deon. He said he was a dangerous guy and that I needed to keep my daughter away from him. He told me that, eventually, we would see the kind of person he was, and then when Deon disappeared, he told me why and offered me a promotion and to move to keep you safe."

My jaw fell slack. "What?!"

"Christian, how could you not tell me that?" my mom asked.

"I thought I was protecting my family." My dad reached across the island and put a hand on mine. "Cherri, I'm so sorry."

"Was it just because he felt scorned by Deon? That he'd be willing to do something so harmful to his own son?" I asked. "He's even more psychotic than I thought."

My parents and I sat in silence for a while, and eventually I made an excuse to leave the kitchen. I couldn't believe that my parents knew so much more about Connor than they'd let on. My mind was going a mile a minute thinking that every aspect of my life from the moment I arrived in Postings had been so manipulated by Connor and his games. He played with my life and the lives of everyone around me.

I was so angry I could breathe fire.

Just like I promised I would, I went up to Gus's room and climbed into his bed. He was asleep, so I snuggled in behind him, and he turned without waking to curl into my arms. I held him close and thought about how much more damage Connor could do if we didn't end him soon.

When I went back to The Royal Court the next day, it was going to be with renewed veracity. I wanted Connor Loche down, and I wanted him down for good.

18

DEON

From casual walks with Concrete to working in the backyard, all outdoor activities for me had come to a complete and total halt. If everything that had happened at the roadshow wasn't enough to convince me that I needed to stay inside, Felicity felt she had no choice but to come clean to Venom about what we'd done, and we both got an earful.

"I mean, fucking honestly," he snapped over speaker during his call with Felicity. "The two people I care about most in the entire fucking world are out there doing shit that could get them killed. I feel like I'm talking to my goddamn cell wall. Did I *not* tell you to let me handle this shit? There's a reason I'm saying what I'm saying. It's not to fucking leave you two out of it, it's because I've seen Connor at work. He's a fucking snake, and he wouldn't hesitate to put a bullet in either of you. And what, he wasn't even fucking there? If he'd killed you, D, he wouldn't have even been the one going down for it. I mean…" He growled. "Shit. Just stay fucking still. I'm not gonna tell either of you again."

Getting really and truly scolded for the first time ever by the man I'd come to see as my father was equal parts upsetting and enlightening. There were people out there who cared about me. People were expecting me to be smart about the decisions I was making and ensure that I was still alive at the end of the day, and I let my hubris and wanting to end Connor for good get in the way of that. I imagined that if Cherri or Nathan knew what I'd done, they'd be just as mad.

I owed it to the people I loved not to be so dumb.

So I was sitting at home. My anxiety was through the roof, and I found myself peeking through the windows on a near constant rotation, because I'd managed to convince myself that I led the people chasing me back to Felicity. They didn't see her face, and if I were to take a guess, they didn't know it was her beneath the mask. That didn't ease my fear. Venom was right, Connor knew how to dig shit up even if it was twelve feet deep. It probably wouldn't take him long to figure out we were together if he was given the smallest hint. By now, he knew that someone was helping me, and he was probably already working his resources to figure out who.

"Deon?" Felicity called out as she walked back into the house. It'd become a bad—or maybe good—habit of ours to call out to one another whenever she was coming or going.

"I'm in the living room," I called back.

I heard Concrete's collar shaking, and a few seconds later he came bounding into the living room, followed closely by Felicity. If it weren't for the fact that she had a job and Concrete turned into a monster whenever he didn't get his walks, Felicity would probably be condemned to the house too, but she at least had a hidden identity, at least for now.

"How's your leg?" she asked.

It'd been a few days since I got shot, again, but luckily the second time around wasn't as bad as the first. "It's sore, but other than that, it's fine. It grazed me really. I took more damage from the fall and then giving it a goddamn seawater bath." Just mentioning it made my wound sting, like the saltwater was still licking at the open sore. "I'm okay."

"Did you change the bandages already?" she asked.

"I just did," I replied. "I'm okay, mama. Really."

She gave me a half-lidded gaze and then flopped onto the couch. Concrete jumped up next to her and curled up, falling asleep almost immediately. "I can't get your father out of my head."

"Me too. We really let him down and I hate thinking that, on top of everything he's already worrying about, he has to add a fear that the two of us are misbehaving to the list," I said.

"Well that too," Felicity said. "But also because I'm not gonna listen."

"What?" I said. "What do you mean?"

"I'm gonna go talk to Nico. Before shit went sideways at the show, I got a good lead on a vendor Connor may have used to secure locations in Postings to hide out. If we can get in touch with the man aiding him, we may be able to find where he is. It's the closest we've ever gotten," Felicity said. "I can't just not do it."

"You cannot leave this house," I ordered. "I'm sorry, I know in the grand scheme of things we haven't known each other that long but I love you like a mom. Not only that, but Ven—my dad was clear that he wanted to take care of this on his own. We should trust him."

"I do, Deon, but I'm panicking now. Every day I think I'm gonna wake up and find you dead in your bed or hear that Venom's been shanked behind bars." Felicity's eyes were low and her voice was strained. "I need to protect my family, you included. Besides, Nico and I… let's just say we go way back. He wouldn't hurt me, and he wouldn't let anyone else hurt me. I'm going straight there and coming straight back, that's it."

I didn't know what to say or do. Felicity seemed so determined, but if Venom found out that I let her go, *he'd* be the one trying to kill me. "If he asks me, I'm not going to lie to him," I said.

She scoffed. "You'd sell out your own step-mother?"

"To not get my ass kicked? In a heartbeat," I said, then I smiled a bit and Felicity returned the sentiment. "I just want you to be safe."

"And I will be," she replied. "I called him while I was walking Concrete and set up a meeting for later tonight. You'll be on your own for dinner, but there's still leftover lasagna."

"I mean… there isn't, because I ate that already, but I'll figure something out," I said.

Felicity nodded. "Thanks."

The rest of the afternoon was tense as Felicity showered, cooked me dinner despite the fact that I told her I could do it myself, and then got ready to go. She wore something much more enticing than I was expecting her to for such a visit. She had on skintight, dark blue jeans, a black crop top, and wore a magenta, sleeveless, anorak-style parka over it, with black stilettos to finish the ensemble off. The outfit showed off lots of skin and she pulled her braids down so that they hung partly in her face. She looked more like she was headed out for a date than to a shady meeting.

"You look good," I said. "Do you usually put this much effort into back-alley conversations?"

She rolled her eyes at me. "It's like I said, Nico and I go back a ways. I haven't seen him in a while, but I'm hoping our... history can work to our favor."

I didn't like the insinuation in the way she murmured "history," but I didn't pry for anymore information. I wanted to have plausible deniability if something came out later. Felicity gave me a quick hug, promised to be back in two hours tops, and then walked through the door to the garage and out of sight. I listened as the garage door opened and her car started, then it closed again, and I was alone once more.

I did just about anything I could think of to busy myself while I waited. Deep cleaning the house and playing video games were two of the things on the list, but those got old fast. Needing something to take my attention for a long time, I decided to try my hand at making a white chicken chili recipe that Felicity had taught me, then I packed the chili into containers and froze it for eating at a later time. Of course, I worked out, but that got old too, and eventually I found myself on the computer, flicking through the social media accounts of The Royal Court once again.

It was white noise across the board as far as they were concerned—a post here and there for optics, but otherwise no activity. Nathan must have instructed them to mostly stay *off* of social media in case Connor was watching. Smart. I would have done the same thing. My head started to droop as I looked through the accounts, and eventually landed on Avery's page. She had posted recently about college and her future, and it made me wonder.

What did my future look like?

If I could get out from under Connor and get back home, what did the days ahead hold for me? I leaned back in my chair and closed my eyes and tried to imagine it. College didn't entirely seem like the right path for me, but that could just be because I'd never considered it before. Cherri was in my future, obviously, but was there anything in particular that I wanted to do?

"Deon?" a voice called out.

I opened my eyes and looked around. "Fel—"

I wasn't at the kitchen table anymore. Somehow, I was in bed, but not the bed in my room at Felicity's house. The room I was in was decorated with plants and I was laying in a sleigh bed that I didn't recognize. My heart started to thump faster.

Did they get me?

The door to the bedroom opened and a head peeked in. "Deon?"

My jaw dropped. Cherri was looking around the door. Her long blond hair flowing down over her shoulders, and a bright smile on her face. "Cherri?"

She giggled. "Were you expecting someone else?"

It was Cherri, it was really Cherri. Was I imagining things? Did I get drunk and not remember? How was I suddenly in an unfamiliar home with Cherri smiling at me like everything was fine.

"N-no," I replied.

"Well, you slept through your alarm, so you're

running late. I'm working on breakfast; you get up and get ready for work," she said, and then she disappeared from the doorway. "Nathan will be here to get you in like ten minutes, so hurry," she called out as she retreated.

"Um… what?" I said to no one.

Alarm? Work? Did I set an alarm? Where did I work? Nathan was coming to pick me up?

Uncertain, I climbed out of the bed, and though my mind had no idea where I was or what was going on, my feet moved with confidence into a walk-in closet. There were suits hanging from white racks fastened near the top of the closet and I reached out and grabbed one. It felt like I didn't have control of the body I was in, so I just relented to its movements. I pulled a tie and socks from a dresser closer to the door of the closet, then walked out and into the bathroom. I took a shower, washed my hair, and then finally got a glimpse of myself when I got out.

My face was totally shaven, and I was back to how I looked before I even went to prison. I touched my face with some trepidation, but my reflection mimicked me and I could plainly see it was me.

What was going on?

"Deon!" Cherri's voice called back into the

room. "Nathan's here!" Again, the body moved without my command, out of the bathroom, through the bedroom, and down a flight of stairs into a foreign kitchen. Nathan was sitting at a kitchen island working on a plate of breakfast foods that had been placed in front of him, and Cherri was in the act of setting another one down on the counter. "Good morning, baby. Breakfast. Hurry so you two aren't late."

Nathan smiled up at me. "Hey bro."

"Hi," I replied.

He was dressed in a suit similar to mine, but didn't seem nearly as put out as I felt. I sat down next to him and started to eat the food Cherri had provided for me. All I could do was watch her as she flitted around the kitchen, and finally, I smiled.

Maybe it had all just been a horrible, drawn-out nightmare.

"We have the board meeting today, remember," Nathan said. "God, I don't want to."

"You say that about literally all of your meetings," Cherri responded. "I thought you liked your job?"

Nathan shrugged. "Sure. I like the job itself and working with my brother, but those meetings are so boring. Right Deon?"

I had no frame of mind to know if the meetings

he was discussing were boring or not, but my lips still parted and said, "They're awful."

Was this my real life? The one that I'd had all along? It seemed pretty nice. Living with Cherri, getting to work with my brother. Those were all things I'd dreamed of.

A pounding on the door had all of our heads whipping around. Cherri walked around the island and disappeared from the kitchen, and after giving Nathan a confused look, we stood up to follow. We were just about to pass through the door frame when Connor rounded the corner. He had an arm curled around Cherri's neck, damn near choking her, with a gun pressed to her head.

"Cherri!" I bellowed.

"I've had just about enough of this." Connor moved his gun briefly and shot at Nathan. Two bullets sunk into his chest, and he crumpled to the ground. I looked down at him laying on the ground, his eyes wide open, but he was unmoving and blood was spilling from his chest.

He was dead.

I looked back at Connor. "I'm gonna fucking kill you."

I stepped forward, but his gun went back to Cherri's head. "No, I don't think you will. I'm going to kill you, and then I'm going to kill her." He ran his gun along her face, pushing some of her hair back. "Though, maybe we'll have a little bit of... fun first."

"I'm not going to let you hurt her!" I screamed.

Connor pointed his gun at me. "You don't have a choice."

His gun fired and a bullet flew at me. "Deon!" Cherri screamed.

My head whipped up just as Felicity's computer went smashing to the ground. Concrete let out a loud bark. The screen had a litany of colored lines flashing over it, and pieces of the casing were scattered across the kitchen floor. I'd broken it for sure.

"Fuck," I said.

Images of Nathan's dead body and Cherri being held by Connor were permanent fixtures in my mind. It was just a wonderful dream turned into a shitty nightmare, but I was shaking and sweating. Carefully, I started to pick up the pieces of the laptop and put them on the table. I'd have to offer to buy Felicity a new one once I was no longer on the run. Hopefully her stuff was backed up.

I glanced up at the clock above the microwave to see how long I'd been out and my heart stopped.

It said it was just after three in the morning.

"Felicity?" I called out, but there was no response.

In an instant, I abandoned the laptop and opened the door to the garage, but Felicity's car wasn't inside. She wasn't back home yet, and it had been six hours. I rushed around the house checking all the rooms just in case, but there was no doubt about it, Felicity hadn't yet been home. Dread filled my body as my mind started to imagine the worst.

Did someone trying to find me figure out that Felicity was the one helping me, and if so, did they snatch her or simply kill her?

19

CHERRI

To say that I was overwhelmed by the information my parents had given me would be an understatement. After everything The Royal Court had all learned and unearthed together, there was still so much we didn't know about just how wide a net of manipulation Connor had cast. From my friends to my parents, he'd poisoned so many waters that I was beginning to think I'd never swim safely again.

But I wasn't going down without a fight.

"Good morning, angel," my dad said sweetly as I walked into the kitchen. "Mom and Gus are gone already. They had already planned on breakfast with one of Gus' friends and his mom."

"That's okay," I said. "I would have felt bad if

their plans got canceled because of me. I gotta get back to Nathan's anyway. We've got a few new leads to follow."

My dad was looking over his phone at the coffee pot, but glanced up at me at that. "Leads?"

"Yeah. We're trying to find Deon and stop Connor." I sat down at one of the bar stools. "Some people Nathan knows had some useful info, and my friend Sicily is trying to zero in on where Deon may be using an unknown number he was calling Nathan and me from."

"Cherri, that sounds dangerous. If you have information, you should give it to the police and let them take care of it."

"Connor has pull with the police. Any information we give them would just get back to him, and besides, Deon is still on parole from when the police conveniently assumed *we* had something to do with that dead body. If they catch him, they'll drag him back to prison, and that's only if they don't turn him over to Connor first."

"But—"

"Dad, I know this isn't going to make you feel any better, but we've already been through much worse. We stick together and have people helping us. I'll be okay. This is just something I have to do."

My dad watched me with anguish, likely feeling

both guilty and helpless. I got up and walked over to where he was standing and gave him a hug. He squeezed me so tight it started to hurt, and even when I tried to pull away, he held on.

Finally, he released me, but kept a hand resting on my arm. "Please be safe."

"I will, and I'll visit again really soon, I promise." I stood up on my tippy-toes to kiss him on his cheek. "I love you."

"I love you."

With one last quick hug, I gathered my keys and phone and left.

Avery said she'd come back and get me, but it was still early and I didn't want to bother her. I took a cab home instead. When I got inside, everyone was sitting around in the living room, apart from Sicily, who I assumed was upstairs.

"Hey," Avery greeted as I walked in. "I told you I'd come back for you."

"I know, but I wanted some alone time. The conversation with my parents did not go as I expected it to." I flopped down onto one of the couches next to Avery.

"Did they take it really hard or something?" Alistair asked.

I looked across the room to where Nathan was

sitting on the ground in front of Nikita. "Turns out, your dad handpicked me to be your trophy."

The statement sucked the energy out of the room. "What?" Nathan said. "I picked you. To hurt Deon."

I chuckled. "That's what he let you believe. I'm not sure why, but Connor wanted to hurt Deon long before you did. Maybe because of what his mom did? He promoted my dad and moved us near Deon, then he told my dad *before* Deon got arrested that he was unsafe, and that they needed to keep me away from him. Even his mom. Then not long after Deon went to prison, he promoted my dad again, and moved us out here to be near you."

"You think Connor had something to do with Deon going to prison to begin with?" Colette asked.

Nathan sighed. "I've been thinking that could be the case for a while, but if he met and picked you out *before* that, he had something premeditated for long before I got mad and wanted to get my revenge on Deon."

"Jeez," Kyle said. "How long has Connor been manipulating all of our lives?"

"Since before birth," Nathan hissed. "And I played right into it."

"You didn't know," Nikita and I said in unison.

Colette leaned forward. "Yeah. Besides, you couldn't have—"

"Yes! Yes! Yes! Yes!" All of our heads turned at the sudden exclamation, followed by the pounding of feet down the stairs. Sicily jumped down into the living room, skipping until he was dead center in the group, and then he started to dance. "I'm good. I'm so good," he sang. "I'm good. OH! Who's good?"

He pointed at Brayden, who apprehensively said, "Uh, Sicily?"

Sicily did a pelvic thrust. "That's right! It's Sicily! I am so good."

"Hey, Mr. Good?" I asked. "Why are you so good?"

"I'm glad you asked, gorgeous." He held up a piece of paper. "I found Deon."

I jumped up. "What?!"

"Are you serious?" Nathan asked.

"Yeah!" Sicily yelped. "He's in Maine!" We all stared at him blankly. "What?" he asked.

I walked over to Sicily and punched him in the arm. "We already knew he was in fucking Maine!"

Sicily rubbed his arm, beyond used to my tendency to swing when I got annoyed. "You didn't let me finish."

I backed away from him a little bit. "You have five minutes."

"Alright, so. Anisa and Cobalt brought me the phone of the two guys we captured—cakewalk to break, by the way—I found messages from some people who had captured him at some point, but he got away," Sicily said. "The places they were discussing are near a handful of the pings from when Deon was calling you and Nathan, meaning he started in that area and stayed in that area. About an hour from here, near the prison. At first I was afraid that the calls may have stopped because he went back to prison, but I searched the database, and he's not listed. More than likely that means…"

"He visited," I finished.

"Exactly," Sicily said. "So I'm thinking he might have made a plan to go there and get some help and then ditched his phone."

"Venom," I said.

Sicily nodded. "That's what I'm thinking. So technically, I don't know *exactly* where he is, but I'm guessing he does."

"Who?" Nathan asked.

"There was a guy who took Deon under his wing when he was locked up and made sure he got his education so that he could rejoin high school when he got out," I explained.

Sicily nodded. "Deon told me Venom was like a dad to him. I hate that it took all of this for me to realize it, but if Deon needed help and he couldn't come back here for it, he'd go there for sure."

"But Deon's on the run. He couldn't just walk into a prison," Colette said.

"From what Deon told me, Venom sort of has his run of the place. He might have known who to talk to in order to speak with Venom without being tagged," Sicily said.

"It's worth a shot," I said. "We should go and talk to him and see if he knows anything."

"There are visiting hours tomorrow," Avery said, and I looked over to see she was already clicking rapidly through her phone, "but only one person can visit at a time."

"Shoot," Nathan said. "I hate the one-on-one thing lately. It always feels like there's some information that gets missed when only one person can represent."

"I get it, but there isn't anything we can do, and because I'm the crux between you guys and Deon, I feel like I should be the one," I said.

Colette shivered in her seat. "At the risk of sounding like a spoiled, rich princess, I can't imagine going and sitting in a prison. You're so much braver than me, Cherri."

"Believe you me, the thought doesn't inspire sunshine and rainbows, but we don't have any other choice. Venom could be the one person who can get us in touch with Deon, and for him, I'd do anything." I imagined being able to see Deon soon, or even just hear his voice. There was nothing that could scare me enough to keep me away from following that lead.

"Next stop, prison?" Kyle said with a chuckle.

I nodded. "Yep. Next stop, prison."

20

DEON

I was trying to decide how long I should wait before going out and looking for Felicity myself. Yes, I'd promised her that I would stay in the house and not risk anything else happening to me, but I also promised Venom that I would look after Felicity just like she promised to look after me. I never should have let her go to visit Nico on her own. I could appreciate what she was doing, especially because she was doing it for me and for Venom, but regret was washing over me like poison.

The sun had been up for hours, and it was getting close to twelve hours since the absolute latest I would have expected Felicity to come home. Something was terribly wrong.

It was a good thing I'd fallen asleep at the table, because otherwise I wouldn't have gotten any sleep. I still felt groggy as I stood up off the couch in the living room and patted my leg to call Concrete to me. He rushed over, tail wagging, excited to get out, but I was bringing him along as backup. I imagined Felicity had to have guns of some type hanging around her house, so I did a sweep of the place looking for one. I checked every nook and cranny I could think of, but nothing turned up.

Maybe in her car.

Rushing out into the garage, I grabbed the keys for the more 'suburban mom' car that Felicity had and ran over to the door. I unlocked it and climbed in with Concrete right behind me and started to search all over the car for a weapon of any kind. Worse case scenario, I could run back in for a butcher knife or the axe she kept to chop wood for her fireplace, but I didn't relish walking into a possible fight without something that would help me long range. Any of Connor's thugs would be strapped to high hell, and it didn't make me comfortable to imagine literally bringing a knife to a gun fight.

"There has to be one in here, Concrete," I said. "I wish you could help me look."

Concrete just stared at me, though some of his

jovial mood had left him—he must have been able to read my panic. I dug my hands into the glove box, under the seats, in the center console, and even checked the trunk, but there weren't guns of any kind.

"Dammit," I growled. "The axe it is, I guess."

Sliding out of the car, I started back towards the door into the house, when suddenly the garage door started to open. If someone snatched Felicity, they'd have her keys and garage door opener; hell, that car was programmed to take her straight home just by asking it to. Anyone with access to her car would have no trouble getting in. My eyes scanned the garage for the best weapon to defend myself with, and landed on the barbell to my bench press. I rushed towards it, pulled the weights off as quickly as I could, and whipped around with the barbell in hand.

Just to see Felicity driving her car back into the garage.

I didn't know if I was angry, relieved, or stunned. Her hair and makeup were a mess, almost as if she *had* run into some trouble, but when she parked the car, pressing the button to close the garage as she did, she looked over at me like *I* was the lunatic.

"What are you doing?" she asked, stepping out of the car. "You gonna hit me or something?"

"At the risk of sounding totally disrespectful, where the *fuck* have you been? You told me a few hours when you left last night," I hissed. "Did something happen?" She walked around the car and I noticed that her clothes were a little more disheveled too. There were a few dark spots around her neck, and the more I started to realize what had happened, the more I was wondering if it would have been better if she'd just gotten into a fight. "Did you… cheat on Venom?"

She let out a sigh. "I keep thinking I'll be able to do stuff without having to explain it to you, but you're too on the ball for that." She waved a hand as she turned to walk inside. "Come on. I need some coffee for this hangover and I owe you some answers."

My heart dropped into my stomach. For a moment there, I was dreading having to explain to Venom that I let Felicity leave after he explicitly told me not to do that, and something bad happened. Was I going to have to reveal his wife's affair? He meant more to me than most people in my life, and even though I'd developed quite a love for Felicity as a pseudo-mother, I couldn't just sit by and say nothing if she was sleeping around behind Venom's back.

I set my barbell down and walked back into the house, following the sounds of Felicity already putting together a cup of coffee. She was still wobbly as she worked, so I walked over, took the can of coffee from her, and pushed her lightly towards the kitchen table. She didn't argue, and dropped into the seat, setting her head down on the table's surface.

My hands were shaking as I brewed the coffee. Was it fear? Was it disappointment? No one likes having the people they care about disillusioned, but it was worse than that for me. Felicity loved Venom, that was obvious. Did she do what she did just to get some help in our plight?

"I know what you're thinking," Felicity started. "And it's not that. What I did has nothing to do with you, Venom, or finding Connor. It was a happy coincidence."

I looked back over my shoulder at her. "I wouldn't call it happy."

"Garrett's been in and out of lockup damn near our entire relationship, Deon," she said. "The first few times, he'd say 'Aw, baby. I don't expect you to just wait around for me. You're a woman, you have needs too,' and I always thought it was insane, because I'd committed myself to him. Even before I got married, he was the only man I wanted. I wouldn't dream of doing anything behind his back."

I pulled a mug out from the cabinet as I listened to Felicity's story. As soon as the coffee was done brewing, I poured some from the pot into the mug, not bothering to add any creamer. Carrying it over to her, I set it down on the table and then sat down across from her. She took a long sip in spite of its heat, and then let out a sigh.

"I figured you'd need it black," I said.

She held up the mug cheers-style. "This is good. Thank you." She looked up. "It was around the fifth time Venom went in. It was just a small stay, he wasn't even upstate, just in the county jail, but I was struggling. He'd been so busy leading up to it, he hadn't touched me in two months, maybe three? Then he went and got arrested. I thought I was going to lose my mind." She grimaced at me. "Sorry. This probably isn't what you want to hear about your dad and step-mom."

"I think I'm far, far past an ordinary relationship with anyone at this point," I replied. "And I think my best chance for feeling better is if you tell me everything."

"He told me to do it. Garrett did. Nico and I

have known one another almost as long as I've known Garrett, and we've always had a little thing for one another. Nico wouldn't dare even look at me, but when Garrett told him it was okay, we just sort of fell into something. It was comfortable, like being cared for by a friend. He doesn't expect anything more from me and I don't expect anything more from him. I really did give him the info I got from the road show, and he really did pass it on to hopefully get us a lead, but once the business was over, he poured me a glass of wine, then another, then another, and…" She waved a hand through the air. "I feel horrible. I fell asleep because with all this shit going on, the level of stress relief it provided me knocked me out. I woke up with a bad hangover, so I still had to wait a couple of hours to be okay to drive. I wanted to call, but you don't have a cell phone."

"Not by choice," I said. "This is convincing me that it needs to change."

Felicity shook her head. "You don't want them to be able to track you in any way. Trust me, this is best."

"Well then you at least need to write down your cell phone number so I can keep it on me," I said. "If I'd been able to call *you* at least, I wouldn't have panicked."

"I can do that." She took another heavy sip of her coffee. "The thing is, though your dad *did* tell me it'd be okay, whenever he finds out it's happening, it kills him, so I don't tell him. I know you love him, I do too. He's my husband, and if the circumstances were any different, I'd never, but—"

I held up a hand. "While I don't like the idea of lying to Venom, I understand your position. It probably makes him feel better to think that you're being taken care of without knowing the details, so I'll keep it to myself."

Felicity let out a sigh of relief. "Thank you. Do you think differently of me now?" she asked.

"No. If anything, it just makes me more angry that this isn't all sorted out yet. I want everyone to be able to get back to their lives. You too," I said. "You said you gave your info over to Nico?"

"I did, and he was over the moon. He's pretty sure that the information I got is going to be the missing link to tracking Connor down, or at least someone who has helped him recently. He's pretty sure it may take us back to Postings though," Felicity said. "A two-hour hike into the lion's den. If Garrett finds out we're doing that, he's going to go bat shit."

"Well, there may be another option if it comes to that," I said. "My brother is still there, and

Cherri, and their friends. Nathan is probably the only man up to the task of facing Connor head on, so if we really do get a lead that takes us back to Postings, maybe you can make contact and give them what you know. We can leave me out of it, just in case, and Nathan can follow it up on his end. When it's all set, I can go home and explain the rest."

"That's not a bad idea," Felicity said. "Although, if your brother really is as smart as you say he is, he'll probably be able to figure it out."

I nodded my head. "Oh, there's no question Nathan will know the second you call him that I'm with you. All we can do is continue to deny it and let him finish the job. If he thinks I'm safe and that getting the job done will make it so I can come home, he'll do it without question."

Felicity smiled. "You have a lot of faith in your brother."

I let out a little snicker. "Yeah. It's kind of weird. In the grand scheme of things, I don't actually know him all that well, but that one year we spent together, I loved being around him. Once I went missing, I'd call him and it felt more like having, you know, an actual brother. I put all the mess with Cherri out of my mind, because I know Connor manipulated him the most of any of us. I can't imagine what he went through after I left. It still gives me guilt to this day."

"I'm sure he feels guilt too," Felicity said. "It'll be good when this is all cleared up so you two can hug it out. You'll need it."

The thought of hugging Nathan made me feel awkward, but she was probably right. "Come on. Finish your coffee. I'll get you a glass of water, and you're going to bed."

She laughed. "Yes, mom."

I helped a very wobbly and hungover Felicity up to her bed and set a glass of water on her bedside table. She sat down on the bed and fell back fully clothed, and I laughed. "Don't stay like that."

"I won't," she snapped. "I'm the mom. Quit bossing me around."

I shuffled Concrete into the room to snuggle with her while she slept and then I left the room and pulled the door closed behind me. Relief didn't cover how I felt about knowing Felicity was okay, but if it was possible, this just raised the stakes. Every day that we didn't catch Connor, things got worse. If we didn't hunt him down and stop him soon, everything was going to be damaged beyond repair.

21

CHERRI

I should have expected that I would struggle to sleep the night before the prison visit. I changed into my PJs, climbed into bed and turned off the lights as if I was actually going to be able to sleep, but nothing could be further from the truth. One hour passed, two, three, and I still hadn't drifted off. All I could think about was talking to Venom and the possibility that he would be able to help me find my way back to Deon.

In spite of the fact that I knew almost instantly that I wouldn't be getting any sleep that night, I gave it a solid try until just after midnight. I'd drift off for twenty minutes and then come back to, praying I'd actually slept through the entire night, only to be sorely disappointed. I looked out the window from my bedroom into the night sky and figured if I wasn't going to be able to sleep, at least I could enjoy the beautiful South Postings evening sky. It wasn't as light-polluted there as Postings Proper and the stars were actually visible. It was just shy of a full moon, and it had been years since I'd taken any sort of night dip in the pool, so I climbed out of bed, changed into my bathing suit, and left my room in the interest of a swim.

As I was passing Kyle's bedroom door, it opened, and Brayden walked out. He was too busy trying to sneak that he didn't notice me standing there until he turned and came face-to-face with me.

"Hi," he said.

There were a thousand things I could have said in that moment, but it was clear Brayden still wasn't comfortable with discussing his and Kyle's relationship, so I settled for a simple, "Can't sleep either?"

His face actually registered a little relief,then he leaned against the wall and shook his head. "No. I've been trying, but I just can't make it happen."

"Same here," I said, then I motioned to myself in my bathing suit. "I've decided to wash my worries away in the pool. Wanna join me?"

Brayden and I had been far from besties before The Royal Court went through all its shit, and ever since I'd returned, we'd only spoken here and there out of necessity. We talked a bit more while Brayden was helping us try and find where Connor was dragging him off to. Since that turned into a dead end and we were relying more on other avenues, a passing comment was all either of us spared. Brayden was, however, a kindred spirit. Our torrid feelings for Nathan, whatever they were, had left us both in precarious positions, and with me trying to move into more of a sisterly position with him, and Brayden trying to back down to be a true best friend, we were both being awkward as hell around the man.

"Sure," Brayden said. "I just have to change."

He started off down the hallway and I followed, waiting outside his room while he quickly slipped in to get changed. A few minutes later he came back out, and we both walked down the stairs and out the back door to the pool. Instinctively, I headed towards the utility shed near the pool to crack on the lights and turn on the auto-heat, but then I noticed the glow of lights from the area already.

"Someone's out here I think," Brayden said.

We walked down the path to the pool and saw that there was already an occupant. Nikita was sitting on the edge of the pool's deep end, just in front of the bar, with her feet in the water, flicking through her phone. When Brayden opened the gate to let us in, she looked up and tilted her head.

"Wow," she said. "I don't typically have visitors for late night dips."

"Do you come out here often?" Brayden asked.

"Once a week I'd say. During the warm months anyway," Nikita replied.

Brayden walked around to sit on the edge next to Nikita, while I opted to wade into the shallow end of the pool, grab one of the floating noodles, and swim to the deep end. I kept myself aloft with the noodle under my arms and splashed around in the warm water.

"Couldn't sleep?" Nikita asked.

"I'm too anxious for tomorrow," I said. "The fact that we may get an actual, solid lead on where Deon is has me on edge."

"That makes sense," Nikita said.

"You?" I asked.

Nikita shrugged. "I don't sleep well in general. In a weird way, whenever we sleep in Nathan's house instead of our room in the main house, I sleep worse. I think it's because I'm constantly afraid I'm going to wake up to find you guys all dead or missing or something. Being at the pool gives me a clear shot of the house just in case."

"I think that's kind of my problem too,"

Brayden said. He gave Nikita an awkward look, but decided to press on regardless. "You know, when Nathan's not under the same roof it makes me nervous something's going to happen when we're not all around to help out."

"I mean, Nikita could kick just about anyone's ass," I said.

Brayden nodded. "I know. Plus, he's not all that weak himself, it's just…" He kicked the water. "Old habits."

"We're a group, aren't we?" I said with a laugh. "We're so fucking dysfunctional we can't see straight."

Nikita laughed. "Yeah, and *I'm* in therapy."

"Maybe we need a good, old fashioned clearing of the air," I said. Both Nikita and Brayden looked at me strangely, and I rolled my eyes. "Oh come on. Are we *not* going to acknowledge the big-ass, Nathan-shaped elephant in the room?"

They looked at each other, then back at me, and Brayden was the first to break, oddly enough. "Being around you two really freaks me out. I mean, I was so jealous of you, Cherri. Then I was jealous of Nikita. I'm not really all that jealous at all anymore, but I don't know how to get my mind off of it, you know? It's like…" He looked at me. "We're clearing the air, right?"

I swished around in the water. "Let it out."

"I hated you. I mean, I fucking *hated* you. Whenever Nathan would be trying to run around behind your back, even though I *knew* it was because he didn't really have feelings for you, I encouraged it. I wanted to torpedo your relationship."

"That's not really news to me," I said.

He shrugged. "Then he started going out with Nikki, and I was happy for him, but I had these feelings too." I could see Nikita sitting as still as I was. It was the most open about his feelings Brayden had ever been, at least with anyone other than Kyle. "I don't really think I feel that way anymore, but still when he walks into a room my heart… does the thing."

"Maybe you still do have feelings?" Nikita said.

Brayden shook his head. "I don't, though. Nathan was like… the one who helped me realize it, but now…" His voice faded away.

"Kyle?" I said.

Brayden's hands came up to his face. "I've never felt this way before."

Nikita smiled widely. "That's awesome."

"I'm so scared though. Like, terrified."

"True love is scary," I said. "Right Nikki?"

Nikita rolled her eyes. "Horrifying. Seriously. It fucking sucks."

We shared a quiet laugh and a moment of mutual understanding for one another. "Can I tell you something else, Brayden? My heart still does the thing too."

Both Brayden and Nikita looked over at me. "Really?" Nikita asked.

"Yeah. For four years he was my boyfriend. I always stood closest to him or would kiss him or whatever. I'm still very drawn to him, just not romantically. I think that's why my stomach gives out a little, because I don't know how to reconcile what I want our relationship to be with what it used to be."

"Yeah!" Brayden yelped. "That's it exactly."

"I've talked to him about it, and I think you should too. Trust me, he'll be super understanding," I said.

"Plus, he *loves* you," Nikita said. "Not that way, but he really does. You two were so close, and the wedge between you now, he feels it and talks about it often. I know it'd make him feel so much better if you guys could take steps back towards where you used to be." Nikita looked at me. "You too."

Something between relief and excitement filled the space between us. "Yeah."

"And maybe if you do that, you two can stop being so goddamn weird with me," Nikita said. "I want to be friends with you guys, for real." Then Nikita's eyes widened and she looked over at me. "Oh my god, you know what I just realized?"

"What?"

"If I end up with Nathan, and you end up with Deon, which I think is where we're headed, we'll be sisters-in-law."

"Oh shit! That's true!" I splashed the water out of pure excitement. "I've always wanted a sister!"

"Can I have a really big role in your weddings?" Brayden asked. "For friendship reasons, but mostly because I like attention."

I started to laugh. "Fuck. I nearly forgot what a tool you are."

"You can be my ring bearer," Nikita said.

"Oh!" I clapped my hands. "You can be my flower girl!"

Brayden pointed at me. "Yes!!"

"You're right. That's so much better than mine. Start practicing," Nikita said.

Brayden kicked his legs in the water. "I'm actually so excited."

The rest of the morning was a downright delight. None of us made any attempt to go back to our rooms to go to sleep and just committed ourselves to sleeping when we're dead. After some coaxing, Nikita and Brayden eventually got in the pool and we hung out and talked until the sun came up.

It was amazing.

I'd gotten to know them so little because of the obvious barriers between us, but those things didn't exist anymore, and it turned out we had much more than Nathan in common. When I finally realized it was after seven, we got out of the pool and broke apart briefly, only long enough to get dressed, and met back down in the kitchen just as the daily breakfast foods were being delivered. We continued to laugh and talk as everyone else filed down, and then in no time at all, the moment had arrived to drive to the prison.

"So, who all is going?" Alistair asked.

"Well, I could go," Nathan said. "I know I can't go in, but—"

"Actually," I looked at Nikita and Brayden, "I think I'll have Nikki and Brayden come with me."

Everyone else exchanged confused looks, including Sicily, who'd spent the night and was pretty much planning on going.

"Uh," Nathan looked at Nikita. "I guess?"

"Yeah. I'm there for you," Nikita said with a smile. "Sisters stick together, right?"

I nodded. "Right."

"And flower girls," Brayden said, and the three of us burst out laughing.

Alistair raised his hand. "Is anyone else uncomfortable?"

"You good?" Kyle asked. "To go, I mean?"

Brayden turned and looked at Kyle and gave him a warm, inviting smile. Kyle's face lit up at it, his own eyes sparkling. "Yeah. Cherri needs me, so I'm gonna go."

"O-okay," Kyle said. "Great."

Brazenly, Nikita reached across the island and gave Brayden a high five, and then Avery raised her hand alongside Alistair. "Yep. I'm uncomfortable."

"Too bad," I said. "We're all fucking friends now. So deal with it. Let's go, guys."

Nikita and Brayden stood up from their spots and followed me towards the front door. The last thing we heard before we left was Colette. "Never a predictable day around The Royal Court."

I smiled, confident with Nikita and Brayden by my side.

No, there was not.

22

CHERRI

Approaching the prison where Deon had been locked up for four years just to protect me was daunting to say the least. Even with Nikita and Brayden sticking close to me, the giant, imposing, cement facade and barbed fence encircling it made me want to turn tail and run. Deon spoke very highly of Venom, but there was absolutely no guarantee that he was as kind as he'd said. Maybe he cared about Deon, but he had no reason to talk to or be kind to me at all.

My heart thundered as we walked through the doors at the front of the building, and we were immediately met with the sight of dozens of people waiting for the visiting hours. There were single parents, both moms and dads, with children running around them while they waited. Elderly parents or maybe even grandparents, and a handful of isolated teenagers like us who appeared to have shown up to see a relative of some sort.

Nikita, Brayden and I must have looked incredibly out of place, because they all looked up and zeroed in on us. Some of them whispered to one another, and then some of the people who didn't appear to be there together, turned and looked at each other and nodded off towards us. Probably several of those people, whether they knew one another or not, were used to seeing each other at visiting hours, and we were new.

"Over here I think," Nikita said.

We turned right from the front door and walked over to a high counter with bulletproof plexiglass separating us from the uniformed people on the other side. We walked up to the counter and the man at the window we approached looked us up and down. "Can I help you?"

"Uh, yeah, we're here to visit someone," I said.

"Are you registered for visits?" he asked.

"I am," I said, grateful that Avery had realized an application was necessary to visit inmates and helped me fill it out after we made the plan to come.

"Which inmate are you visiting?" he said.

I looked at Nikita and Brayden as my heart sank.

I didn't know his name.

Deon always called the man he was aided by 'Venom,' but I assumed that wasn't the name on his birth certificate. "Um," I said. "I only know his nickname?"

The officer crossed his arms. "If you don't have a legal name, how am I supposed to know who to call to come down?"

That was a fantastic question. Still, Deon had made it seem like Venom had his run of the place. Maybe they'd know him by name. "His name, or the one I've always known him by, is Venom."

Behind the glass, the officer took a step back. He looked left and right at the other officers behind the counter, then he looked back at me. "What's your name?"

"Cherri," I said.

He looked at the female officer to his left and nodded, and she put up a 'Be Right Back' placard at her window and disappeared behind a door. The cop looked at us, keeping a curious gaze on us, but said nothing. Had I made a mistake name-dropping Venom? His nickname was probably listed alongside his real name in some public record, somewhere. Why didn't I think to look it up first?

We didn't let the tension scare us and stayed standing in place. At one point, I must have been shivering and didn't know it, because Brayden pulled off his zip-up hoodie and slung it around my arms. I smiled at him and Nikita rubbed my back. Even if Avery and Sicily had come with me, I wasn't sure they'd have offered the same kind of support Brayden and Nikita were. The fact that we *weren't* all that close kept them from doing too much. They just offered quiet support, which was exactly the kind I needed.

After what felt like an hour, but had only been around twenty minutes, the female officer came back. She pulled the officer we were dealing with back, and whispered something to him. He nodded at her, then turned around and faced us. He grabbed a clipboard with a paper on it, scribbled something on it, and then slid it through the window to me.

"Fill this out. I've already done the inmate name for you. Do you have an ID?" he asked.

I nodded. "Yeah."

"Okay. When you turn that form back in, you have to give me your ID too. I'll hold it while you visit and return it when you're done."

"Okay. Thank you." I grabbed the clipboard, and filled out all of the necessary information, then

I pulled out my ID, clipped it to the clipboard and slid both the form and the ID back. I took a note of the inmate name on the paper before sliding it back.

The man I was there to see was Garrett Williams.

"Find a spot to sit and wait for the guard to call for visiting hours. You'll have to go through the metal detector and you can't take *anything* with you. No phone, no keys, no wallet, no nothing. I'd give that hoodie back. You'll be cold back there, but deal. We don't like baggy clothes here."

"Fine," I said. "Thank you."

We went and found a couple of open seats and I handed my cell phone, wallet, and keys over to Nikita and returned Brayden's hoodie. We waited for about thirty minutes, then a guard came and stood at a door to the left of the room. The regulars must have recognized him, because a representative for each group started standing before he said anything, and as they were lining up he called out, "Line up for visiting hours!"

"Okay," Nikita said to me. "We're right out here. Good luck."

I smiled. "Thanks."

Brayden gave my hand a squeeze as I stood up and left them behind to get in line. One cop was standing on our side of the door, that, when opened, gave me a clear view of the metal detector on the other side, behind which a cop was standing with another, handheld metal detector.

"Remember, folks. Visiting time is one hour long. You sit across from your loved one and talk using the phone. Any attempt to tamper with the glass, phone, chair, or booth will result in immediate termination of all visitation rights for the duration of your inmate's stay."

For a moment, I imagined visiting Deon while he was there. How I'd be one of the people in line ahead of me, moving on memory, used to doing this all already. I was glad that Deon and I reconnected after, even if I was sad to have been separated from him all those years. If it would have helped him at all, I would have visited him.

But thank god it didn't come to that.

Once we were through the metal detectors, the same female officer who'd helped me earlier appeared from a door and led us down a long hallway. We entered a totally cement room with about a dozen seating booths lined along the center of the room. Plexiglass separated our side from the other side, and dividers separated each booth from the next one over. Each booth only had one chair, and I hesitated in the door, wondering if I needed to go to a specific booth, but everyone appeared to just be sitting down, so I went to the booth way at the end and sat down.

A loud buzzer echoed through the room, and a door at the end of the other side we were separated from opened and a different officer led in inmates who were cuffed at their wrists and ankles. They sat down at the booths as they passed the ones they were meant to be at, and I watched as one man's eyes locked on me. He wasn't as tall as I had imagined, but he was twice as built. His arms looked like he could punch right through the concrete if he wanted to, and his shoulders were so broad, they completely blocked out the view of anyone behind him. He had chocolate skin, and a bald head and walked with an overconfident swagger that made me feel like I wasn't worthy of talking to him.

He walked to the end of the booths and sat down in front of me, then a prison guard stepped forward and unlocked the handcuffs around his thick wrists. He reached up and grabbed the phone hanging on his side of the booth, and I did the same.

"Cherri, right?" he said.

I nodded. "Yeah. Are you Venom?"

A huge smile crossed his face, unexpectedly kind. "Yeah. Call me Garrett."

"Okay," I replied. "Hi, Garrett."

"Now, you are one of the most beautiful women I've ever seen," he said. "My kid's got good taste."

Deon had mentioned he thought of Venom like a dad. It was sweet to see that Venom thought of Deon the same. I remembered Anisa and Cobalt loving Nathan like parents, and I was happy to see that Deon had found something similar in Venom. "Thank you."

"Now, Cherri, I'm not sure if you know this, but anything you and I say into these phones can be replayed and listened to by anyone." His eyes narrowed at me. "Anyone."

I didn't have to guess what he was trying to say. Connor had contacts everywhere, and if we said anything about or pointing towards Deon, he could find out. "I understand."

"So. What can I do for you?" he asked. "I assume you're on a bit of a hunt."

"I am," I said. "Am I your first visitor?"

Venom's smile grew. "Smart too. I love it. No, you're not. Someone else came and saw me about, oh, three months ago now. Needed a lawyer, so I put them in contact with my wife, Felicity."

"Felicity?" I said. "Williams?"

"Yep," he replied. "I'm sure she gave them some information and I'm sure she can do the same for you. I'll give you her address. You shouldn't attempt to call her. Prying ears, you know."

"Right," I said.

He looked over his shoulder at the prison guard standing right behind him and flicked his head, and the guard walked away. He said Felicity's address into the phone while looking away from me, towards the wall, then he turned back and smiled at me. "You won't forget it will you?"

"No," I said. "It's the most important thing."

He nodded. "Felicity will get you straight. Don't you worry."

"Thank you," I said. "Thank you so much."

"No. Thank you. You're a good woman, just like my woman. I'm glad my kid has you. Take care of him for me."

"I will, I promise," I said. "We'll be back."

Venom blinked a couple of times and then nodded. "Well now, that makes me incredibly happy."

He nodded towards those doors. "You don't have to stay the whole time. Go. Go find out what you need to know."

"Thank you, Garrett."

"Nice to meet you, Cherri," he replied, then he hung up the phone and a prison guard was behind him within seconds to start locking up his wrists again.

I walked over to the door and stood next to it, and the officer on our side looked at me. "You ready? Can't come back 'til next hours."

"I'm ready," I said.

She nodded, then she opened the door, did a scan of the room, nodded at one of the other officers on the visitor's side, and led the way out. She brought me back down the hallway, back through the metal detector, and returned me to the room where Nikita and Brayden were sitting waiting. They noticed as soon as I walked in the room and stood up to come over to me.

"Well?" Nikita said. "That was fast. Did you talk to him?"

"Yeah. We couldn't say much because…" Then I looked around. "Let's actually get out of here first." We went back outside and climbed into Nikita's car, me in the front passenger's seat, and Brayden in the back. "He gave me an address."

"Whoa!" Nikita said. "To where Deon is?"

I shook my head. "No. He just said it was his wife and she should be able to give me the same information she gave Deon. Hopefully she'll know where he's staying though."

Nikita handed me her phone. "Enter the address. Let's go."

"Wait," I said. "Just… go? What about the others?"

"Do you wanna go back first?" Brayden said.

I really didn't. This lead could bring me to Deon, potentially within the day still. I wanted to be fair to my friends who'd stuck with me through everything, but I also wanted to get to Deon as soon as possible.

"No. I don't," I said.

"Then let's go find him," Brayden said. "We'll ask for forgiveness later."

I looked at Nikita, who had the same look of determination, and then I smiled. "Thanks guys." I grabbed Nikita's phone. "Let's go."

The address Venom had given to me was about two hours from the prison, but that didn't seem to shake Nikita or Brayden's confidence at all. We swung by a gas station for a horrible lunch of gas station snacks and sodas, then set out on the drive. We listened to music and talked the entire way, and I was surprised how comfortable it felt, like I'd been friends with them forever. Once again, I was struck by how much I missed being so caught up in my own deal both before I left The Royal Court, and during my crazy rebellious phase. I was an incredibly lucky woman for the people fate had intertwined with my life, or at least the ones Connor had. He was a villain in every sense of the word, but I wouldn't have Deon or my friends if it weren't for him.

Maybe I'd thank him before punching him in the face.

Eventually, we got to Ushuru, Maine, a Japanese-inspired town near the coast. The address we'd gotten from Venom led us to a large and beautiful home. Nikita parked her car in front of the house and we got out, and not a moment passed before four people jumped out and had guns pointed at our faces.

I held up my hands. "Shit. Was it a trap?"

"Who are you?" One woman demanded.

"We're here to see Felicity. Garrett sent us," I said.

The gunmen exchanged nervous glances, then pulled their guns down. The woman stepped forward and motioned us towards the door. She knocked for us, and a dog started barking on the other side. After a few seconds, the door opened, and a gorgeous woman with long, braided brown hair and cocoa skin answered the door.

She looked me up and down and then a bright smile found her face. "Oh my god. You're Cherri."

My eyes widened. "Yeah. How do you know that?"

She was damn near exploding with joy. "Come in." Nikita, Brayden and I shuffled inside, and then the woman grabbed my hand. "I'm Felicity. Come with me. You two, we'll talk when I get back. Make yourselves comfortable in the living room." Brayden and Nikita didn't even get a chance to answer before Felicity dragged me towards the stairs and pulled me up. "This is insane," she said. "We'll discuss the details later."

"Er, no… I'd really like to talk right away. If we could," I replied.

She didn't respond, but instead stopped in front of a door. Side-glancing me, she gave me a huge smile and said, "I've been waiting for this moment." She opened the door and my heart dropped straight from my chest, through my stomach, and into the floor.

Passed out in the bed, shaggier than I remembered, was Deon.

Tears filled my eyes as I carefully walked into the room. "I wouldn't expect him to wake up. I gave him a little scare yesterday and he was up late."

"That's okay," I said. "I need the sleep too."

Felicity put a hand on my back. "Like I said,

we'll talk later. I'll get details from your friends." She left me then, leaving the room and closing the door behind her.

I couldn't stop the tears from flowing down my cheeks as I climbed into the bed next to Deon. He was on his back, so I was able to lay on my stomach and snuggle as close to him as I could get. So many questions ran through my brain, but I didn't care about the answers to any of them for the time being.

For now, I was back in Deon's arms, and with that emotion overwhelming me, I quickly drifted off to sleep.

23

DEON

The fact that I could see the sun shining in through the window meant that I'd slept straight through the afternoon and into the morning. I could smell breakfast being prepared and knew that Felicity was already working on something delicious to start the day with, but for some reason, I just didn't want to get out of bed. I was normally pretty warm under the down blanket that Felicity dressed my bed with, but there was something particularly warm and enrapturing about it that morning. If I didn't get up right away, Felicity would just throw my breakfast in the microwave to warm up when I finally did.

I was pulling my first ever "five more minutes!" card.

Gripping the blanket, I attempted to roll over, and that was the first time I felt a weight settled next to me. At first, I thought it was Concrete, but then I looked down. What I saw made me think I was on some sort of psychedelic drug.

"Cherri?" I said quietly.

There was a woman laying across my chest, snoozing away quietly. Her hair was different from Cherri's, short cut, with brown hair at the roots and fading to blond at the tips, but some of the naturally blond roots were starting to show right at the top of her head. For a moment, I tried to convince myself it wasn't her. She looked slightly more rugged than the Cherri I remembered, but then I looked at her face. Those cheeks, those lips.

It was definitely my Cherri.

The dream I'd had with Nathan and Cherri in it crossed my mind, and I quickly realized the same was true here. Maybe my mind was forming some new image of Cherri to account for how much time had passed since I'd last seen her. I had dreams like that all the time in prison. Because it was impossible that Cherri was actually laying in bed with me, it was easy to draw the next natural conclusion.

I was dreaming.

My other dream felt so real too, and I actually had a chance to touch and kiss her then, and I didn't. I wouldn't miss my opportunity the second time around. If the only way I got to enjoy Cherri was in my dreams, then enjoy her I would.

Twisting my arm around to comb into her hair, I was surprised by the silken feeling of the strands between my fingertips. My brain was going the distance with the dream. I curled her head towards me and ducked my head down so I could kiss her. Her lips were sweet and warm and I wrapped my other arm around her waist to pull her even closer. At first, she was still asleep in my arms, but then she blinked and groaned and slowly came to. Her pristine blue eyes opened and met mine, and my heart slammed in my chest.

"I love you," I said.

Tears carried to her eyes. "I love you, too."

Her lips were back on mine a moment later. She pressed her body flush against mine and laced her arms behind my head and into my hair. The way she lightly tugged at my hair had the animal in me trying to break through to the surface. My tongue left my lips in search of hers, and she opened her mouth to allow me entry. It all felt so intensely real. I ran my hands along the bend of her waist and the arch in her back. I could only pray that my dream would allow me enough time to refamiliarize myself with every inch of her.

Like a flip had been switched within us, we turned the dial up on the fire. Cherri's hands slipped from around my neck and down under my shirt to drag along my skin. The coolness of her fingertips somehow burned, and I hoped they would leave marks. She pushed until my shirt was bunched around my neck and I had no choice but to break away from her to take it off. Her eyes flashed at the sight of me, and I smiled. Having a woman like Cherri look at you like Cherri looked at me could give a man a dangerous amount of confidence.

I pushed against her to pin her back against the bed and hovered over her. She was wearing a dark blue t-shirt that clung to her form, and as sexy as the simple look was, I wanted it off. I grabbed the hem and dragged it upwards until I was able to toss it off of her. My hands quickly traveled then to the front clasp of her bra and undid it. Her perfect, round breasts came free, and I dipped in to take a taste. Her body was hot and her peach skin was flushed red.

A body blusher—one of the sexiest things about Cherri.

"Deon," she squeaked in my ear as I sucked one of her pert nipples, and when I switched to the other she arched her back upwards. Her hands dropped between us and grabbed at my pants. "I need you, baby."

I hugged my arms around her back and held her tight. "I don't want to rush," I said.

"I've missed you," she complained. "Please."

But I knew how dreams worked. All I had was until just before the end. The sooner I got inside her, the closer I got to exploding, the quicker I approached the end of my dream. Just before I came, I'd wake up and Cherri would be ripped from my arms again. I couldn't handle it. I had to hold onto her for as long as I could.

To my surprise, tears filled my eyes and I simply set my head on her chest. "I can't. I don't want this to end."

"End?" Cherri questioned. "Why would it end?"

"I'll wake up," I admitted. "I have to make it last."

"Deon," Cherri said in a serious voice. "Look at me."

Part of me was too embarrassed to listen. Not because I was crying, but because it was all just a manifestation of my imagination anyway. Was I going to cry to myself and beg myself not to go? Cherri was back in Postings somewhere. I was getting high off a placebo.

But I twisted my head back anyway, placing my chin on her chest and looking up into her eyes. She put her hands on my face and rubbed my cheeks gently. "Baby, I'm real. I'm here. This isn't a dream."

I smiled. "I wish that were true."

She pulled, bringing my face up to hers and pressed our lips together again. Her mouth caressed mine, taking a passionate kiss, at the end of which she bit down on my bottom lip. It stung, and I grunted.

But it stung.

I leaned back a little bit, setting my fingers to my lip to feel the spot, and there was a small bump forming there. Cherri put each of her hands on my arms, and pinched spots that hurt as well.

They hurt.

I wasn't dreaming. Cherri was lying beneath me, looking at me with the eyes I'd longed to look into every single day. "Cherri?"

She nodded. "Yeah."

It shifted me sideways, out of my own body. Anything in me that wasn't focused on Cherri had to take a back seat. I wrapped my arms around her and lifted her off the bed. There was an armchair in the corner of the room, and I backed up until I was sitting in it. The sun glinted in through the window and bounced off her perfect skin, giving her an angelic glow. She undid the button of her shorts as I slid my lips along the curve of her neck. It only took a little bit of shifting to slide our pants off, and then I was standing at attention between Cherri's legs.

Cherri grabbed me and stroked me a little. "So is it okay to jump ahead a little?" she asked with a coy smile. "We've got all the time we need to double back."

"Fuck yes," I said.

That was all the go-ahead Cherri needed. She lifted off of me just enough to brace me at her entrance and then slowly started to lower herself onto me. It was so much hotter than I remembered, and I had to grip her hips to stop her.

"What?" Cherri said.

"I forgot how fucking good it feels," I replied. It had been close to nine months since I saw and got to be with Cherri last, and being on the run didn't afford a ton of time for helping myself out. Even since I settled down at Felicity's, we spent most of our time together, and I had a tendency to pass out at the end of the day. "I'm not gonna last long this go round."

"That's okay," Cherri said, setting her hands on

my face and kissing me. "Like I said, we have plenty of time."

With that assurance, I released Cherri's hips and she continued to fall. She sucked me in, enticingly slow, reminding me of exactly what I'd missed in the past eight months. The way we fit together, as cheesy as it sounded, felt like it was fated, and when she was finally fully sitting in my lap, we both threw our heads back, breathing in the ecstasy of the moment. The bed couldn't have offered this forced closeness, and as I wrapped my arms behind her back and pulled her snug to me, I pushed even past what the chair was demanding to get closer.

Her lips found mine again and we stayed latched that way while she started to raise and lower herself in a hypnotic rhythm. Each time she pulled me all the way in, she squeezed on me, and a grunt huffed out of me. She moaned into my mouth and the vibration of it sent a wave of chills down my spine.

"I love you," I said to her again, looking up into her sparkling eyes.

There were tears in them. "I love you too. I missed you so much."

I squeezed her even closer. "I missed you too."

As if intended to make me lose the little bit of control I had, Cherri sat all the way down and then started to rock her hips back and forth. I dragged along every part of her inside, pulling even sexier noises out of her.

"Shh," I said. "We'll be heard."

"I don't care," she said.

Finally, I had no choice but to dig my fingers into the milky flesh of her ass and hang on as she dragged me closer and closer to the edge. The gentle rocking got faster, the friction got more intense, and the steam whistle inside me started a low hum. Cherri alternated between rocking and moving up and down, and eventually that whistle started to blow.

"Shit, Cherri," I growled.

The beautiful woman on top of me exploded, her moisture drenching me in a firestorm of pleasure. She clenched down on me and shuddered, and the power of it finally pulled a finish out of me. The noise that came out of me was something between a moan and a roar, and as Cherri pushed on, continuing to pleasure herself on top of me, my entire lower half started to tingle.

She expired, going limp against me. I leaned back in the chair, taking her with me, and did the best I could to catch my breath. I smoothed my hands over her skin, halfway afraid that she was going to disappear exactly as I'd feared, but she remained beneath my fingertips. She was soft, and warm, and real. If I had my way, we'd continue to stay that way forever.

We settled for a few more hours.

There wasn't a piece of furniture in the room that we left unsoiled by our antics. We were insatiable, and even though I still didn't understand how or why she was there, we never had enough of a moment to discuss it. We rolled into each other again and again, until it felt like we were going to start losing our ability to walk or talk.

Then we went into the shower and did it once more.

When we finally left the bathroom, I was exhausted but happy beyond measure. I wouldn't let her more than a few inches from me, before pulling her back and kissing her more.

"I know," she said. "I want more too, but we probably should show our faces to the others. Even if there's no hiding what we've been up to anymore."

"Others?" I said, tilting my head to the side.

She smiled. "Yeah. I only brought a couple with me, but I bet everyone's arrived by now." She grabbed my hand and led me out of the room.

We went down the stairs and I was immediately met with a murmur of voices. We walked into the kitchen and my heart jumped up into my throat. Felicity was standing in the kitchen, chatting away with a few women that I recognized as Nikita, Colette, and Avery from The Royal Court, and Alistair, Kyle, and Brayden were sitting at the kitchen table, chatting over a plate of pastries and coffee, but standing directly across from me, with smiles rising to their faces when they saw me, were two other people I'd missed more than I was willing to admit. My best friend Sicily…

…and my brother, Nathan.

24

DEON

When Cherri and I entered the kitchen, all eyes turned to us. Across from me, and much to my surprise, Nathan looked like he was on the brink of tears. Everyone's glances bounced between us, and even as uncomfortable as it made me, I had to admit it was good to see him. He took a step forward and so did I. He shook his head with a little chuckle and held his arms out for a hug.

And then Sicily jumped in front of him and threw his arms around me.

"Deon!" he whined. "It's really you! I've been dreaming of this day!" Even though there was damn near a foot between us, he squeezed me tightly. "I kept looking for you! Your best friend never gave up."

"I heard," I said, finally managing to put a wedge between us to push him back a few feet, but I set my hands on his shoulders. "Thank you. You took care of Cherri, you never gave up on me. You really are the best friend a guy could ask for."

What I'd learned about Sicily in the limited time that we had to develop a friendship was that he didn't do emotions very well. He was a natural jester, and when his feelings started to get the best of him, he did what any good jester did—he played it off with a joke. His feelings about being reunited with me must have gotten the best of him, because he started out kidding, but in the wake of my earnest statement, I watched all of his inner jokester fade away.

"Deon," he said in his serious tone, an octave lower than his usual jubilant tone. "You're like, the first real friend I ever had, and as much as I hated thinking you were out there in a ditch somewhere, if that hadn't happened..." He looked past me to Cherri. "I wouldn't have made the second real friend I ever had."

Cherri stepped forward and slid between Sicily and me to pull him into a big hug. When she released him, I pulled her back so her back was against my stomach and put a hand on Sicily's head. "You're the first real friend I ever had too.

When I went missing, you looked after the most important people in my life, my queen…" I looked across at Nathan. "And my brother."

In an instant, Sicily turned back into the class clown, and his typical tone was back. "Oh! He called me his friend! Nathan did." He looked back at him. "Tell him."

Nathan nodded. "I did say that, and I've regretted it ever since."

Everyone chuckled a little, then Cherri stepped aside and dragged Sicily with her. I finished crossing the kitchen, and doing something I honestly never thought I'd do, I pulled Nathan into a huge bear hug. I closed my eyes and breathed in the moment—actually bonding with a brother I hated. We had something that bonded us more than anything else ever could.

The manipulation of Connor Loche.

"So," Nathan said, pulling away. "How about that dad of ours?"

I shrugged. "I don't see him as my dad."

Nathan nodded. "Oh good, I don't either."

Colette raised her hand. "Don't you have to acknowledge that he's your dad to some extent? Otherwise you wouldn't be brothers."

"No," Nathan and I said in unison, and it brought that concept to an end in a flash.

"He's done all he needed to do in making us brothers by spreading his seed," Nathan said.

I nodded. "And now it's time to stop him so he can't bring that level of harm to anyone else."

Cherri and I were understandably hungry given our torrent for the past few hours, so after Felicity made us a full breakfast each, despite it being nearly lunch time, we all adjourned to the much roomier living room. I took my normal armchair, and when Cherri tried to sit on the floor in front of me, I pulled her down in my lap instead. Nathan, Nikita, Colette, and Jaxon all squeezed on one couch, while Kyle and Brayden sat next to one another on the other, with Felicity in her regular spot at the end of that one. Sicily sat on the floor and Avery and Alistair joined him, though they quickly curled into each other as expected, and I noticed how close everyone else seemed.

"So, everyone's paired off then?" I said.

Kyle looked around nervously, "Well—"

"Yeah," Brayden said. "Everyone's paired off."

Kyle looked at Brayden with glowing eyes and it brought a smile to my face. I never suspected that Kyle was into guys, but it also didn't shock me. He was never the kind of guy who seemed to give a shit about stuff like that when it came to who he chose to spend his time with. The fact that he was into

Brayden as an individual was a little more surprising, but it seemed Brayden had mellowed out at least.

"Is that an admittance?" Avery asked, leaning in. "Is that what that means?"

"No," Colette said quickly, then looked at Brayden. "No, right?"

Brayden shrugged. "It doesn't have a title or anything, but…"

Avery clapped her hands. "Yes! Yes!" She stabbed a finger out at Colette. "Suck it, Bentley!"

Colette crossed her arms. "Fine. I owe you $50."

"Did you bet on us?" Kyle said with his nose wrinkled up. "That's pretty shitty."

Colette sat up straight. "Oh no! We didn't bet on your success or anything. We all knew that was happening. It was more a matter of how long it would take you to come out and say it." She put a hand on her chest. "*I'm* the better friend, because I wasn't going to rush you into anything."

"You are not. You said they'd keep flip-flopping between who would be willing to say it," Avery said.

"Rude," Colette snapped. "That was supposed to just be between us."

"Technically, that's what happened," Alistair

said. "I mean it was Brayden who confirmed it just now, not Kyle."

Avery turned around and looked at Alistair. "Whose side are you on?"

Alistair shrugged. "What? I'm just saying—"

"WAIT!" Sicily screamed, bringing all the attention to him. "You two are together?!"

Colette looked over at Avery with a grin. "Ooh, I *do* believe that brings us back to even."

"Goddammit, Sicily," Avery hissed. "Did you *really* not know?"

"No," Sicily whimpered, deflating. "Dang it. So I really am the only single one? No love for ol' Sic?"

"You'll find someone, Sicily. You're so wonderful," Cherri said.

"You really are," Avery tacked on. "I meant what I said at the beginning of the summer."

That seemed to light Sicily up. "Really?"

"Wait," Alistair said. "What'd you say?"

"Yeah," Avery replied, totally ignoring Alistair. "You're a catch."

Alistair poked Avery in the back. "Avery, what'd you say?"

"Oh! Do you mean when you said you'd put him on your list?" Nikita asked.

"Nikki!" Avery yelped.

Nikita slumped further into the couch. "Oh… is that not what we're talking about?"

"List?" I asked.

"A list of people other than your partner that you can sleep with, but it's usually celebrities that you'd never meet," Cherri explained quietly to me before looking at Avery. "Did you really say that? I thought you were talking about when you said if it wasn't for Alistair—"

"Oh my god! Both of you shut your fucking mouths!" Avery hissed.

"No, no. Please continue," Alistair said with a stone-serious face.

Avery looked back at her boyfriend. "Honey, I meant like, if I wasn't *madly* in love with you."

"Deon, your friends are funny," Felicity said, petting Concrete and enjoying the show.

Alistair was leaning away from Avery and wouldn't even look in her direction. Avery tried to give him a couple of kisses on the cheek to help, but he couldn't be swayed for the time being. Avery turned and gave Cherri and Nikita each a death glare. "Great. Thank you both for this."

"Huh," Brayden said. "It's rare that I'm not causing the fighting." He smiled at Kyle. "It's nice."

Kyle wrapped an arm around Brayden and pulled him close, and I simply laughed. "Damn.

The Royal Court has changed quite a bit. I don't even recognize you." Nathan was leaning his head against his hand on the arm of the couch. "You aren't gonna do your weird king thing and simmer 'em down?"

"I no longer have control of this train. I just have the prestige honor of sitting in the driver's seat so that I'm the first one to hit the wall when we crash," Nathan said flatly.

"Damn," I said again. "I was about to ask what I missed, but I'm not entirely sure I want to know."

"I'll tell you what you missed," Sicily said. "Avery would put me on her list." He winked at Avery and smacked a kiss in her direction and Alistair shifted immediately. Sicily scrambled away with a yelp and sat next to the couch where Felicity and Concrete were. "It was a joke. Just lightening the mood."

"Getting back to your question Deon," Felicity said. "It sounds to me like your friends have been on quite the hunt for you. Some of the tactics they tried, I hate that I didn't think of them first."

"Really?" I asked. "All of you?"

Sicily nodded. "Colette has been my little tech monster. The rest of them have helped, but she and I have been checking pings off your unknown number for weeks trying to track you down."

"And Brayden has put in a ton of work trying to find Connor," Cherri added in. "Everyone is doing their part though. We've been working nonstop, it feels like."

I looked at Colette and Brayden, the two people I might have previously considered the snobbiest, shallowest members of The Royal Court, and they were looking back at me with nothing but smiles. In fact, I could see it in all of them, they were *happy* to see me. The Royal Court had not been my group of friends before everything went ass up. I had Cherri, and through Cherri I'd begun developing something of a friendship with Avery and Alistair, but other than that, I thought very poorly of all of them, Nathan included.

In just that one day, the one where everything changed, I realized that my understanding of The Royal Court wasn't just skewed, it was totally off. When push came to shove, they dropped everything to rush to Nathan's aid. Even Cherri, who had just had a horrible experience with Nathan, was committed to finding and saving him within 24 hours. These people, whether they realized it or not, were committed to each other in a way most people never found.

The fact that they extended that commitment to me when they barely knew me was a true tell of the wonderful people that they were. "Well, I'm appreciative," I said. Squeezing Cherri around the waist, I smiled. "You guys kept my girl safe, you kept my brother safe, my best friend. You've been trying to stop my shithead sperm donor, and you've been looking out for one another. I couldn't thank you as much as I wanted if I tried. How *did* you eventually find me?"

"That was a combo effort between Sicily and Nathan," Cherri said. "Nathan had a couple of Connor's goons being held by some people he knew and they were able to swipe their phones. Sicily was able to break in and compare the info in their phones to the info he and Colette had gotten from the pings off the number you were calling Nathan and I from, and we realized you'd been near the prison. Once we realized you hadn't gone back to prison, we guessed you must have visited and both Sicily and I remembered you mentioning Venom, so I went and spoke to him. He gave me Felicity's address and here we are."

"You met my dad?" I asked. "What'd you think?"

"He's pretty great," Cherri said. "He was super helpful and really nice. He loves you a lot, Deon."

It gave me a warm, fuzzy feeling in my stomach

knowing that Cherri and Venom had the chance to meet.

"Did you get anywhere with Connor?" Felicity asked.

"Not far," Nathan said. "Like Cherri said, Brayden sort of broke his back trying to sort out his connection to Connor, but it led to a totally cleaned out warehouse in North Postings."

Both Felicity and I sat up a little straighter. "A place Connor had been before?" Felicity asked.

"Yeah, but he'd completely cleared it out, even tore the walls down, by the time we got there," Cherri said.

I looked across at Felicity. "Would this be helpful to Nico?"

She nodded. "Definitely. If he knows a specific place, he could find the guy."

"Who?" Kyle asked.

I looked straight at Nathan. "Felicity and Venom know a guy that has about as many connections as Connor does. We currently have him hot on Connor's trail, and he's getting close. Knowing an actual warehouse that Connor had used though. That's golden information."

"Can you write down the address for me?" Felicity asked. Nathan immediately pulled out his phone and started flicking through it. When he found the info, Felicity gave him her number and he sent the info over. She smiled up at me. "As soon as we're done, I'll go tell Nico."

That was when it hit me. These were my friends and the brother I was so desperate to get back to. They'd managed to stay out of Connor's clutches up to that point, and even if they hadn't, adding me to the mix wasn't going to make them any *more* of a target—they already had Nathan.

"Done," I said quietly, then looked at Felicity. Cherri was in my lap, and I knew I couldn't be separated from her again. Nathan was there, and I was excited to be back around him again. "I'll be going back with them, won't I?"

Felicity nodded. "I've been talking to them about everything. How safe they've managed to stay and the fact that they're taking Connor head on, and I think that would be best. You've been wanting to go back to Cherri and Nathan this entire time, now you finally get to." For some reason, that left a knot in the pit of my stomach. Cherri must have noticed it, because she started to rub my back and rested her head on top of mine. Tears slowly rose to Felicity's eyes and I had to bite back my own emotion. "Dammit, Deon. I cried in the bathroom about this for like twenty minutes this morning just so I'd be okay. Don't look so sad, it's heartbreaking."

"I am sad though," I said. Concrete was snoozing in Felicity's lap despite the loudness in the room, and Felicity looked so normal in her spot on the couch. "I liked this life too."

"Getting shot aside?" Felicity asked.

"What?" Cherri and Nathan yelped at the same time.

Felicity looked at them both and then groaned at me. "Sorry."

"That's okay. I'll explain all of that to them later." I tapped Cherri's leg and she climbed out of the chair so that I could stand up. Felicity moved Concrete's head out of her lap and stood up as well and we walked to meet each other in the middle of the room. I wrapped my arms around her and hugged her tightly. "I've loved being here with you for the past few months."

Felicity sniffed against my chest. "I've loved having you. Promise me you'll visit soon."

"Oh I'll be back. We've still got a man to break out," I joked.

Felicity finally pulled herself away, her eyes drenched, and said, "I'll go pack your stuff," before fluttering out of the room. Ordinarily, I'd fight her on something like that, but I knew she'd need a minute.

"You okay?" Cherri asked, wrapping her arms around me from the back.

I rubbed her arms, loving that she was that close again. "I will be. Felicity's become like a mom to me. I'm gonna miss her." I walked over and knelt in front of Concrete and rubbed his ears. "I'm going to miss you too, you big oaf."

Concrete slobbered a lick up my face, and I scratched his favorite spot behind his ear. "These two are my family now and their lives have been just as affected by Connor as ours have."

"How so?" Nathan said.

"Like I said, I've got a lot to explain to you, but not here. If we don't leave soon, I may never leave."

The rest of The Royal Court went ahead of us, leaving only Cherri, me, and Nathan behind. Felicity eventually brought down the bags of things I'd amassed since living with her—all the things I only had because she loved me like a mother and bought them for me.

"Your weights," she said weakly.

I shook my head. "Keep them here for when I visit."

She nodded. "Okay."

We embraced once more, that time for much longer. When I pulled away I smiled down at her. "I love you, mom."

She laughed. "I love you too. Be safe in Postings. You're still wanted, remember that."

"I've already made certain arrangements," Nathan said.

Felicity exchanged glances between Nathan and Cherri. "You two take care of my boy."

Cherri nodded. "We will. We promise."

25

DEON

Most of the ride back to Postings, I slept in the backseat. Every few minutes, I'd come to and hear Cherri and Nathan talking as if they had always been best friends and nothing had come between them. Nathan was less snotty than he was when I spoke to him last, and Cherri was much more of a spitfire. There were times in the drive that I felt like I wanted to 'wake up' and join in, but it was actually nice to see the woman I loved and my brother getting along so well, especially considering all of the reasons they had to not. From what they talked about, it sounded as if The Royal Court had quite the journey of introspection and had changed dramatically for the experience.

Glad I wasn't the only one.

Eventually, we made it back to Postings, and Nathan drove us back to his family's estate. The last time I'd been there, I was brazenly flirting with Cherri in the back gazebo despite knowing she was dating Nathan at the time. Something about the energy of the place simply felt different. There were several cars parked out front, and when we walked in, all the members of the Royal Court were hanging around, Sicily included.

"Hey!" Colette said when we walked in. "Welcome home!" She fanned her arms out and stood in the entryway where we couldn't walk past her.

"What the fuck are you doing?" Cherri asked.

"Oh nothing," Colette responded. "Just welcoming you back."

"We're done!" Avery's voice called from the living room.

Colette dropped her act. "Oh, thank god. Come on!"

She turned around and led us towards the living room. I saw colorful balloons and a welcome home banner. There was a cake sitting on the table that also said "Happy Birthday," and I tilted my head. "Whose birthday is it?"

Brayden scoffed and dropped onto the couch. "Well, that was anticlimactic."

"Deon," Nathan said. "It's your birthday."

I stood in silence for a moment, trying to wrap my head around that information. The last time I celebrated my birthday, I was still locked up, days away from getting out. Venom got cupcakes from the commissary and pretended the wrappers were candles because we couldn't have real ones. He even forced me to blow out the fake flames.

Had it already been a year since that happened?

"Today's the fifteenth?" I asked.

"Uh huh," Avery said, then she fanned out towards the table with the cake on it and a single present. "Happy birthday, and welcome home."

"Wow," Cherri said. "I didn't realize at all." She looked at me. "Happy birthday."

I leaned down and kissed her, thinking that being reunited was about the best gift she could give me. "Thank you."

"Actually, none of us really realized it was already that late in the summer. Sicily still thought it was June," Nathan said.

"For like three minutes," Sicily grumbled.

"I opened my phone when Nikki called me to tell me where you guys were and I saw the reminder on my calendar. So we threw this together. It's not much, but I hope you like it," he explained.

I set a hand on Nathan's shoulder. "It's awesome. Thank you."

Like them, the day of the year had been totally lost on me up to that point. Part of me felt bad for denying Felicity the joy of celebrating with me, but maybe her not knowing made it at least slightly easier to let me leave.

I approached the table and a smile slowly came to my face. The present was a very small box, and I picked it up and turned around to face the group. Nathan nodded his head at me and said, "Open it," and I lifted the top off. Inside was a key ring with several different keys on it. I pulled it out and Nathan walked over. "This key," he said as he grabbed a brand new silver one, "is for the front door here." He grabbed the next one. "For Nikki and my house in the back." The next key was a wider, brass key. "This is the key to your office at L.C.E." Then he grabbed the last key. "And this is the key to your new Tesla. It's still registered in my name until your name is cleared, then I'll transfer the title."

"Wow," I said. "I… wow. Thanks."

"Hey, uh, Avery, Ali. Would you guys be willing to bring me to visit with my parents?" Cherri asked suddenly. "I'd like to let them know we found Deon.

Nikki, Brayden, will you guys come too? I want them to meet you."

Alistair nodded. "Of course."

Brayden and Nikita both smiled at me and gave their own nods of affirmation. Cherri walked over to me, gave me a quick kiss, and then the four of them left without another word.

"I'm exhausted, so I'm gonna go nap for a bit," Kyle said, leaving the room shortly thereafter.

"Sicily, we probably should clean up our mess," Colette said. "Jax can help."

Jaxon let out a frustrated sigh. "I guess."

"Yeah. Let's do it!" Sicily led the way out of the room, tapping me on my shoulder as I passed, and then I was left with just Nathan.

"That wasn't subtle," Nathan said.

"No, but whatever," I responded.

Nathan pointed outside. "Wanna go talk?"

"I think that'd be good."

Nathan led me over to the sliding glass doors in the back of his house, then we walked down the winding path to the very same gazebo where Nathan had caught Cherri and me before. It was one of the nicer gifts he'd ever given her, knowing that she loved a quiet, natural place to sit sometimes, so it didn't surprise me that he'd kept it.

"I'm honestly a little shocked to see you still

living here," I said. "After your mom and Connor, I'd have thought you would have left a you-shaped hole in the wall."

"I thought about it," Nathan said. "But I don't hate it here. I completely renovated the inside and it's sort of the official house of The Royal Court now."

"You're like one of the social media groups that all lives together and films crazy videos," I said.

Nathan nodded. "I never realized that, but it's pretty on brand for us, honestly."

I snickered. "Maybe y'all. Not me."

"Well, there's a room for you up there too, so get used to it. You're one of us now, whether you like it or not," Nathan said.

I sighed. "Is it weird that I sort of like it?"

"To be fair, I *did* offer you a position in The Royal Court before," Nathan said.

"Oh, you mean when you cleared out an entire classroom, sat on top of a desk like some sort of shitty dictator, and threatened me?" I said. "Can't imagine why I turned that offer down."

He rolled his eyes. "Fair."

"I've learned a lot about our father," I said. "Venom, our meeting behind bars wasn't just random. He used him to frame me for the death of some random guy. Apparently Felicity is one of the many women he'd manipulated and he was able to use her to get to him."

Nathan's nostrils flared with anger. "I shouldn't be surprised. I'll do you one better. He handpicked Cherri *years* before you met her. He moved her family here, intentionally near you. It's still uncertain if his original plan was for her to be with you, or if he always intended to have me snatch her from you, but regardless, he'd been in control over her family from even before she moved here."

"God," I barked. "This guy is a fucking piece of shit."

"No disagreements there, but I do have to say, sometimes I find myself being a little, I don't know, grateful. I mean, if it weren't for him, Cherri wouldn't be here. I wouldn't know any of my friends. Hell, who knows if you and I would have ever met. For all his fucking around with us, he did leave a *little* bit of good in his wake."

"I suppose," I said. "I'm not acknowledging that to him though."

"No, never," Nathan replied. "No, next time I see him, I'll be taking him down, and that'll be it."

"We have to keep him alive," I said, and Nathan's eyes widened at me. "I know, but he's the reason Venom is locked up. The only way he'll be able to get out is if we can prove that Connor was on bullshit when he was working with Venom. If we kill him, there will be no way to do that."

"I really want him dead, Deon," Nathan said. "He killed my mom."

"I'm not saying anything specific, I'm just saying, once he's locked up, Venom's men will have access to him and it probably won't be pretty. I want him six feet under too, but if we jump the gun, we'll never be able to clean up all the messes he's made."

Nathan sighed. "I guess I'd better get started on trying to come up with a new way to entice him to do what we want, if it's not going to be a barrel down his throat."

"Thanks," I said.

"Wanna hear something else insane?" Nathan asked. "You are an officer of our company."

"What?" I said.

"Oh yeah. Your name is on an office there. That key I gave you is no joke. Deon Keane, you are the Chief Executive Officer of Loche Corporation Enterprises."

That dream I had with Nathan and Cherri came blasting back into my mind. Was it just a freaky premonition? "I'm the C.E.O.?"

"Seems dear old dad had some plans up his sleeve that even I didn't know about. From the day the company was incorporated, I've been listed as Vice President and you've been listed as C.E.O." Nathan kicked the dirt on the gazebo floor. "It's been a pain in the ass getting them to function without us, but I told them they need to just toe the line until we can figure all this shit with Connor out."

"So, what? After all this is done, you're gonna go and be an 18-year-old Vice President of a Fortune 500 company?" I asked.

"Pretty much, although I'll technically be President now," Nathan said. "I plan to go to business school and eventually get my MBA, but Connor had me studying that shit when I was ten, so I know how things go." He looked over at me. "What about you? Will you join me? Vice-president?"

"I never considered myself much of an office guy," I replied.

"I'll let you keep the Grizzly Adams beard," he joked.

I ran my hand along the scruff. "It's something, isn't it? Do you think I should cut it?"

"At the risk of sounding *so* creepy, no. Cherri likes facial hair," Nathan replied, then he held up a hand before I could quip back. "No, don't comment on it. Let that be the first and last time that ever happens."

"Deal," I said. "I don't know. Maybe I'll join you. Currently, I'm still a wanted man, so I have to get all that sorted out first."

"Yeah," Nathan said. "I've been in contact with your P.O. I never let on for a second that we were looking for you or anything, only asked what we would have to do if it turned out all of this had been manipulated by Connor. Turns out, he'd been threatened by our old man a time or two, and would be willing to look the other way—in exchange for money, of course. He's pulled your warrant back and is currently reporting visits to keep you in good standing. You can't run around robbing gas stations or anything, but at least for the time being you aren't actively being hunted by the cops."

"Wow. Thanks, Nathan," I said.

"Yeah."

I thought about what the coming days were going to hold for us and imagined getting to just settle down and be some office guy with my brother and go home to the love of my life every day. It felt like too boring and normal a life for me to deserve. I'd fight for it if I could have it, though.

"Well, if it's okay with you, I really want to go and see my mom. I can't imagine how much she's gone through these past eight months," I said.

"Cherri took pretty good care of her," Nathan said. "They lived together for about six months."

"Cherri and my mom did?" I said.

Nathan nodded. "Yeah. Cherri like… flipped her shit at the beginning of our last semester and got kicked out of her house, among other things. She went to stay with your mom until The Royal Court got the band back together and she came to live here."

I remembered seeing my mom talking about her roommate leaving about a month ago. That was Cherri. "Wow."

"Your family has missed you quite a bit, Deon. We had to cope by just being there for each other," Nathan said, and I was slightly surprised he included himself.

"Well, I'm home now," I said.

"That's right, you are." He stood up. "Come on. I'll show you to your room."

Nathan and I went back inside the main house and grabbed my bags. We carried them up stairs and down a few doors to one on the left side. He opened it and I was smacked in the face by Cherri's delightful, inviting smell. Her things were scattered all around the room and I immediately felt like I truly was *home*.

"My old room?" I said.

"Yeah," Nathan said. "I remodeled it, made it special for you guys. Cherri's been staying in here already, as I'm sure you can tell. I'll give you the rest of the tour later. For now, go and see your mom."

I set my bags down, then turned around and pulled Nathan into a big hug. He wrapped his arms around me, and with all prying eyes gone for the moment, we shared an extended hug. Brothers reunited after all of Connor's best attempts to put space between us. I really did love my brother. Hopefully the future held plenty of opportunities for us to get to an even better place.

"Alright," Nathan said, pulling away and flicking a tear away. "Get out."

I laughed. "You got it."

Walking around him, I made my way downstairs to the cars parked in the lot in front of the house. I clicked the button on my keys, and a white Tesla flashed a couple of times. A whistle came out of me as I climbed in and started up the car. I honestly never thought I'd have a car like that of my own. That was what awaited me if I *did* take my position at the company. I could get my mom into a nicer house, get her a nice car, and make sure she'd only have to work if she wanted to.

Yeah, that was the life I wanted.

The drive from South to North Postings was plenty of time for me to come to the realization that business school and working with my brother seemed like a damn good future. I'd pretty much written off getting to have one, but if fate was suddenly offering, I wasn't going to say no.

The lights were on, shining against the early evening sky as I pulled up and parked in front of my mom's house. My heart was beating wildly for some reason as I walked up the walkway and pulled my hand up to knock on the door.

It opened before I even made contact.

"Deon," my mom said breathlessly, tears gathering in her eyes and sliding down her cheeks. "My baby."

My throat tightened and tears were in my eyes a moment later. I held my arms out and she ran into my embrace. "Mama," I said with a smile. "I'm home."

26

CHERRI

"Ugh, Cherri, I love these two new friends," my mom said. She squeezed Brayden close. "You're such a pumpkin!"

"They were around before," my dad said. "But it seemed like you didn't really like them before."

"Gee, thanks dad," I said with a chuckle.

Brayden was excitedly leaning into the snuggle with my mom. "I mean, it isn't as if we didn't know that."

"True," I said.

Alistair leaned back in his seat and rubbed his belly. "There is nothing like your home-cooked meals, Rebeccah."

"It's so true," Avery said. "I don't think I've ever seen Nikki this food-happy."

Nikita was half-asleep in her chair, with a lazy smile on her face. "I don't think I've ever *been* this food-happy."

"Thanks for doing it on such short notice, mama," I said to my mom, who saw four hungry young adults walk through her front door, and took the challenge head on.

"Are you kidding? I live for this," my mom replied. "I knew that I had a promise to Alistair and Avery, and a few extra mouths only made it that much better."

"I cannot wait to rub this in everyone else's faces," Brayden said.

"Aw," I said. "Glad to see you getting back to your roots, Brayden."

He smiled over at me. "What can I say? There's a jerk streak in me that I've been ignoring for far too long. It's time for my inner ass to re-emerge." Then he looked at my mom. "Sorry, inner butt."

My mom waved her hand at Brayden. "It's okay. We're a family that *staunchly* believes in swearing."

Avery leaned forward and her eyes started to sparkle. "Wait, really? So *that's* where Cherri gets it from."

"Oh no," my dad said. "Did we raise a potty mouth?"

"Fuck no," I said, and everyone at the table started to laugh.

Avery's smile only widened. "This whole time we've been seeing this darker side of Cherri and hearing her swear more often, and I've wondered where it came from. I don't think I've ever heard either of you swear."

"Well, we try to do the right thing around you kids, but Cherri has obviously been around us her whole life, so." My mom shrugged. "What can you do? Sometimes your kid gets your sailor mouth."

"I cannot imagine having to get up and actually go home," Alistair said. "We would have to move and walk and stuff and ugh." He fell back in his chair. "I don't wanna."

"Sorry guys, but I'm pretty anxious to get back to Deon," I admitted.

"I'm still angry you didn't *bring* Deon," my dad grumbled, something he'd been complaining about since I first arrived to tell them that he was alive and well.

"He had to reconnect with his brother, dad. I think that takes precedence over being interrogated by you literal *hours* after he was brought home from being on the run for eight months," I said.

My dad rolled his eyes. "Fine."

"I'll bring him by soon, I promise," I said.

"We'll be just fine," my mom said. "You kids go. Tell Deon we're glad he's okay, and we're looking forward to seeing him soon."

"I will. Maybe don't tell Gus that he missed me," I said.

"Yeah, because we were looking forward to hearing him whine all night," my dad grunted.

"Chris," my mom hissed.

"Oh my god," Avery yelped. "It's so cute. You're just like them, Cherri. I never knew!"

"Welcome to a look into where I get it from," I said, then I tapped Alistair on top of his head. "Come on, buddy. It's time to go."

In dramatic, flubber-like fashion, Alistair rolled to the side so far that it looked like he was going to drop onto the floor, then he stood to his feet. He leaned all the way back, his long blond hair dragging behind him, and dragged himself towards the front door. Avery, Nikita, Brayden and I opted for a much less showy departure, each giving my parents a hug, and saying our goodbyes before heading out into the night. We all piled back into my car and made our way back to Nathan's house.

Inside, Nathan, Kyle, Sicily, Colette and Jaxon were sitting in the kitchen working on a platter of sandwich ingredients. My heart dropped a little when I realized Deon wasn't among them.

I opened my mouth to say something, but Nathan held up his hand before I could get it out. "Relax. He's with his mom."

I let out a sigh of relief, but I still wanted to make sure. I pulled my phone out of my pocket and quickly dialed Ciara's number, just to curb my own fears. The phone rang a few times, and then it picked up. "I'm okay, gorgeous."

Deon's voice filling my ears immediately made me feel better. "Okay. I just wanted to make sure you made it okay. I won't bother you again."

"You are never a bother to me," Deon replied. "I love you."

"I love you too," I said.

There was a rustle and then a new voice came across the receiver. "Cherri?"

"Hey, Ciara," I said. "How is it having your baby home?"

"I can't believe it. You really found him. You brought him back to me," she said, sounding like she was on the brink of crying. "Thank you so much. Thank all of your friends for me."

"I will. Enjoy your time together," I said. "I'll see you soon, I promise."

"Okay, sweet girl. I love you loads," she said.

"I love you too. Bye."

The call ended and I went and sat around the

kitchen island with everyone else. Despite being stuffed from dinner at my parents, I grabbed a couple pieces of cheese from the platter and started to nibble on them. It was pure stress eating. I believed that Deon was just fine at his mom's house, and I knew Nathan had made certain arrangements to keep Deon out of the eyesight of law enforcement for a while, but after everything we'd been through, I'd always be anxious when Deon wasn't at my side, at least for a little bit.

"Don't let me do that shit again," I said to the group in general. "I don't want to be *that* girl."

"It's okay for it to make you a little nervous for a while though, Cherri," Avery said. "He literally went missing for eight months. If that happened to Ali, I wouldn't want to let him out of my sight."

"Literally, at one point during our last semester, we initiated a buddy system, and we always had to be with one other person in the group, right after Brayden went missing," Kyle said. "We even tried our best to always keep you and Sicily in our line of sight at all times. With Connor out there literally snatching people off the street, we've pretty much committed ourselves to always staying together."

That actually made me feel much better. "Thanks."

"Deon told me that my dad manipulated even Venom," Nathan said. "I guess Felicity was one of those women like Ciara and Miss Abrams that he was using to his advantage. He was able to exercise control over Venom that way, and he was actually the one who killed and dropped that body in front of you all those years ago."

My jaw dropped. "I can't believe that."

"Fuck!" Brayden snapped. "It seriously feels like the more we find out about Connor, the more we learn that he's been pulling strings since forever. What in our lives *hasn't* been masterminded by him?"

"Not much," Jaxon said. "I fucking hate that guy."

"Still, the other thing Deon and I were talking about is how none of us would be here if it weren't for him. Maybe a few things here and there *might* have happened, but the reason The Royal Court exists, the reason Cherri made it to Maine, it's all because of him. I really think we need to start viewing this as a silver-lining," Nathan said. "For as much bullshit as he put us all through, he also brought us together."

"We should never, ever, say that around him though," Cherri said. "I'll be damned if I'm going to give that *dick* the satisfaction of thinking he did anything positive in our lives."

"Agreed," Avery said, and everyone else nodded along as well.

"Deon's stuff is up in your room, and I think he's planning on coming back tonight, so I think it's just a matter of waiting now," Nathan said.

We sat and chatted for a little while, some of us eating, others not, and eventually, Deon came back home. He walked into the kitchen and straight over to me, putting his hands on either side of my face and kissing me. "Hey, my love."

I smiled at him. "Hi. I'm glad you're home."

"I'm glad to be home," he said. He sat down on the stool next to me and started putting together a sandwich. "So, what are we doing next? You said you've been working nonstop right?"

"Well, right before we came to find you, we sort of hit a wall. I think the next thing we're waiting on is—" Nathan's phone rang at that exact moment. He picked it up and held it out. "Is this."

"That's not the first time that we've gotten perfect moments down to the second like that," Colette said. "I swear our lives are so weird."

"Hello?" Nathan answered. "Yeah, hey Felicity, what's going on?" He went silent for a minute and then said, "Oh sure, hang on." He pulled the phone away from his ear, pressed a button, and set it flat on the counter. "Go ahead."

"Deon?" Felicity said.

"Hey, mama," Deon said with a smile. "Miss you already."

"Same here. I'm not even going to send you this video of Concrete walking in and out of your bedroom looking for you. It'd break your heart," she said.

Deon frowned. "Yeah, please do not send me that video."

"What's going on?" Nathan asked.

"I heard back from Nico," she said. "With that info about the warehouse you found and the lead we already gave him from the road show, he was able to track down someone quickly. There's a guy there in Postings, who only goes by 'T.C.' and operates out of a night club there called the Black Star Night Club. It's 21 plus from what I could see online, so I don't know how you guys will get in, but Nico set up a meeting with him tomorrow night at 9:00 pm."

"That sounds like a job for…" Sicily stood up off of his stool and put his hands on his hips like a superhero. "Super Sicily!"

"Oh yeah, Sic?" Felicity asked. "Fake IDs fall under your purview, huh?"

"Fake IDs were, like, freshman year," Sicily replied. "I'll have 'em done by morning."

Felicity laughed. "Nothing like having a shady agent on your side."

"That's right," Sicily said.

Deon chuckled at Sicily. "I missed you, man."

That seemed to double Sicily's excitement. "Thanks, man. I missed you too."

"Well, I'll text you all the info so you have it in writing, Nathan. Please be careful. You have no idea what you're walking into. Be smart," Felicity said. "Deon, don't tell your dad."

"I won't if you won't," Deon replied.

"I love you, kid," Felicity said.

Deon smiled. "Love you too."

"Bye guys," Felicity said.

"Bye," The Royal Court echoed.

Nathan pressed the button to end the phone call and pulled his phone back. "Okay. Well, now we know what's next. The Black Star Night Club."

"I've heard of that place," Jaxon said, and it didn't surprise me at all that he was the one who knew it. "Apparently the security guards there are all cops who are paid to look the other way for the dirty dealings."

"Have you ever been, Jax?" Colette asked.

"Nah. It's a little too on the nose for me. A real

pop music and tight clothes kind of place," Jaxon said.

Avery smiled. "Sounds amazing to me."

"Well, we've got a long night ahead of us tomorrow, and Felicity is right, we don't know what we're walking into. Some of us have had crazy sleep patterns," Nathan said, looking at Brayden, Nikita and me specifically. "Some of us have had crazy eating patterns, and we don't have room for any of that. Eat up, get some rest, and I'll make sure tomorrow's meals are protein-packed."

"Given that it's a shadier place, do you think we can get our guns in, Jaxon?" Kyle asked.

Deon's jaw dropped. "Guns?"

I looked sideways at him. "Yeah. You find once you've been attacked by grown-ass men you gotta keep yourself armed. We're all licensed carriers."

Nathan pointed at Deon. "You will be carrying no guns. You're in a good spot right now, but you can't carry on parole. Just let us do the heavy lifting."

I could see Deon shifting uncomfortably at the concept, but I put my hand on his back. "Please?"

Deon looked at me and nodded. "Yeah, okay." He picked a chip up off his plate and popped it in his mouth. "Damn, if someone had told me that I'd be holding back and letting The Royal Court of all people carry instead of me, I'd have punched that person in the face."

"We're sort of The Dark Royal Court now," Alistair said.

Nathan smiled. "I like that. The Dark Royal Court."

27

DEON

The Black Star Night Club was situated in Downtown Postings, ironically not far from where Loche Corporation Enterprises was located. I couldn't help but feel like it wasn't chance placement, and I imagined that Connor Loche had done more than one shifty deal in the bowels of the place. The outside was painted black brick with gold stars painted all over it, so it stuck out like a sore thumb from the modern, sleek buildings that were situated on either side of it. Postings was a manufacturing city, so most of the downtown buildings were offices to support all the commerce coming into Maine from the coast. There were a few night clubs and bars, as any city had, but it seemed Black Star Night Club was the club of choice. When we got there, there was a line of people around the block.

"Wow," Cherri said. "Packed to hell."

"I mean," Colette said from the back seat. "We're not *normal* people. We should be able to throw our names around and get in, right? We'll be standing in that line long past nine."

Cherri was driving a car with her, me, Sicily, Colette, and Jaxon in it, and Kyle was driving in front of us with Brayden, Nathan, Nikita, Alistair and Avery.

"That's going to be up to Nathan, I think," Cherri said. "He's the one with all the clout at the end of the day."

"Excuse me, Colette has clout," Jaxon said.

I turned around and looked backwards at him, and saw that his face was stone serious. I laughed and looked at Cherri. "It's unexpectedly adorable."

"Oh I know. I can't get over it," she replied.

I took a moment while we were stuck in traffic to look Cherri's outfit over once again. She was wearing a high-waisted, black leather skirt and a black, ruffled crop top. Her hair was down, and she'd applied a layer of dark makeup with black lipstick and a deep purple eyeshadow. She looked good enough to eat.

"Stop it," Cherri said. "We're never going to

make it all the way through this night if you keep looking at me like that."

"Fine by me," I joked, glancing sideways at her, but she just shook her head. I loved the slight blush that rose to her face.

Eventually, Cherri's car phone rang, and she answered, "Hey."

"Hey," Nathan said. "We're not standing in this line. We're gonna go park in the L.C.E. parking lot and walk over."

"Okay," Cherri said.

We followed Kyle's truck around the block and into the parking garage that was attached to Loche Corporation Enterprises. We all climbed out of the cars and walked across the street and back down the block to where the line was beginning. Nathan strode right past the line, and I shook my head at how entitled he looked, not even making eye contact with the pissed-off people glaring at him from the line. If the situation were any different, I would have demanded we wait in line like everyone else, but we didn't have time for that.

When we got to the front of the line, the thick-armed, broad-shouldered security guard looked us up and down. His lip curled up as he hissed, "This isn't a fucking daycare. Run along, tykes."

Nathan reached into his suit jacket pocket and

pulled out a few things. One of them was a white card that I couldn't read, one of them was the fake ID that Sicily had made, and the last was a flush of hundreds. He handed all three things over to the security guard and waited.

The security guard flipped through the handful of hundreds and then looked at the card and ID. He looked up at Nathan, scanned him over, scanned the rest of us, and then looked back down at the card. Finally, he pressed the button on the walkie talkie on his chest pocket and said, "Got eleven coming in. Let 'em by." He grabbed the velvet rope that was separating the outside of the club from the inside, and waved us by. "Come on, before I lose my fucking job."

We didn't hesitate at all. We all slid inside, past the line of swearing club-goers waiting to get in, and past the second security guard inside. Flashing our IDs, we finally left the waiting line behind and entered the club. Music was pumping and directly opposite the door was a massive dance floor, sunken lower than the main level we entered on, and to the left and right were staircases that led up to a second floor with bars on it, overlooking the dance floor. Lights were flashing and fog machines were raining down on the dancers, spurring them on.

"I wanna go!" Colette yelped. "It looks like so much fun."

"We have work to do first," Nathan said. "Partying afterwards."

I looked up to the balcony that was overlooking the dance floor and could see a line of purple, velvet curtains hanging down, separating what looked like V.I.P. booths. "Up there."

All of The Royal Court's gazes shifted up to the balcony, and then Kyle turned and led the way up the staircase to the left. There was a glowing bar situated along the wall at the top of the second floor, and once we were up there, we could see that the area with the velvet curtains was roped off and guarded. With Cherri's hand clasped in mine, I stepped through to the front of the group and led us over to the roped area. A guard noticed us immediately and crossed his arms, preparing to face us when we reached him.

"You got a reservation?" he growled.

"We're here to see T.C.," I said. "Tell him that Nico sent us."

The guard eyed me for a minute, but then turned around and walked all the way down to the booth at the far end of the line, and slid the curtain aside. He poked his head in and stood that way for a few minutes, then he turned around and came back down. He unlatched the velvet rope and motioned us through.

"All the way down," he said. "Last one."

I led the way down the row of private booths and stopped at the last one. Another security guard took over and slid the curtain aside from the inside when he got there. We walked past the security guard and into a deceptively large room. It had a set of seats encircling the walls, and a couple of tables were in the middle, topped with food and booze.

One man was sitting in the center of the couches, opposite the curtain, arms crossed and glaring at us. He had tanned skin, a clean goatee, and wore a suit. "Well now," he said as we walked in. "Nico thinks I do work with babies now. Seems you all came in search of information."

"You helped Connor Loche recently," Nathan took over, stepping up to stand at my side. "You helped him secure a warehouse in North Postings."

T.C. looked around at some of his guys, seemingly a little flabbergasted at the gall eleven barely-adults had entered his space with. "Maybe I did, maybe I didn't. I don't typically give information away for free."

"What would you charge Garrett?" I said. "I would assume I'd get the son discount."

T.C. leaned forward a little. "What's your name?"

"Deon," I said. "Keane."

"Well hell!" T.C. said, his entire demeanor shifting. "You didn't say you were Venom's kid, get in here!" He motioned to the couches. "Sit. Do you want drinks? Food?"

"We're good, thanks. We just need to know about Connor."

T.C. looked around at his men, then nodded towards the door. They all filed out. The only one who remained on the side of the booth we were on was the security guard who let us in. T.C. was working on a beer and lifted it to take a sip. "Yeah. I've been helping him out. It's been a bitch working with him too. He comes in here every other week asking for a new warehouse space to hole up in. When the show is over and he's ready to pack up, he pays my men to clean house. Even tear down walls."

"Yeah, we saw one of those places," Cherri said.

"You've seen him recently?" Nathan said.

"Yeah. Last place he asked me for, he came in about a week ago for it."

"So he should still be there," I said.

"Yeah. I'll give you the address, so you can go

out there and take care of things yourself. Leave me out of it," T.C. said. "Just make sure you tell Venom I helped you out."

"I'll let him know right away," I said. "Thanks."

"Wow," Colette whispered from next to me. "Deon just went and found a *different* dad with pull."

Still, Nathan pulled out his wallet and took out a wad of cash. "Consider it a tip and to make sure this information doesn't get back to Connor."

He threw it to T.C., who caught it and nodded at Nathan and tossed a piece of paper back at him. I assumed that was the address. "Your secret is safe with me." Then he looked us over. "Well, did you need anything else?"

"Not unless there's more you think we need to know," I said.

"One last thing," T.C. said. "Part of the deal with Connor was always security. He has the place bugged to high hell. If you're planning on showing up at the doorstep, he'll know you're coming before you even get through the door, and you'll be dead before you get past the doormat."

"Don't you worry about that," Nathan said. "We've got it covered."

T.C. held up his hands. "Well, here I thought

you were just a bunch of angry toddlers. Well, good luck, kids."

We stood up and left the booth, passing T.C.'s cohorts outside the curtain. They walked back in as we walked out. Once we were beyond the rope that divided us from the booths, we all looked at one another.

"I'm kind of sad that it went so well," Colette said. "I wanted some action."

"Well, going after Connor won't be that easy," I said. "Be careful what you wish for."

"That's it for work, right?" Avery said. "Because I *have* to hit that dance floor."

"The fun stops tomorrow," Nathan said. "So let's live it up tonight!"

Everyone cheered and Nathan quickly hunted someone down to secure one of the V.I.P. booths for us to use. Liquor was brought in after we flashed our very convincing fake IDs, and Kyle, Brayden, Nathan, and Nikita stayed behind, while Avery, Alistair, Colette, Jaxon, Sicily, Cherri and I left to head down to the dance floor.

"There's gotta be someone here who wants an attractive, younger man," Sicily said as we walked down the stairs. "D, you gotta wingman for me."

"Alright," I said. I hooked Sicily's collar, found a gorgeous woman standing with her friends and working on a drink, and shoved Sicily straight into her.

"Deon!" Cherri yelped.

Her drink popped out of her hand and went spilling all over her dress, and Sicily looked up, horrified. "Uh, oh my fucking god," Sicily said. "I told my friend I thought you were hot, and he thought the best plan of action was to shove me into you."

The woman blinked a couple of times down at him, then a smile crossed her face. "You owe me a new drink then."

Sicily snagged a couple of napkins like a pro from a nearby table and held them out to her. "I've got plenty up in my booth, if you wanna join me."

She nodded. "Yeah."

Everyone apart from me stared in shock as Sicily led the beautiful blond up the flight of stairs and out of sight.

"I hate that it worked," Avery said.

I just shrugged. "He's like a cat, that one. You present him with an opportunity, even if it's razor thin, he'll make the most out of it."

"I've noticed that about him, actually," Colette said. "It's so weird."

"Well, Sicily's pretty weird," Alistair said.

Avery grabbed Alistair's hand. "Whatever. Let's go dance!"

Avery and Alistair, and Colette and Jaxon threaded into the crowd and Cherri grabbed my hand and dragged me in as well. Guys immediately started to size her up, so I was throwing glares in all directions as we got further in. Eventually, however, we found a good spot, and Cherri turned to face me. She grabbed my face and turned my attention to her, and her eyes had a seduction behind them.

"Just focus on me," Cherri said.

It was like she was a witch with insane, super-natural powers. "Yes ma'am."

The first song we danced to was upbeat and had Cherri swaying her hips back and forth. Her hair flicked around her head, and she laughed and sang along. I wasn't much of a dancer myself, but grooving along with Cherri felt worth it. The pumps she was wearing gave her ass an incredible lift, and the clothes she was wearing clung to her form like a glove. She held my gaze and sucked me deeper and deeper in, and soon there could have been twice as many people standing on that dance floor and I wouldn't have known. Cherri was all I could see.

All I cared to see.

After about ten minutes, the light changed to a

moody, deep purple, and the music slowed way down. The crowd shifted almost as a unit, closing in on their partners for the smooth, slow song. I slid my hands around Cherri's waist and set them low on her back and she pulled herself against me. Her hands pressed to my chest and she looked up into my eyes, and I couldn't resist the urge anymore. I ducked down and brought my lips to hers. Cherri waved her hips forward, sliding against my midsection, teasing me. My lips left hers and slid around to latch onto a spot on her neck.

"Deon," she sang into my ear, and it sent a rush of chills down my spine.

When I came back to her lips, it was with more passion, sliding my tongue in her mouth and breathing in her intoxicating scent. I wanted so much more of her than I was allowed to take standing in the middle of a public club.

Cherri pulled back, and her eyes fluttered to me. "Wanna give my keys to Colette and get out of here?"

Everything in me tingled at the resonance in her voice. "Like, you have no idea."

28

CHERRI

Colette was beyond understanding when I searched her out from the crowd and gave her my keys to drive my car home. "You've just been reunited!" she screeched. "Get it girl!"

We exchanged a cheek kiss, and then I sifted my way back through the throngs of people to where Deon was standing at the edge of the dancefloor. I grabbed his hand and pulled him out into the steamy night. My whole body was already hot and it doubled outside in the summer night. I held up a hand to flag down a taxi, but then Deon pulled on my hand.

"I've got a better idea," he said. "Come on."

We walked away from the curb and made our way down the street away from the club. We crossed the street and continued down the block, and Deon finally stopped in front of one of down-town Postings' fancier hotels. He pulled on the door and guided me inside, and my heart leapt with excitement. Deon kissed me, then left me standing in the lobby so that he could approach the desk. I was a little surprised to see him pull out a wallet and brandish a credit card, because it didn't seem like he would have access to those resources yet, but then I remembered a moment between Nathan and I before I went to go and visit with Venom.

"You look tired. Is everything okay?" I asked.

"Yeah," Nathan said. "I've just been getting everything set up for Deon."

"What do you mean?" I said.

"I've gotta make sure my brother is set when he gets back. There's a whole life he didn't get to live that I hope he can from now on."

Nathan worked with Deon's parole officer to get his warrant revoked, bought him a brand new car for his birthday, and made sure he had keys to both the main house and Nathan's house on the Loche estate. It wasn't a major jump to think that Nathan made sure Deon was set financially as well. If I knew Nathan at all, and I'm pretty sure I did, he probably loaded a card with hundreds of thousands of dollars and told Deon it was his share of their family funds. The fact that neither of them told me that was actually a little enlightening and encouraging. If they had brotherly things, they were developing a trust in one another, and that was good.

After about ten minutes, Deon came back with some paperwork and a couple of keycards in hand. He had a huge smile on his face and snickered when he got to me. "I don't think I've ever indulged in something like this before. It was weird."

"Yeah, getting used to being rich is strange," I said.

He closed in on me and placed a hand on my head and pulled me up into a kiss. "It's worth it for this though." His voice got low and unbelievably enticing. "Don't expect me to be as quick to fire as I was last time."

I smiled. "I'm looking forward to it." We walked over to the elevators and climbed on. Deon swished his card key in front of the scanner on the elevator, which allowed him to press one of the top buttons labeled for the suites. "A whole suite?"

"This is the kind of stuff I always dreamed of doing for you," Deon said. "A night out, ending in a beautiful hotel room overlooking the city. This is me just trying to get back to where we were supposed to be. To make up for lost time."

The elevator reached the floor we were riding to, and Deon had to set the key card in front of the scanner again to get the doors to open to let us out. The doors slid apart and opened into a stunning hotel suite overlooking downtown Postings. The lights from the buildings below were lit up and were casting a beautiful glow into the hotel room. We walked through the front hall and into the living room. There were a few couches situated around a fireplace against one wall, and a chaise sitting in front of the windows that viewed the city. There were a couple of other doors that probably led to a bathroom and bedroom, but Deon and I wouldn't know that for some time.

We tossed the few things we had on us onto one of the tables and then Deon led me over to the chaise. He laid down across it and pulled me down on top of him and I blanketed myself over him. His hands threaded into my hair and I smiled at him.

"I love you so much," I said.

"I love you," he said. "I hope you're okay with not getting much sleep tonight."

A smile rose to my face. "You have no clue how okay with that I am."

My lips found his in the darkness lit only by the lights from outside, and his hands slid down my back and over my ass. He squeezed as I curled against him, already feeling his arousal poking up. My hands dipped between us to fiddle with the buttons of the button-up shirt he'd donned for the night out. At first, I was just trying to get the buttons undone, but then I got annoyed. I sat up enough to get a hand between a couple of the holes and I yanked, snapping the buttons and sending them flying around the room.

"Holy shit," Deon said.

"I was over those fucking buttons."

I unwrapped the shirt from his torso and slid it away, then grabbed the base of his undershirt and pulled it up and over his head. If it was even possible, his abs, arms, and pecs were even *more* defined than they were when he first got out of prison. Maybe it was just because I was so excited to see him when I first got to Felicity's, but I hadn't registered that before.

But everything was registering now.

"You know," I said. "You've never been properly punished for making Nathan convince me you'd died. Do you have any idea how much that hurt me?"

Deon looked up at me through sad eyes, shocked at the sudden turn. "Cherri, I—"

I set a finger to his lips. "Shh." I stood up off the chaise and walked over to the button-up I'd already destroyed and brought it back to Deon. "Rip the sleeves off of this."

Deon did exactly that, grabbing the long sleeves of the button up and tearing each of them from the shirt. I tied the ripped sleeves together and then looped them around Deon's eyes and tied them behind his head. He tensed up a little bit, but I noticed him growing larger in his pants and figured the frustration was probably more with still being sheathed than not trusting me to blindfold him.

Still, I wanted to make sure. "You okay?" I asked.

"Yeah," his voice was gravelly and low and it sent a wave of chills crashing over my body.

"Good." I leaned in and kissed him as I grabbed one of his arms to pull him to sit up on the chaise.

I kicked my shoes off and then sat on the chaise between Deon's legs. I took his hands and guided them to my stomach, and he took over, sliding them up under my shirt. His big hands were enough to wrap fully around my breasts, which he did. "Skipped the bra, huh?" he said.

"And the underwear," I replied.

"You're really not gonna let me see?" he asked.

"Not this time," I replied. "Use your imagination."

He squeezed down on my chest, and I let out a moan before grabbing one of his hands and moving it to the hem of my skirt as well. Once again, instinct kicked in, and Deon slid his hand up my skirt and between my legs. While one hand worked my breast, the other started to massage my center. Though moisture had already started to develop there, it doubled when Deon's fingers started to flick over the bundle of nerves at my crest. I leaned backwards against him and closed my eyes, letting myself go in the feeling of his hands working me over, knowing that I had total control.

For too long, I'd had to react to everything that was happening to me. Tonight with Deon, at least on our first round, I wanted to dictate everything that was happening. I wanted to help him bring me the ultimate pleasure and bring him the same as well.

Deon's hand slid lower between my legs and poked at my entrance there. "Yes, baby," I said.

He slipped his fingers in and I let out a moan so loud it echoed off the window and bounced back to me. Above, his fingers were flicking one of my nipples, while the other below was stirring me up inside. My mind turned to mush, made worse when Deon leaned his head forward enough to latch onto my neck. He bit down before kissing at the spot gently, and unexpectedly, I came.

"Ah," Deon said. "You like being bitten."

"Maybe," I said.

"Duly noted."

He continued to work even through my barreling orgasm and then sunk his teeth into my shoulder and held on while he brought me to a second climax almost immediately. My legs shuddered at the intense feeling, never before having experienced what it felt like to tell someone exactly what I wanted and to receive it.

It was unfair how heavenly it felt.

I sat forward a bit from Deon, and he pulled his hands away from me. He dragged my top with him as I pulled away, snatching it off, so when I stood up again, I wriggled my skirt down my legs and off. I knelt in front of Deon and widened his legs then, snickering at his length stabbing straight up, a darkened spot showing through his pants. Instead of pulling him out, I ducked my head down and started to nuzzle along the length. Deon tensed up again, his hands balling to fists at his side.

"Don't tease me, Cherri," he demanded.

I rubbed his shaft through his pants. "I told you, this is a punishment."

He growled, but didn't fight me. My teasing continued, rubbing him through his pants, until I felt I'd caused him enough strife. Pulling his pants and boxers off first, I shoved both articles away, then I went back to just mouthing along the shaft. I didn't close over, at least not until Deon threw his head back in frustration. Finally, I stuck my tongue out and licked up and closed over. Deon let out a loud grunt and his hands came to the back of my head. He didn't push or do anything that would suggest his control over me, and it allowed me to totally move at my pace. It was a nice reminder of just how impressive Deon's length was, and I enjoyed tasting him.

He continued to let out sweet grunts and groans as I worked, never taking more control. I got slightly lost in it, loving the feeling of him in my mouth, but then he started to swell and twitch in my mouth. His gentle thrusts deeper into my throat suggested he was close, and I wasn't ready for him to finish just yet. I popped off, keeping a hand in place to stroke him, and smiled up at him even though he couldn't see me.

One of his arms flipped across his face. "That was mean."

"Don't worry," I said. "I'll give you something better." I stood up and returned to the seated position I'd been in before, only this time I slid back until I was sitting in his lap and his member was resting like a hot iron against my thigh. "Remember earlier?"

He offered a dark chuckle. "Ah. You were training me." One of his hands wrapped around me and grabbed at my breast, and the other dipped between my legs. "Whatever you want."

I lifted up a little, and Deon grabbed himself and guided himself into my waiting hole. I lowered over him and his hand settled right at the top of my most sensitive spot and started to rub. What had been pleasurable earlier was now pure ecstasy, as Deon's hands worked in tandem with his lower half. I rocked my hips back and forth, dragging him along the deepest parts of me until he was targeting a sweet spot deep inside. I let out a moan, and Deon started to fire against the spot, lifting himself into me.

"Yeah, baby," I moaned. "That's so good. I'm—"

I was cut off by my own orgasm. It was the most powerful one I'd ever experienced, with twinges of rapture snatching at me from all angles.

"Fuck," Deon hissed. "Cherri, I can't."

"That's okay, baby. Let me have it," I demanded.

Deon slammed up into me and I rocked my hips backwards to meet his movements. Whether my orgasm never stopped or another ran into me before the last one had completely subsided, I wasn't sure, but I could no longer make sound, only hold my mouth open and try to keep myself conscious. Deon's legs started to shake, then he dropped and I rutted down against him, and he exploded, growling in my ear. He flowed into me, and I sang out with pleasure as he filled me up.

Thank god I made the last minute decision to start birth control at the beginning of the summer.

We both went limp, and the only sound in the room was that of us trying to catch our breath. Deon's hands squeezed me, and I could feel his heart bashing in his chest. When we'd recovered enough, we moved our antics to the bathroom, where I kept Deon blindfolded for another couple of rounds before finally letting him take it off so we could run a bath in the giant jacuzzi tub and settle in for a soak.

I made myself comfortable between Deon's legs

and leaned back against his chest. He wrapped his arms around me and nuzzled his head against mine. "That whole 'you in control of me blind-folded' thing," he started. "The whole thing just works for me."

I giggled. "I'm glad. I was a little scared you wouldn't like it. Thank you for trusting me enough to do it."

"Of course. I'd trust you with my life, Cherri." He kissed the top of my head. "That was the best by far."

"I think so too. It's exhilarating asking for what I want," I said.

"You should always do that," Deon said. "Ask for what you want from me. In or out of the bedroom, if I can give it to you, I will."

I snuggled back against him. "I love you."

"Hey, can I ask you for a favor?" he said.

"Of course."

"Tomorrow, when we go in search of Connor. Can you stay back?" he asked.

I turned my head so I could look up at him. "Stay back? Why?"

He curled his arms tighter around me. "I don't want to lose you. If he hurts you, I don't know what I'll do."

"No," I said. "Deon, I'm coming with you wherever you go. I'm a ride or die."

"Yeah, but I don't want you to die," Deon replied.

"I won't," I said. "I can take care of myself, and besides, you're not going to let anything happen to me and neither are our friends. The only one who should be scared as shit is Connor."

Deon didn't seem to like that answer very much, but nodded. "I'd sooner die than let anything happen to you."

"Well, no dying for you either." I repositioned myself and leaned back against Deon's chest and closed my eyes. "We're going to do this how we should have been doing it all along. Together."

29

DEON

"Woo hoo!" Colette said, starting a round of applause as we walked into the pool area where the entire Royal Court was hanging out. "There they are!"

"Hey, how was the honeymoon, you two?" Kyle asked, snickering.

Brayden, who was floating in the pool between Kyle's legs, smacked his knee. "Hey, that's not okay." He looked over at Cherri and I. "No wedding without the flower girl."

Cherri and Nikita immediately broke out into laughter, along with Brayden, while everyone else just stared in confusion. "I don't get it," I said.

"None of us do," Sicily said. "This is an inside

joke the three of them have that they *refuse* to let us in on."

"I'm sorry," Cherri said. "I know we probably would have gotten started sooner, but we were… preoccupied."

"Even this morning?" Alistair asked.

I shrugged. "Checkout wasn't until 11."

"Yeah!" Avery said. "Get it, Cherri!"

"Well," Nathan said. "As much as the sexual exploits of my brother and ex-girlfriend interest me, I would love *nothing* more than to shift the topic as far away from that as possible."

Nikita tapped Nathan's leg, chuckling. "That's fair."

"Let's shut this pool party down then, and head inside to make a plan. We have a crazy man to shut down," Alistair said.

Those few people who were in the pool started to climb out, and everyone else stood up from the lounge chairs and barstools scattered around the pool. We all made our way back inside. Even though my back and legs were sore in the best way, I did my best to look unaffected by my long, lovely night with Cherri and kept her close to me as we walked in.

Those who were wet went up the stairs to get

changed, while the rest of us sat down in the living room. Cherri and the other members of The Royal Court bounced casual conversations off one another for a while, and I still felt a little out of place. I'd judged The Royal Court so harshly back before I went to prison. Though to be fair, so did Cherri. As shitty as Connor was, he'd presented us all with an opportunity to grow as people and become more honest with one another, and as I watched people like Cherri and Sicily chat happily with people like Brayden and Colette, I knew that the universe was hard at work trying to give us back what Connor Loche had stolen from all of us.

Once everyone was in the living room, Nathan stood up and leaned against the fireplace at the front of the room. "Okay. This is it, guys. This is everything that we've been working towards. We got Deon back and now it's time to take Connor Loche down."

"Nathan?" a voice called out.

"In the living room!" A few seconds later, a shorter, fit-looking woman and a taller, buff man rounded the corner into the living room. "Hey!"

"Who are they?" I whispered to Cherri.

"The woman is Anisa and the man is Cobalt. They used to work for Connor, but quit when they could no longer take how he was treating Nathan. Now they love him like they're his parents. It reminds me of you with Felicity and Garrett."

As Cherri was explaining it, Nathan walked over and gave them both big hugs, and Anisa held Nathan's face just like a mother would. Nathan had been pretty muted since I returned, but when Anisa and Cobalt entered the room, he lit right up. It made me happy to know that there were some people loving Nathan like the parents he never had. He deserved that.

"I invited Anisa and Cobalt because I figured it was time for us to stop storming into dangerous situations alone."

"You just decided that right *now*?" Colette said.

"Anisa and Cobalt are retired as far as the muscle aspect is concerned, not just because Anisa only has use of one eye now, but because my father convinced them to take up a pacifistic lifestyle. But I asked them if they would be willing to make an exception for us."

"And of course," Anisa said. "We'd do anything for you."

"You're still mostly going to be stealth," Nathan said. "T.C. said that the place he set Connor up with is bugged, so we need your help to get us in. Although, I'll admit, once we're in, I'm not sure what we do. If Connor knows we're there together, he's most likely to just run. I think that most of The Royal Court, Anisa, and Cobalt, could be watching any visible exits, but knowing Connor, he's got a hidden way out. That was probably just as big a part of the deal as all the security."

"For sure," Brayden said. "The place he brought me to always had tons of ways in and tons of ways out."

"Right," Nathan said.

"Actually, though, I think I might have a plan," Brayden said. "I could be bait."

Nathan raised an eyebrow. "What?"

"Do you guys still have those two guys?" Brayden asked Anisa and Cobalt.

"Yeah," Anisa said.

"I say we have those two guys blindfold me and tie my wrists and bring me to Connor like they used to do. They can say they escaped and captured me or something. If Deon and Nathan can sneak in behind them, then as soon as Connor's out, you make the jump."

"I don't like that plan at all," Kyle said.

"I don't either," Brayden said, "but it would work. Connor thinks he can manipulate me, probably still. If I appear in front of him, with those two that worked for him saying they captured me, it'll be enough to coax him out. He'll think that, through me, he can get to you. Either by force or by thinking he could control me again."

"Brayden," Nathan said. "I can't ask you to do that."

"You didn't," he replied. "I want to do this. For once, I want to be the one turning the tables on Connor."

"If you do," I said. "We'll owe you our lives." I looked past Brayden to Kyle when I said, "I'd protect him with my life."

It was clear Kyle and the rest of the Court were uncomfortable with the plan, but no one could deny that it was probably the best course of action. If Brayden was dangled in front of Connor as a way to find Nathan and me, he'd absolutely take the bait.

"I'm not weak," Brayden said. "I appreciate you saying that, but I know how to protect myself, and it's time for me to play my part in all of this. I want to play an active role in ending Connor for good."

"Okay," Nathan said. "If you're sure."

Brayden nodded. "I'm sure."

"We can get you close, no problem," Anisa said. "We'll drive ahead and scope the place out and call you with the points to take. We'll grab those two morons on the way as well, and fill them in on the plan."

"Out of curiosity," Jaxon said. "What's keeping them from blowing everything up in our faces? They could flip out of pure spite."

"They won't," Cobalt said, cracking his knuckles. "You can trust me on that."

Jaxon looked at Cobalt as if he didn't trust that he could muscle his way through it, but he didn't say anything. His gaze traveled further to me and we locked eyes. He nodded at me as if to say, 'Make good on your promise to protect him,' and I could see that, in spite of how little Jaxon spoke, he cared about The Royal Court as much as the next person over.

"We're going to get ready. I'll send you the address we got from T.C.," Nathan said. "Everyone take a few minutes to breathe. This is the calm before the storm, and we want to be ready for whatever is waiting for us. This is it. It's time to end Connor Loche's reign of torment."

30

DEON

The address T.C. had given us led us to a business park in South Postings, not far from the high school. It gave everyone more than a few willies to know that Connor was holed up so close, but because he was, it meant we could walk to the location instead of drive. Anisa had called Nathan to let him know the best way to enter the park without being seen, and we found ourselves sneaking in from a small forest behind the park, closest to the door to the building Connor was supposedly hiding in.

Everyone was together apart from Brayden, who met up with Anisa and Cobalt to be handed over to Connor's thugs and carry out his plan. My heart was pounding as we watched Brayden approach the front door, and next to me, Kyle was up on his tiptoes, ready to pounce if need be.

"Okay," Nathan whispered. "Once they're through that first door, we can sneak along the building and follow them in. Deon and I will slip in and call if we need help."

"You're not going in there without us," Nikita said. "Cherri and I will be right behind you."

Both Cherri and Nikita had a burning look of determination on their faces, and I knew it would be fruitless to argue. Nathan must have seen it too, because he simply watched Nikita for a moment and then let out a sigh of defeat.

"Fine. The four of us are going in with Brayden. The rest of you should man any possible exit you can see. If you spy Connor making a run for it, call for Anisa and Cobalt."

Everyone nodded and not a moment later, a buzzer pierced the night silence. The men dragged Brayden in faux restraints through the door, sticking a pipe in the door jamb as they entered. Nathan, Nikita, Cherri and I left the treeline of the forest behind, slipped up to the side of the building, and slid along the popcorn walls until we were at the door. Nathan held it open and we slipped inside, leaving the pipe in the door jamb, just in case.

"Well, well, look what we have here," an evil voice that sent a chill down my spine began. "If it isn't Brayden? You disappeared after you failed me."

We snuck to the corner and peered around, and there he was—the devil himself. Connor looked worse for wear, no longer a silver fox, now a sickly thin man with greasy, wispy gray hair and sunken eyes. He still looked as smug as I remembered, but it looked out of place on him now, like a little boy wearing a hat that was too big.

"I did what you told me to," Brayden said. "It's these idiots that fumbled."

"Well, all three of you have been missing in action, so I'll ask plainly, where have you been?"

Then it went silent. Call it intuition or having dealt with my fair share of shady people lately, but I knew something was off. We couldn't hear anything, but Connor was intently staring at his men as though they were giving a soliloquy.

That was when it hit me.

At the road show I went to with Felicity, those people seemed to have the ability to communicate silently as well. Exactly as Jaxon had feared, the men were turning on us.

"Go around," I whispered to Nathan, then I

charged around the corner and out into the clear view of Connor.

"Oh. You figured you'd turn on me, Brayden, is that it? You think Deon alone can stop me?" Connor asked.

"He's not alone," one of the goons said. "This whole thing is a setup."

I took a few steps forward, but Connor pulled out a gun and pointed it at Brayden. "Ah, ah, ah. Why don't you stop right there? Unless you want me to—"

A gunshot cracked into the room, piercing the leg of one of thugs, sending him clattering to the ground. I looked over my shoulder, but no one was there, and that was when I realized the shot had actually come from Brayden. His restraints were applied in such a way that he still had total mobility, and he was able to pull his gun out and shoot. He quickly turned on the other guy, but he'd already let go and was ducking for cover.

Connor fired, but Brayden managed to duck out of the way. Exactly as we expected he might, Connor turned and started to run towards a door near the back, but the second he opened it, he came face to face with the barrel of Nathan's gun. Nathan backed Connor back into the room with Nikita behind him, who then blocked the door.

Brayden passed me, saying, "I'll guard the front," and crossed paths with Cherri walking in, her gun drawn as well.

"It's the end of the line, Connor," Cherri said.

"Isn't this cute?" Connor said. "A double date? You were just going to storm in here and the power of love was going to help you defeat me?"

Resounding clicks pierced the sky, as several men appeared as if from nowhere, all with guns cocked and aimed at us. Behind me, Cherri yelped as one of them got hold of her, and one appeared behind Nikita, capturing her as well.

Connor walked over and sat down behind his desk at the head of the room. "Tsk, tsk, tsk. I honestly expected a little more from you boys, but I suppose you're just children at the end of the day. Only children are stupid enough to think the bad guy just sits around in his office unarmed, waiting to be jumped. This isn't a hero story. That's not how it works. Deon, I half-expected this from you, but Nathan. I taught you better than this."

"You did," Nathan replied. "You taught me well. I'll admit, finding you was a pain in the ass, making sure you were cornered was something else I wasn't sure about, but going tit for tat with you—I'm a master at that."

"A master?" Connor scoffed. "Look around

you. You've got no cards left to play. I'm going to kill that pretty girlfriend of yours in front of you, then your brother. I'll hunt all your friends and end them too, keeping only that one." He smiled at Cherri. "I knew ever since I first laid eyes on her that I had to have her, one way or another. How will it feel, knowing she suffers everyday because of you?"

Rage filled my body, not just because Connor was disregarding me, but because he was threatening Cherri in the process. Something in me snapped and I whirled around and punched the guy holding Cherri in the face. He went down in a single hit, as did the two guys standing closest. I pushed Cherri behind me and put myself in front of her. If anyone else touched her, I'd see to it that they stopped breathing.

"I'm sick of this. Why don't we get the ball rolling?" Connor stood up and held a gun out towards me. "Goodbye, son."

A gunshot popped out from Connor's gun and I braced myself for impact, but felt nothing. A fear bubbled in my stomach and I looked behind me, but Cherri was still standing there. I turned around and looked forward and halfway between me and Connor, was Nathan. He was still on his feet, but there was blood dripping from him.

"Nathan!" Nikita and Cherri both screeched.

My brother had put himself between me and a bullet. I glared past Nathan to Connor, and saw for the first time, that flash of regret on his face before he went cold again.

"You *will* regret that," I growled. "Just like you will regret all the shots you took at me and missed."

31

CHERRI

Deon reached his hand behind himself and shoved me off to the side. He ducked down and snatched a gun out of one of the gunmen's hands, and in the distraction, I retrieved my gun from the man who had taken it. Immediately, I lifted it to shoot and hit the guy holding Nikita straight in the shoulder. He released her and she finished the job, throwing her head back and headbutting him unconscious. The remaining guards broke out, firing their guns in our direction. I slipped behind some filing cabinets and fired back, giving Deon enough of an opening to grab Nathan and drag him back.

Nikita backed into the hallway for protection, and eventually she disappeared. I figured she must be running back around, but it only took a handful of seconds for them to get around the first time, and in that same amount of time, she didn't appear.

Either way, I trusted Nikita to take care of herself, and Deon dragged Nathan back behind where I was. I knelt down next to him and was glad to see the bullet only grazed his stomach.

"Deon," Nathan said. "You know what you have to do. Just get their attention."

Deon was firing into the fray, keeping himself mostly blocked by the cabinets. "Yeah, they're all fucking firing at me and Connor is making a break for it."

Suddenly, the shooting stopped and I watched as the remaining three shooters crowded around Connor and filed him towards the door Nikita had gone through.

"Shit," Deon hissed, then he stepped out again. "Who here has a daughter named Cynthia? A wife, Angelique?"

The men stopped. Two of their gazes shifted towards one man, who was seething. "Keep their names out of your mouth."

"Connor used them, right? To get to you?" Deon took another couple of steps forward.

"Threatened to release scandalous photos and videos?"

"Do not listen to him," Connor demanded. "If you know what's good for you."

Next to me, Nathan shifted and started trying to get to his feet. My one attempt to hold him down failed, so I braced an arm under him and got him to his feet instead.

"I have all those videos," Nathan said. "Each one of you who has been blackmailed into working for my father, I hold the key to deleting any sensitive information for good."

"He's lying," Connor said. "I'll prove it to you."

He grabbed a remote from his desk and turned on the television hanging on the wall behind it. He pressed a few buttons, navigating to a folder on the smart TV, and pressed it, but the second he did, an alarm started to blare from the TV.

I smiled as Sicily's face appeared on the screen. "Oh, hey. If you're seein' this, you been Sic-hacked." He started to snicker. "Sic-hacked. That's good stuff."

"No!" Connor yelped. He backed out and pressed the folder button again.

"Oh, hey. If you're seein' this—"

He tried over and over, each time getting Sicily's dumb grin.

"My dad doesn't have any power over you anymore," Nathan said.

Deon glared at Connor. "Just like he doesn't have any power over us."

"You see, Dad," Nathan said, stepping away from my hold. "You taught me my most important lesson. You're only as powerful as what you have to offer." The three men stepped away from Connor and turned to face him instead. "And you have nothing."

Nikita came running back into the room via the back door with Jaxon behind her, but stopped short when she saw that the tables had turned.

"Tell me, Connor, did you know that you can legally be reported missing, if you're absent for six or more months?" Deon asked, and any smugness Connor had left evaporated from his face. "In order to protect any abandoned family members, assets are adjourned to the next of kin. Crazy, right?"

I smiled at Deon's arrogance. So *that* was where he got the money.

"Your company, assets, estate, and even your offshore accounts are now held in our names," Nathan said. "You don't even have the money to pay these men." He pulled some cash from his pocket and held it up. "But I do."

The men pulled their guns instantly, but this

time trained them on Connor. Nathan and Deon stepped forward, so Nikita and I followed as well. Nikita snatched Connor's gun from his hands, and I clocked him in the face, sending him down to the ground. After years of his torment, it felt good.

"Now here's what we're gonna do, *dad*," Nathan hissed. "You're going to prepare a few directives. One will keep all of your assets in our names. One will inform Garrett Williams' legal counsel that you were fraudulent in violating his parole. The last will inform a judge that you framed Deon for murder… Twice. You will call for his record to be totally expunged and then you will willingly hand yourself over to law enforcement, by which I mean, you'll surrender when we bring you there."

"You can just kill me if that's your plan," Connor said. "I would never."

"Very well, then we'll draft some directives of our own," Nathan said. "First, we will liquidate L.C.E., second, we will sell your estate, and third, we will donate any money to a charity."

"And I'll burn your fucking business degree out of spite," Deon snipped.

"Everything you worked for will go up in smoke, and we'll keep you alive just long enough to watch it all happen."

"Then we'll auction off putting a bullet in your

brain to the highest bidder and live off of that," Deon said.

"Whoa!" Nathan said. "You are most *certainly* the brawn to my brain. That's sick. I love it."

"Seems like your boys *do* take after you, Connor," Nikita said. "If you don't want a very nasty taste of your own medicine, I suggest you comply."

The look on Connor's face was so satisfying, it required a picture, so I took one. When Deon and Nathan realized what I was doing, they jumped behind him and posed like they were taking a silly photo with a buddy from Spring Break.

It was glorious.

After that, Connor was shoved down into his desk and furiously scribbled out the directives Nathan had demanded. Eventually, the rest of The Royal Court entered the office. We watched as the man who had tormented us for years was finally punished for what he had done. Once he was done with the orders, Anisa and Cobalt dragged him off, and it was a delight to see Cobalt accidentally smack his head against several walls as he pulled him out.

Any men that had attacked us were given pardons because, if there was anything The Royal Court had learned, it was how Connor's influence

could make you do things you wouldn't otherwise
do. An ambulance arrived to patch up Nathan and
anyone else who had gotten injured, then we finally
limped ourselves back to the clubhouse.

"I mean, *our* story sounds WAY cooler," Colette
said. "We fought like fifty guys between us."

Alistair pinched the bridge of his nose. "It was
like eight."

"No, it was definitely at least fifty," Avery said,
then winked at Colette.

We all collapsed onto different couches, leaning
against our significant others, apart from Sicily who
leaned against a table leg and said, "Aw, babe. You
worried too much. See? I'm fine."

"So what now?" Brayden said. "We don't have
to save any kidnapped friends or stop any psychotic
dads. What do we *do* with our time?"

Sicily raised a hand. "I say everyone works
together to find Sicily his dream girl."

"Work together? I'd rather compete," I said.

Nathan pointed across at me. "Now *that* sounds
like fun."

EPILOGUE
DEON

Just when I thought I'd finally tired Cherri out, she rolled over and got on top of me. She looked so beautiful in the morning sunlight that I was relatively powerless to do anything to stop her. If a girl that looked like Cherri wanted more, how could I not give her more?

"Good god," I said. "Someone ate their Wheaties this morning."

She reached down and curled a hand around my length and began stroking it to bring it back to full size. "What can I say? You asked me what I wanted for my birthday. This is what I want."

"This feels more like a birthday present for me," I said.

Cherri giggled. "Happy birthday to *you* then."

She was just bending over to kiss me when there was a knock on the door. "Enough already! There are *more* people that want to celebrate you, you know!" Colette screeched.

"Yeah, Cherri, come on out! We've got presents!"

Cherri looked down at me with a frown and I tapped her ass a couple of times. "Don't make such a frustrated face. They put in a lot of work. Besides, we can pick up from where we left off later," I said. "Maybe with the handcuffs?"

"Ooh, on you or me?" she asked.

I sat up to kiss her. "However you want it, baby."

Cherri squeaked with happiness. "Deal." She finally climbed down off of me, grabbing the blanket to wrap around herself, then she went over to the bedroom door and cracked it. "This better be good. You just interrupted some amazing fucking sex."

"It *will* be. Just get dressed and come down-stairs," Avery replied.

I heard a party horn, then a rain of glitter burst through the door and sprinkled down over Cherri. She laughed and closed the door and I couldn't help but stare at her a little bit.

"Nope, no. Don't look at me that way. You were

the one who convinced me to stop, so just avert your eyes."

"Why did we stop again?" I crossed the room towards her. "I can't remember."

"It's because we have a whole fucking party planned!" Nikita screeched, then there was a hard bang on the door. "Knock it off and get down here!"

Cherri and I shared a silent chuckle, then I yelled, "Alright, we're coming!"

I pecked Cherri on the cheek and then turned my back to her before I really did lose my resolve and drag her back to bed.

We took separate showers for obvious reasons, and then each got dressed and went downstairs. At the bottom, I clasped my hands over Cherri's eyes and guided her outside and down the path to the pool. The entire area was decorated with lime, pink, and sky-blue balloons and streamers, and the pool had been adorned with brand new floaties to match the color scheme. I smiled at some of the faces standing around, and the table piled high with presents. It made me feel guilty for monopolizing so much of Cherri's time that morning.

Finally, I pulled my hands from around her eyes and everyone screamed, "Surprise!"

Cherri's hands came up to her mouth. "Oh wow!"

Cherri's mom, dad, and brother were standing near the shallow end of the pool, each with hats on and horns in their mouths which they were blowing excitedly. Back by the bar, Felicity, Anisa, Cobalt, and my mom were standing, with drinks in their hands that they held up to cheers to Cherri. Standing closest to us were all the members of The Royal Court, all dressed in nice clothes, wearing party hats and holding a mix of horns and blowers in their mouths.

"Happy birthday!" Nathan said.

"Honestly," Avery said. "I didn't think you were going to make it out until Ali and I were leaving for New Haven."

"Don't be so dramatic. You still have a week," Cherri replied.

"No. Kyle and I have been in school for a whole semester now," Colette said.

Cherri put her hands on her hips. "Alright. Enough with the drama. I'm ready for my party!" She looked over towards her parents and Gus. "Hi, Mama! Hi, Daddy! Gus!"

"Happy Birthday, baby!" Rebeccah, Cherri's mom, said. "In all seriousness though, if you and

Deon have so much trouble waking up in the morning, you should set an alarm."

All the murmurs of voices went silent as all gazes shifted to Rebeccah. "Y-yeah, mom," Cherri said. "That's a really good idea. Let's have cake!"

Nathan led us over to a table that had been set up between the bar and the pool, where there was a tiered cake and platters of food. There was a tiny model of Cherri, with her short brown, fading-to-blond hair, wearing a leather jacket and jean shorts sitting on top of the cake.

"It's so cute," Cherri said. "I love this so much."

"It's white cake, with raspberry filling and lemon buttercream," Avery said. "Made from scratch, by your personal baking crew, me, Ali, and Brayden."

"That's awesome. Thank you guys so much!"

"Happy birthday to you!" Sicily randomly started singing.

"What are you doing?" I asked. "The candles aren't even lit ye—"

He held his hands up above his head. "Happy birthday to you!"

All the rest of the guests threw their voices in awkwardly, joining Sicily mid-song and finishing it out with him conducting everyone like they were a choir. When the song was done, Sicily clapped his hands, and Cherri walked over and squeezed him.

"I wouldn't have had that any other way. I love you, you fucking weirdo," she said.

"Love you too," then he skipped over to the present table and pulled a small box off the top. "Open my present first."

I eyed Sicily. "Why are you like this? We just finished singing 'happy birthday' and she didn't even get to blow out the candles."

"Shhh," Sicily hissed at me as he handed the box over to Cherri. "Go ahead."

Cherri took the box from Sicily, and lifted off the top. She reached her hand inside and pulled out a necklace. It had a pendant hanging at the bottom that was a circle with three teardrop shapes that looked as if someone had dragged a toothpick through them and bled them together.

"Woah," Cherri said. "This is beautiful."

"It's the Greek symbol for strength," Sicily said. "I saw it a couple weeks ago and I thought of you instantly. You're the strongest person I know."

Cherri's eyes started to sparkle with tears and she reached out and pulled Sicily back into a hug. "Thank you so much. This is beautiful, I love it."

"Okay. If we wanna light candles and do things the normal way, we can," Sicily said. "I just had to give it to her. I bought it two weeks ago and I almost blew that I bought it like twelve times." He tapped Cherri on the shoulder. "Happy birthday, kid."

"He went from so sweet, back to good old Sicily in no time flat," Nikita said. "What a national treasure."

"Well," Alistair said. "I guess we're moving onto presents. Come on over here and get 'em goin' girl!"

Cherri walked over to the table and Kyle brought a stool for her to sit down at and then she smiled and started to go through her presents. She had several presents from her family, and a whole host from The Royal Court, so she had quite a few to get through. I had a present of my own for Cherri, but I wanted to give it to her in private, so it wasn't stacked in the pile.

Avery had helmed control of taking all the pictures and videos for social media, so I slid over to where Felicity and my mom were standing and gave them each a big hug.

"So. Mom, what do you think of my other mom?" I asked my mom.

My mom smiled at me. "I think very highly of her. She took such wonderful care of my baby when I couldn't. I'm forever in her debt."

"It's me in *yours*," Felicity said. "I got to share your amazing son. He's truly something special."

My mom put a hand on my face. "He is, isn't he? I can't wait to meet this man who he sees as a dad."

"Well, turns out that may be happening sooner rather than later." Felicity pulled out a letter and handed it to me. "I know it's Cherri's birthday, but here you go."

I opened it and smiled at all of the information regarding Venom's granted appeal of his revoked parole. Based on the letter that Connor wrote, the judge agreed to reopen the case, and a date had been set for a couple of months down the road. "This is amazing."

"Yep, and while he's still behind bars, he's making sure that Connor receives a nice, warm welcome for all the harm that he's caused his kid," Felicity said with a sly grin.

"Thank god," my mom said. "I hope whatever happens to him behind bars is painful and permanent for all the pain he's caused our families."

"Oh, don't you worry, Ciara. Garrett's men are bound to create issues for Connor long after Garrett is gone," Felicity said.

Over near the table, Cherri shrieked as she opened one of her presents. It was a Yale letterman jacket. Cherri wasn't going to Yale, but Avery would be leaving in a couple of weeks to start her stint there. "I love it!"

"I knew you would!" Avery said. "This way, you have something to keep me in your mind and in your heart until you come visit."

"Plus it's *so* cute," Colette said. "With a pair of leather pants you are going to make that jacket look like it belongs on the runway."

Cherri finished opening her gifts, enjoying her cake, and eating the delicious food that had been laid out. She took some specific time to talk with her parents, Felicity, my mom, and Anisa and Cobalt, and had made sure to spend a good amount of time playing in the pool with Gus. Though I still wasn't much of a people person, it made me perfectly happy to sit back and watch her enjoy the party that her friends had put together just for her. She had a smile on her face the entire day, which was all I could ever want for her.

Eventually, the sun started to set over the horizon. Gus was so tired he could barely stand up, so Cherri's parents left first, taking him home, and Anisa and Cobalt left shortly thereafter. My mom and Felicity hung out a little bit longer, admittedly so that they could spend more time with me, but then they eventually gave Cherri a huge hug each, and left, promising to visit again soon.

Finally, The Royal Court was left alone once again.

"You guys," Cherri said, sliding down onto my lap in one of the outdoor chairs that was surrounding the pool. "This was absolutely amazing. I can't think of any way I would have rather spent my birthday. Everyone I loved was there, and all the gifts were perfect."

"I'm so glad you liked it," Nikita said. "We all played our own little part in it. Kyle wanted to do like a creepy escape room thing as a joke because we haven't had to chase around after Connor for over a month, but he was overruled."

"No I wasn't, I just bought tickets to take Cherri some other time," Kyle said.

Cherri giggled. "And I can't wait."

"What'd you get her, Deon?" Avery asked. "I mean, apart from breaking your bed frame this morning?"

I chuckled. "I actually haven't given it to her yet. I kind of wanted to do it in private."

"More bed breaking?" Colette said.

"No," I replied. "Well, yes, but no. It's just something special to me and I kind of wanted it to be an intimate moment between us, if that's okay?"

"Oh, sure." Colette stood up. "Well, let's go, gang."

I held out a hand. "Oh, no, I didn't mean—"

But it didn't matter. Everyone was already getting up from their respective seats and filing inside, leaving Cherri and I alone in the cool, summer evening air. Cherri just laughed and snuggled against me. "Gotta be careful what you say to these assholes."

"I guess so," I said. "But, I'm not going to turn down the moment. Can you get up for a sec?"

"Oh. Sure."

Cherri stood up out of the chair and I stood up to stand across from her. I grabbed her hands and held them. "Cherri, you are the love of my life. I know we're only 19, officially today, but there's not a question in my life that I want to be with you forever."

Cherri smiled. "Yeah. Me too."

"I know it would be insane to propose to you, at least at this point. Not just because we're still so young and have a lot to figure out, but because I know how I want to propose and it doesn't involve any of this stuff."

"Ooh, what does it involve?" Cherri asked.

"Nice try, Slick," I said.

She shrugged. "It was worth a shot."

"Even if I'm waiting a little bit longer to propose, I do want you to have something as a promise of what's to come. I know that sounds cheesy, but I do."

I pulled the small, silver box in my pocket out and tipped back in the case. Inside was a modest ring with a purple crystal at the heart of it, and a couple of small diamonds on either side. It wasn't extravagant, by design. Even though I could afford more now, I wanted to start simple so that there was room to grow.

Just like with our relationship.

"It's beautiful," Cherri said. "I love it."

"Now that I'm officially going to be working at L.C.E. once I get my G.E.D., and then going to business school, I'm vowing a few things to you. One: to build a beautiful life for us that's earned from *my* hard work. Not Connor's, not Nathan's, but mine. Two: to have a house of our very own built. Somewhere nearby, so we still have access to your family and all of your friends, but far enough away that we don't feel smothered. Three: to prepare myself for the family I know you want. In a few years, when we're ready, and I've taken all the necessary steps towards our future, I'll propose to you for real, and our wedding is going to be amazing."

Cherri nodded. "I can't wait."

"So?" I said. "Do you accept?"

"Of course I accept!" She held out her right hand, the typical hand for putting a promise ring on. "I love you."

I pulled the ring out and slid it onto her right ring finger. "I love you, too."

She looked down at the ring for a little bit, and I tried to memorize the genuine, warm smile that rose to her face as she did. I set my lips to hers and she wrapped her arms behind my neck. I still didn't know what the future held for Cherri and I, but I knew with her by my side and the support of our family and friends, there was nothing but happy days ahead.

"One last thing," Cherri said, rubbing her hands through my hair.

"Yeah?" I said.

"Brayden is going to be our flower girl," she said.

I blinked a couple of times absently at her and then just shook my head. "You know what? I'm just going to leave that decision up to you."

"Oh, you are already a pro at this whole spouse thing. Keep subscribing to that concept and you and I are going to make it to the end," Cherri joked.

I held her close to me and still couldn't believe I got to spend every single day of the rest of my life with her. "Anything to make it to the end with you, my love."

"Anything?" she asked.

I nodded. "Yep. Anything."

WANT MORE?

Go to www.RebelHart.net/Stories for a full list of my books.

WANT TO BE A REBEL?

Join my FB Group of Rebels to chat with me and other fans. I'd love to have you there!

Thank you for reading this series!

If you loved it, consider leaving a review on Amazon. Just 1 or 2 lines would be amazing!

Get an alert when I release a new book:

SMS: Text REBEL to 77948 (US only)

EMAILs: join at www.RebelHart.net

ABOUT THE AUTHOR

Rebel Hart is an author of Contemporary and Dark Romance novels. All her books are FREE in Kindle Unlimited. Check them out at author.to/RebelHart.

NEVER MISS A NEW RELEASE:

Follow Rebel on Amazon

Follow Rebel on Bookbub

Text REBEL to 77948 (US only)

Sign up at www.RebelHart.net to get an email alert when her next book is out.

authorrebelhart@gmail.com

CONNECT WITH REBEL HART:

www.facebook.com/groups/RebelHart

ALSO BY REBEL HART

For a full list of my books go to:

author.to/RebelHart

www.ingramcontent.com/pod-product-compliance
Lightning Source LLC
Chambersburg PA
CBHW051156190726
48288CB00006B/1682